HELL HOUNDS DON'T HEEL

BOOK 3 OF THE VALKYRIE BESTIARY SERIES

KIM MCDOUGALL

Published by Wrongtree Press, www.WrongTreePress.com.
Cover and book design by Castelane, www.Castelane.com.
Cover art by Pamela Francescut.
Editing by Elaine Jackson.

Paperback ISBN: 978-1-7772144-5-6
Hardcover ISBN: 978-1-7776401-1-8
eBook ISBN: 978-1-7772144-6-3

Version 1

FICTION / Fantasy / Urban
FICTION / Fantasy / Paranormal

BOOKS BY KIM MCDOUGALL

The Hidden Coven Series:
Inborn Magic
Soothed by Magic
Trigger Magic
Bellwether Magic
Gone Magic

Valkyrie Bestiary Series
Three Half Goats Gruff (Novelette)
Dragons Don't Eat Meat
Dervishes Don't Dance
Hell Hounds Don't Heel

Writing as Eliza Crowe:

The Shifted Dreams Series:
Pick Your Monster
Lost Rogues

The sun set in a riot of grisly purples and reds. I parked my truck at the side of an access road on the southwestern edge of Buzzard Island. A far-away howl broke the stillness as I gazed up and down the road. No one used this route anymore. It led to a beach blanketed in debris from the Flood Wars and left uncleared to protect the tower looming over the shoreline. On top of the tower, the Apex stone funneled power from a ley-line to the ward protecting Montreal. Even people without my sensitivity would be uncomfortable so near that much magic. To me, it felt like a heat rash prickling my skin. I took several centering breaths to reinforce my personal defenses and slipped into the forest surrounding Gerard Golovin's estate.

Spring buds gave me no cover as I crept beneath the trees. I would have preferred to wait until full dark, but it was nearly feeding time and the beast I stalked would be more manageable if it was hungry.

I made it over the ten-foot wall surrounding the property without encountering anyone, but I didn't let that lull me into complacency. Polina, the witch we had inadvertently freed from her bloodstone prison last fall had shacked up with Gerard, a man we already suspected of darker schemes. And she brought along her security of an otherworldly nature. Ghost sentries might not sound like an effective way to guard anything—they couldn't use physical weapons after all—but they could raise an alarm, and most people wouldn't see them coming.

Most people weren't me.

I crouched in the shadows and waited. Two minutes and thirty seconds later—right on time—the spectral guard glided across the top of the wall. It scouted outward, not into the yard it was supposed to protect. The ghost was an old one that had forgotten most of its humanity and manifested only a vaguely human form. It drifted by a few feet from my hiding spot, then stopped. I willed the forest to close its protective arms around me. I'd been practicing green magic. It was an effective camouflage even against those who saw with more than their eyes.

The ghost turned to survey the gloom of the yard. I slowed my pulse. The sockets that should have been eyes were blank hollows, staring right into my hiding spot. I breathed as quietly as a tree. The ghost paused for a long minute before moving on. I stood on shaky legs.

One hurdle down, one to go.

I snuck past the house, a sprawling three-story monstrosity of pale gray brick. Massive Greek-style columns flanked the front entrance with a stained-glass window hanging above the door. Only security lights shone outside. The windows were dark. That was all right. I wasn't making a social call.

By the time I reached the yard on the north end of the property, the sun had fully set on the moonless night. Only the reddish glow from the Apex stone—some two-hundred feet overhead—gave me any light.

I watched the fenced-in yard for several minutes. It was a large space, easily fifty meters long, with a low building butting up against the tower at one end. Two big doghouses sat in the middle of the yard. A large black mound crouched in the shadow beside one of these.

Another ghost sentry drifted by the fence and disappeared into the trees. By my calculations, I had nine minutes until the next patrol.

As I left the safety of the shadows, a deep growl broke the silence. There was no use trying to hide from this beast. She could smell me coming, no matter how I tried to wrap myself in green magic. But after a dozen visits, I felt like we had come to an agreement. So, I took her growl for a greeting.

"Hey girl." I kept my voice low, barely above a breath of wind.

The growl deepened. The beast's lip curled, displaying one impressive fang. She sprang, jaws snapping, and slammed into the fence separating us.

Maybe *agreement* was too optimistic.

The top of the hound's head reached my shoulder. Her powerful front legs were longer than her back legs, which were made for springing into a sprint. A glossy black mane covered her head and massive shoulders that tapered to slender hips and a whip-like tail. Yellow eyes flashed from a face that was armored in thick hide like plating, and looked like it was painted for war in black and white stripes.

She was beautiful. And terrifying. Her magic felt untamed, like her corporeal form could barely contain it. This was a true hell hound meant for guarding the gates to the nether worlds.

I sat in the dirt beside the fence. She pawed the ground and paced, her growl a deep rumble like thunder heard in the distance.

I hummed an old tune my grandfather taught me and waited for her to settle. The hound's eyes never left me. Was I prey or master? I suspected anyone she met fit into one category or the other.

From my pack, I fished out a chunk of Gita's special sausage. I pushed my fingers through a link in the fence, dangling the meat as bait. So far, I had been unsuccessful in getting her to take food from my hand. This wasn't a mindless beast, driven by hunger. Her intelligent eyes reflected suspicion as she considered my offering. I shoved my magic out in a cloud and let it settle over her. She snarled and tried to dance away, but it clung to her like a stubborn musk until she gave up and lay down with her head on her massive front paws.

"*Bra Jobbe*," I said, settling back into the Norwegian commands Grandfather had taught me for taking care of his hounds. The language came easily, as if I hadn't abandoned that world fifteen years ago.

"*Flink. Kom her.*" Good dog. Come.

The beast inched forward.

"*Bra Jobbe. Kom her.*"

She lunged and snapped the meat from my fingers. It disappeared in one gulp. I pulled out more sausage, lacing it with my magic before offering it to her. Yellow eyes glared. She still didn't trust this stranger.

"You know I've dealt with dragons and chimeras and trolls. You don't scare me."

She reached out with her muzzle. Her lips curled back, revealing inch-long fangs as she delicately grabbed the meat.

The sentries would return soon. I tossed her one more chunk, pushing as much magic into it as I could.

Maybe next time I visited, she'd let me into the yard.

A Hell Hound Tale

January 1, 2081

Happy New Year! I have been thinking a lot about hell hounds lately, and I thought I'd tell you a story about these amazing and often misunderstood beasts.

Once upon a time, a young woman left the only home she'd ever known to live in Asgard, the land of her ancestors. Valkyrie blood ran in her veins, but the Freya of the Valkyrie maidens refused to train her. At eighteen, the girl was too old to learn, and her formative years on Midgard had made her weak.

But the king of the Aesir had a soft spot for his granddaughter and he forced the Freya to teach her. The Freya obeyed her king, but grudgingly. She didn't like to be told what to do. The Valkyrie were her greatest pride, and she didn't want a half-human girl to tarnish their reputation. So she made the girl work twice as hard as other novices. When the girl failed to meet expectations, the Freya beat her. When she was too tired to raise her sword one more time, the Freya beat her. Nothing the girl did pleased the Freya. And even as she progressed, growing stronger and faster, the Freya set higher and higher standards, so that triumph was always just out of reach for the half-human.

The king kept a pack of beasts descended from Loki's great wolf son, Fenrir. These weren't regular hunting dogs. These were hounds that guarded the portals to other worlds. One particularly nasty beast had six legs, a mane like a lion, and the bowel movements of an elephant. Cleaning the kennels was a punishment given to the novice who displeased the Freya the most, and so the half-human girl spent many hours with the howling, snarling pack of hounds.

After watching her struggle to control the beasts, the king took pity on the girl and taught her the words that would make the beasts obey. After that, the hounds became devoted to her, and she spent many wonderful hours running with them in the forest. She never let it slip that she enjoyed working with the hounds, and the Freya continued to use kennel chores as a punishment.

One day, as the girl and the hounds ran through the forest outside the gates of Asgard, they stumbled into a patrol of giants. These were in the days just after the king had signed a treaty with the giants of Jotunheim. They lived only one world over in the branches of the Yggdrasil, the world tree that connects many lands. The treaty forbade the giants to travel within the border of Asgard without an Aesir escort, at least not in any numbers, and certainly not armed.

They would have killed the girl to keep their secret. And one young Valkyrie novice against six giants isn't much of a match. Still, the Freya's training made her brave. She was ready to fight the giants to the death. But one hound grabbed her collar and flipped her onto his back. All she could do was hang on as he ran. Snarls and shouts of pain behind them soon faded into the distance, and she understood the pack was protecting her. Of the dozen hounds that left with the girl that morning, only six made it home. The others stayed back to fight the giants, to make sure the pack had a chance to run. And to live.

The king was angry about the giant incursion, but he was more angry about losing six good hounds. And after that day, the girl was no longer allowed to run free with the pack.

COMMENTS (5)

Hell hounds are indeed misunderstood. They are majestic beasts. And like any dog, they are only as good or evil as the master that trains them. And a merry changing of the calendar to you too!

cchedgewitch (January 1, 2081)

Fun story! I wish I could visit Asgard one day!

HarperHays (January 1, 2081)

> Me too :)
>
> *Valkyrie367 (January 1, 2081)*

Great story! What are those power words? Would they work on a hyperactive black lab?

PercyH (January 2, 2081)

> Sorry, it's just a story. You'll have to find your own magic words.
>
> *Valkyrie367 (January 2, 2081)*

Monday afternoon found me on the edge of the Laval floodplains, chasing down a dozen locusts. Twelve doesn't sound like much of an infestation, but these were each the size of a cat. And their bite had enough venom to put a man in a coma. The first two Hub officers on site were already being treated at the hospital.

A third officer joined me, and we hunted the rest of the giant bugs that manifested from the floodplains. He was fae and knew this border territory better than me. His glamor made him seem perfectly mundane. His hair was between brown and blond. Height: average. Eyes: brown. Features: pleasant, but not handsome. He'd taken pains to be unremarkable, but my keening sensed that his real appearance was anything but bland. When the wind shifted, I got a distinct tang of salty sea air coming off him, and his magic felt big, like a monster was towering over me every time he stood near.

We worked as a team. I keened the critter, and he sprinted across the open ground to catch it. He was bitten twice, but the venom didn't work the same on fae. Around six p.m., he caught the last locust and held it up by one leg. It thrashed and snarled, gnashing the air with sharp teeth. When I asked what he planned to do with them, he licked his lips and said, "Don't worry. I'll dispose of them properly."

I didn't really want to know. The fae had unusual tastes. And it wasn't like I could re-home such lethal creatures.

Critter wrangler rule number seven: some monsters just have to die. It's the way of the world. I couldn't save every noxious locust or fire-spitting lizard.

Some days, I had to just do my job, and if the fae wanted to eat chocolate covered venomous bugs, I could let that be.

This was me. The new Zen Kyra. My sword no longer lusted for blood or souls, and I didn't have to make all the big decisions.

I left the fae officer who seemed happy with his booty and headed back to Hub Station to record the job so I could get paid. At the dispatch counter, I grabbed a tablet to fill in my report. For once, I wasn't covered in mud, blood or feces, so I decided against a shower. Maybe I could even get home in time for a late dinner.

A commotion by the entrance made me turn. Angus walked in, flanked by two Hub officers. His hands were cuffed, and a strap around his chest bound his wings. I dropped the tablet on the dispatch counter and ran to him.

"Angus! What happened?" I reached out, but one officer tugged him aside. It was Tommy Perez. We'd fought together during the opji attack last spring. I'd worked a couple more cases with him since then. He seemed like a nice guy, but right now he was in cop mode.

"No speaking to the prisoner." Perez shoved Angus into the interrogation area.

"Kyra!" Angus called over his shoulder. "Call Dutch. Get Oscar here! Tell them I didn't kill her!"

The door swung shut behind them, leaving me in stunned silence. I turned back to the dispatch desk. Trudy was on duty tonight. She was friendly, but if she thought I had a personal stake in a case, she would shut me out. It was protocol. Luckily, she was arguing with someone on the phone and had missed Angus's entrance.

As soon as she hung up, I asked, "Can you pull up information on an arrest?"

"What name?"

"Uh, Angus…I don't know his last name. They just brought him in." I tried to sound casual.

Trudy scanned her computer. "Angus MacOg. Looks like he killed someone. A Susanna Coulter. Why does that name sound familiar?"

"She used to work here. Last year. I knew her." I forgot all about protocol.

Susanna was dead? And Angus had apparently killed her. That was possible. I hadn't seen Susanna since she walked out of the lab last year, leaving me and Mason at the mercy of Pierre and his mad fantasies. I'd seen Polina several times on the news, usually on Gerard Golovin's arm as he spat out sound bites about the future success of his railroad for the evening news. They were an item now, and he liked to parade his beautiful new girlfriend around like a trophy.

"You know her well enough to ID the body?" Trudy's question brought me back.

"I guess so. Why?"

"They brought her in this morning, but Tommy said her grandmother was too distraught to come to the station right away. And she has no other family. Can you do it?"

This was the point where I should have mentioned that Angus was a friend, and identifying the body of his alleged victim was a conflict of interest.

"Sure. I'll head down to the morgue right now." I turned away before Trudy changed her mind, but she was already taking a call for a new disaster in the busy ward.

The morgue was in the basement. I ducked into the stairwell but stopped to call Dutch before heading down. He listened to my news in silence.

"Angus asked you to call someone named Oscar," I said. "Do you know who that is?"

"Our lawyer. Oscar Lewis." Dutch as always, was all business. "I'll contact him right away."

"Okay. I'm going down to ID the body now. I'll see what else I can find out. And Dutch?" I hesitated. "Is there any way you can get word to Mason? He would want to know."

There was a long silence on the line. Then Dutch said, "I can try."

I exhaled the breath I hadn't realized I was holding. "Okay. Thanks. I'll wait for the lawyer." I pocketed my widget and leaned against the wall, feeling suddenly overwhelmed.

Mason, where are you?

Downstairs, the morgue was busy. Life inside a ward was safer than the alternative of living in the wilds of the Inbetween, but we still had to contend with rogue magic, squabbles between fae factions and humans, and everyday, garden-variety crime.

A busy orderly showed me to the examination room.

"She ain't been prettied up yet," she said. "You sure you don't wanna wait?"

I shook my head.

"Okay, then. But if you have to throw up, try to hit the sink." She checked the toe tags on several bodies before leading me over to the table at the far end. Without ceremony, she folded back the white sheet to reveal Susanna's bloodless face.

"Is that her?" The orderly checked her tablet. "Susanna Coulter?"

I nodded.

"I need to hear you say it for the record."

"Yes. That's her. Can you give me a minute alone?"

The orderly nodded and left, already talking on her widget.

I stared at Susanna. She'd been pretty in life, with blond curls that framed her cherubic face. Now she looked gray and sharp featured, as if death hardened her somehow. A gaping red line was visible under the blood stain on her neck. Someone had slit her throat.

I peeled back the sheet to inspect the rest of her body. Her arms were a mess of cuts, defensive wounds maybe, like she'd blocked several knife thrusts with her bare arms. Another puncture wound marked her shoulder. That one wouldn't have been fatal, but it would have hurt like hell. Bruises mottled most of her chest and shoulders, looking too old to be from the fight that killed her. I recognized that kind of bruising. It was common in the novice Valkyries. Susanna had been training to fight.

I checked the toe tag. She'd been brought in early this morning. It was now nearly nine in the evening. The officers waited all day until Angus woke from his stone form to bring him in. That meant they probably found him at the scene of the crime.

Why would Angus be fighting Susanna?

I covered the body and went back upstairs to wait for the lawyer. I hoped he'd let me in to see Angus. Something was off about this whole scenario, and I intended to find out what.

t pays to be friendly with the dispatch officer. I was sitting beside Trudy's desk when a short gray-haired man hurried through the front door.

"That's your lawyer guy," Trudy whispered to me.

"Thanks." I stood, feeling exhausted from an already emotionally draining day and intercepted him.

"Mr. Lewis? My name is Kyra Greene, I'm…"

"I know who you are, Miss Greene. I'm a big fan of your blog." He pumped my hand enthusiastically. I'd never met a fan before. "Seems like you have quite the menagerie—a basilisk, dervish and even a banshee. I admire your fortitude. It can't be easy to care for so many."

"Thanks. Sometimes I think they take care of me though."

Oscar Lewis resembled an overgrown gnome, balding with a fringe of gray hair, clean-cut round face with startling blue eyes behind thick glasses. His rumpled suit was good quality, but had seen better days. He looked like he'd slept in it. Twice.

"You're here about the gargoyle, I take it?"

"Yes. I hoped to join you for his interview."

"If Angus agrees, it's fine by me. Where is he?"

Trudy showed us to an interrogation room and a few minutes later, an officer escorted Angus inside.

"Are those necessary?" Oscar pointed to the cuffs binding Angus's hands in front of him.

"Standard procedure," snapped the officer, though he released Angus's right hand and locked the left to a ring on the steel table that was bolted to the floor. I waited until he left before reaching across the table to grab Angus's free hand in both of mine. His wings fluttered. At least they'd unbound those.

"Aw, Kyra, don't fret. I've been the rock in harder places than this before."

"What happened?" I asked.

"Wait." Oscar pulled a widget from his briefcase. "Do I have permission to record your statement?"

"Oh, aye. Do what you must."

Oscar fiddled with the widget, then spoke into it, stating the date and interview information. "Miss Kyra Greene has requested to be present for this interview. Do you consent?"

"Of course," Angus looked affronted. "She's family."

His words hit me like a bolt in my chest. I don't know why they surprised me. Angus *was* family. I couldn't stand the thought of anything happening to him.

"Good. Now please start at the beginning and tell us exactly what happened. Don't leave out any details."

"I didna kill her."

"From the beginning, please." Oscar had a tablet to take notes, and he tapped it impatiently with his stylus.

"Fine." Angus leaned back in his chair, breaking my grip on his hand. He looked deflated, like this whole episode had taken the wind from him.

"We've been keeping an eye on Gerard Golovin's place. He has a fine, big house on Buzzard Island, right up against the northwest Apex tower."

"When you say we, you mean the Guardians?"

"Aye. Me and the boys. We take turns. Nothing too prying. We just swing by there once or twice a week to make sure Gerard and that witch he's keeping like a princess aren't up to no good."

"The witch?" Oscar raised an eyebrow.

"Polina. His new girlfriend. And Mason's ex-wife." He growled that out. "You might have heard something about her arrival last year. Around the time Gerard stepped down as prime minister."

"Ah, yes. I've seen her with him at events to promote the new railroad. Quite a strikingly beautiful woman," Oscar said.

Or so beautiful you want to strike her. I kept the thought to myself. Pettiness isn't a good look on anyone.

"Beauty that doesn't break the skin. She's evil. Don't make any mistake about that." Angus shook his head, and the spring leaves in his hair rustled.

"So I was on my usual patrol—"

"Alone?"

"Aye. We're spread a bit thin these days. Berto flew over Gerard's compound the night before and thought he spotted some unusual activity. So I went on a bit of a scout."

"What kind of activity?"

"A mustering, he said. A lot of movement in the yard behind the house, but he couldna get close enough to see who they were. So I snuck in. It wasna easy. There be wall around the place. It's new too. Not a bit of moss or greenery growin' on it. I asked myself, why does Gerard and his witch need such a big wall all of a sudden?" Angus's craggy face looked stern. I could always tell when he got agitated. His accent thickened.

"And did you find out?"

"No. I didna get the chance. Susanna found me in the woods."

"The dead woman?"

Angus nodded. "I don't know how she knew I was there. I must 'ave tripped some alarm. She fell on me from above. I didna even see her coming. And she is…*was* wicked good with a knife. I barely had time to get my blade out before she cut me twice. Here and here." He pointed to his face and his right shoulder.

Oscar leaned in for a better look. "I don't see any wounds."

"Course not. We gargoyles heal with the change."

"That's not good." Oscar tapped his tablet. "We've no proof that she struck you first."

"You've my word!" Angus jumped up, rattling the metal cuff that chained him to the desk.

"Your word is not proof." Oscar's tone was gentle. "But please continue."

Angus sat. "We fought. It was vicious. Susanna was a slip of a girl, but she knew her way around a blade. And she was fast. I cut her a dozen times before she went down."

Oscar frowned. "Be clear here. By 'went down' do you mean you killed her?"

"No! She fell. Tripped on a tree root that I called up."

Oscar looked confused, and I said, "Angus has dryad magic." The lawyer nodded and waved at Angus to continue.

"I'd lost my knife by that point. Magic was the only weapon I had left. I called to the trees and they heeded me. As the roots wrapped around her ankles, she threw her knife. Hit me in the gut. To be sure, if the sun had taken any longer to rise, I'd be a dead man. But she was alive when she fell."

We waited for Angus to continue. He seemed tormented by the memories of his fight. Finally, he said in a quiet voice, "I didna want to hurt her, you understand. She was just a wee girl." He rubbed his eyes. I wasn't sure Angus could actually make tears, but his distress was evident.

"I lay there, bleedin' from the guts, and she was hurtin' too. I heard her grunting, fighting with the roots that had her legs all tangled. Funny, but even though she'd nearly gutted me, I felt bad for her. My magic had gotten away from me by that point. I was too weak to call it back, but I tried to help her out of the mess. She kicked at me, but her wounds were making her weak too.

"And that's when the pair of devils showed up. Gerard and Polina, with their damn dog. It was that beastie that scented the blood, no doubt. Gerard near choked on his own spit when he saw Susanna lyin' all bloodied up. He rushed over and took the girl in his arms." He smiled. "Polina didna like that, I tell you. Not one bit. The look on her face could have soured the milk in a mother's teats. She sent Gerard back to the house for an axe to cut Susanna out. While he was gone…" His voice dropped, his eyes bore into mine. "She took my knife and slit that poor girl's throat. But that's not the worst of it. By Dagda's breath, she drank it! Blood all over her face. Then she pulled out a vial from a chain around her neck and collected the blood. Like the poor girl was a cow in need of milkin'." He shivered and his gaze was bleak. The room fell silent except for the hum of the lighting fixture overhead.

"And when Golovin came back with the axe, she wept big crocodile tears for the granddaughter she lost, even while Susanna's blood was dryin' on her lips." He shook his head, unbelieving.

I couldn't say that Susanna was innocent, or even that I cared for her. She'd played me. She'd also been the catalyst that brought Joran and Pierre to Montreal, the catalyst that caused the deaths and injuries of people I loved. But still, Susanna was Polina's own granddaughter. Or great-great, many greats removed granddaughter. She was the closest thing to family Polina had in this world.

"And why do you think she did it?" Oscar asked. The question caught me off-guard. Wrapped up in the horror of it all, I didn't stop to consider the implications. Mason had called it. He'd said Susanna would live only so long as she was useful to Polina. It seemed that Susanna's services were no longer needed.

Oscar's penetrating gaze was sharp as he prodded Angus again. "Why would she murder the girl?"

"Who knows? She didna like the way Gerard ran for Susanna. Jealousy? Or maybe she saw an opportunity to take out one of Mason's team." He thumped his chest.

"She did vow to see Mason's family destroyed," I said to Oscar.

He nodded thoughtfully, and turned back to Angus. "So why didn't she just kill you too? Sounds like you were an easy target."

"I was. But the sun was my savior for once. I changed just as she came for me. She was mighty pissed about that too. But she could 'ave still done me in. That woman has power. She reeks of it. Wouldna even strain a muscle to blast me into a million little pieces. Instead, she tossed the knife at my feet and walked away. To call Hub, I assume. They showed up some time later and kept me company until they could cuff me at sundown." He rattled the chain attaching him to the table.

Oscar stopped the recording and sat back. His gaze turned inward as he thought over the options for Angus. "So you didn't kill her. You just stabbed her a few times—"

"In self-defense!" Angus protested.

"That we can't prove. This is serious, my friend. No doubt your DNA is all over that girl."

I wasn't sure that gargoyles had DNA, but whatever. Hub would find forensic evidence to link Angus to the crime.

"We have only your word that she attacked you first," Oscar continued, "and let's face it, no jury is going to believe it. You were there snooping, you're twice her size, you have no visible injuries and you're known to work with an unsanctioned vigilante group." Oscar counted off each check mark against Angus on his fingers. "It doesn't look good. I have some favors I can call in to get you out on bail, but I'm afraid this will go to trial."

For once, Angus had no snappy comeback. Oscar rose and shook his hand.

"I'll make some calls to set up bail." Then he left.

"Angus, I'm so sorry," I said.

He shook his head, looking grim. "This is only the beginning. I fear that when Mason returns, his whole house will be gone up in flames."

And I feared that Mason wasn't coming back at all, but I wouldn't say those words out loud. Not yet.

"You think she's targeting Guardians?" I asked.

"Maybe. Or I was just a happy opportunity. Now that she's started, she'll escalate quickly. We have to prepare." He rubbed a rough hand over his face. "I could kick myself for getting caught."

"It's not your fault." I had other soothing platitudes for him, but the door opened and an officer came to escort Angus back to the holding cell. I followed behind them.

"As soon as you're out of here, we'll make plans," I said.

"Don't wait for me," Angus called over his shoulder as the officer hauled him away. "Get your critters and your banshee somewhere safe. Do it now before Polina takes it to the next level."

I was about to answer him when a shriek cut me off.

Polina stormed through Hub's front door.

"Murderer! You killed my baby girl!"

Polina rounded the corner and flew at us. Her eyes blazed fury.

"You killed her!" She raised a hand to strike Angus, but Gerard Golovin held her back. A small dog yapped at her heels, excited by the raised voice. She jerked its leash, and it yelped. Polina sniffled and turned to sob into Gerard's shoulder. He considered us with hate-filled eyes. As the officer pushed Angus down the hall, Polina reached out with fingers bent into claws. She meant to rake his face or cast a spell. I didn't wait to find out which and put myself between Angus and her grasping fingers. The dog snarled, but I'd faced scarier things than chihuahuas. Polina took her eyes off Angus long enough to skewer me with her glare.

That's right, witch. Focus here.

I wanted to give Angus time to get away, but the inept Hub officer stopped in front of Polina.

"Is there something I can help you with, Miss?" he asked with a shy smile.

Polina whipped her gaze to him, then softened. It was like watching her put on a mask. Her features went from livid to coquettish in an instant.

"It's Mrs. Grimaldi or Madame, if you prefer."

"Of course, Madame." The boy squirmed in the light of Polina's glow. "Is this woman bothering you? Shall I have someone show her out?"

Now it was my turn to glare. What in the hells had I done?

"No, thank you. That's very kind. I'm simply overwrought by the death of my dear…my dear…" She folded into Gerard's arms again. He held her protectively until Angus and the officer disappeared through a door at the end of the hall.

Then Polina sniffled and asked Gerard to find her some water. As soon as he left, Polina dropped the act and rounded on me.

"You identified Susanna's body, I'm told." Despite the tears, her makeup was perfect and her blond hair coiffed into a stylish do. The look had to be a glamor, but I couldn't sense it. Instead, my keening picked up a boiling cloud of magic surrounding her like a protective ward. Interesting. What was she? A ghost? A demon? Certainly not human.

"Yes. I identified her." I forced myself to stand still and not back away under her fierce gaze.

"What gave you the right?"

"I was asked to. I knew Susanna when she worked here, and the officers in charge said you were too upset to come in. That's understandable. It would be distressing to murder your own granddaughter."

"Why would I kill her?" Polina pretended to look affronted. "She was my flesh and blood, my little girl…"

"Cut the crap. Angus told me what happened. The only thing I can't figure out is why you would do it. Why kill Susanna?"

"Why wouldn't I? She was nothing to me! A pretentious brat. But you'll never prove it. Mason's pet green man is going to jail. I hear there's quite a nasty little island near here where Montreal drops its worst offenders and forgets them." She meant Grandill, where criminals of the ward were imprisoned to live out their remaining days. Between the murders and the wild beasts on the island, most didn't survive a week. "Angus should bloom like a spring rose there. Or not. Either way, Mason will…"

"Oh, my gods. Do you ever shut up?"

She looked like I slapped her. I took the moment of quiet to lean in and whisper, "I will prove that you killed her. Angus has friends. A lot of them. And we're already working on it."

Polina considered me. "Aren't you cute? You have nothing. Angus will go down for murder." Polina smiled. It wasn't the soft, welcoming smile she used like a spell to entrap every man she came across. This was a reptilian smile that turned her eyes to glass.

"Anyway, he'll soon have company because I plan to send the rest of the Guardians there too," she paused, looking thoughtful. "If I don't kill them. So many ways to make Mason's world crumble! Tell me, where is Mason? I haven't heard from him in months. That's so unlike my husband. I thought for sure he'd try to kill me by now. I'm starting to think that he's run away."

I didn't want to give her anything, but the retort popped out before I could stop it. "He's not your husband."

"Oh, but he is. 'Til death do us part. So tell me, where is he?"

This time, she laced the words with power. I felt it encircle me, prodding me, trying to force me to speak the truth. But I'd been barricading myself behind wards since I was a child. Her simple spell had no effect, and I wagered that she wouldn't try anything too messy here in the Hub lobby with half a dozen officers only a shout away.

When she realized her spell wasn't working, she dropped it and smiled.

"No matter. When he gets home, he'll find his house on fire and his Guardians smashed to dust. I will take everything from him, even you."

Through all this, the dog whined and pawed the floor. The beast looked like a chihuahua had mated with a naked mole rat. Its black eyes bulged from a nearly hairless face with one snaggle-tooth sticking up into its nose. And Polina had topped this monstrosity with a pink bow.

"Princess! Heel!" Polina snapped the leash. The dog snarled, then slunk behind her mistress.

"Your hound could learn some manners," I said. Then I turned my back on her. As I headed for the front doors of the lobby, I felt that itch between my shoulders—the itch you get when someone has you in their sights, about to pull the trigger.

Let her take her best shot. I knew she was coming for me and I would be ready.

C H A P T E R

5

Willow yowled in that particular way cats do when distressed. Something fell with a thunk. I shot out of bed, awake in an instant, and skidded to a halt in the living room as my bare feet hit dirt and broken flower pot shards. Willow flew by in a flash of gray. She crashed into a second plant stand and bounced off the wall before tearing after her prey again. I grabbed the teetering stand before it toppled.

"Gita!" I hollered. The banshee stuck her head out of her closet. When she saw the mess on the floor, she tsked, then went back inside and shut the door.

I scanned the cages to see which critter had taunted Willow into a game of early morning chase and found one empty.

Last week I'd trapped two new rodents at Emil's lodging house. I should have re-homed them to Dorion park, but they were such oddities. I wanted to find out more about their origins. And Gabe took an instant liking to them. So I'd put them in a wire cage, thinking they were secure. Wrong.

Something skittered past my ankles. I grabbed Willow as she zoomed by again and dumped her outside.

Still in the tank-top and panties I wore to bed, I headed through the door to the office, expecting to find it empty at this time of morning.

"It's a little informal for the job." Gabe pointed to my attire.

"I was sleeping." I ran a hand through my hair. "Those rats you like so much woke me up. They got loose again." I scowled. When trying to look dignified in nothing but panties, taking the offense worked best.

"They're not rats."

"Whatever. Just get me a glass terrarium. There's an extra one in the garage under all that junk beside the weapons closet."

I returned to the apartment to clean up the broken planters. A few minutes later, Gabe came in with a small terrarium and a bag of sand.

"Now we just have to catch them," I said.

Gabe let out a series of three short whistles. The rodents skittered out from under the couch and sat at his feet like eager puppies awaiting a treat.

"How'd you do that?" I asked.

"I've been training them."

Gabe whistled again, and the critters turned circles around his ankles. They had long lizard tails, but their front halves were mouse-like with black beady eyes, pink pointed noses and twitchy whiskers. Or maybe hedgehogs, since they had manes of spiky fur that blended into the lizard scales. Either way, they didn't act like rodents. They had none of that knee-jerk prey fear. I had no idea what they were, but I was calling them squamus or maybe squamice for plural.

Gabe picked them up. The one in his left hand was slightly larger. Its white mouse fur and spikes gave way to greenish scales.

"I named her Sweet Pea. And she's Niblet." He held up the smaller one, whose scales had a yellow cast.

"That's it, then. You gave them names. Now we'll never get rid of them." I petted Sweet Pea's head with one finger. "They're kind of cute though." Sweat Pea nudged me with her nose.

"And smart. Look." He pointed to their cage. They hadn't slipped through the wire mesh. They'd piled up the cage toys until they could reach the lid and escape that way. Gabe dumped the critters back in the cage. He held up one finger and moved it to the left. Their eyes tracked it. He moved it again, and they followed.

"Let's set the terrarium up in the office," he said. "I want to study them some more. Who knows, they might come in handy on the job, getting into tight spaces you can't reach. I'm looking into some kind of surveillance equipment that we could attach to them."

"Huh. Rodent scouts. It might work. Take them into the office, then." A sudden thought hit me. "Hey, wait! What are you doing here on a Sunday?"

Gabe looked away. "I wanted to get a start on that pond out back for Hunter."

Hunter was my pygmy kraken. He lived in a tank beside the couch in my living room—a tank that was too small for him and the abaia eel he shared it with. Unfortunately, my place wasn't big enough for a larger tank or even two small ones, so Gabe had offered to build an outdoor pool that they could use during the summer. And next winter? Well, I'd figure that problem out then.

"That doesn't explain why you're here so early."

Gabe flushed, making his golden skin and brown eyes light up. "I…uh… escaped from a bad date in the middle of the night. It was closer to come here than go home."

I frowned. That was the third bad date this week.

"Are you okay?"

"Just tired."

As Gabe left to deal with the squamice, I tried to dismiss my worry. Since breaking up with Dutch, a parade of gorgeous young men and women had lined up to help soothe his broken heart. But so far, none of them were successful.

I sighed. Maybe I should put a cot in the garage. We already used it as a gym, war room, storage and weapons locker. Why not a spare bedroom too?

Since I was up, I went to shower and dress. But first I had to pluck Hunter, sucker by sucker, off the tile where he hung out in the corner of my bath.

After breakfast, I spent time with Jacoby. Gita had built a shrine of blankets and pillows that she ringed in fresh herbs. The fire dervish remained in a coma since being used as a magic battery last fall. At least I thought it was a coma. His breathing was so slow, it was more like a hibernation. I laid my head on his furry chest to feel the faint glow of magic deep within him. Every morning I hoped that today he would show signs of life. And every morning I was disappointed. He never changed. He never moved. He just lay on his pillow like Snow White waiting for her prince.

This morning was no different.

I smoothed the kinky fur around his eyes and adjusted his stuffed bear which was about to slip off the pillow. Maybe tomorrow.

I headed to the kitchen for coffee. Gita was watering herbs under the grow-light. I touched their little spirits with my green magic. The plants were happy and excited about Gita's ministrations. I was learning to incorporate this other magic into my everyday life. It was so different from my keening and the Valkyrie magic that let me create glamors and heat my sword with a touch. Dryad magic was more passive. I had to call to the plants, and ask for an invitation before I could wrap myself in their energy. It was still a struggle, but I now felt confident that one day, my two heritages would no longer clash inside me. One day, communicating with plants would feel as natural as keening.

"I need more clover," Gita said, holding up a pot. "Not enough four-leafers in this bunch." She sniffed.

"I can see what Nesi's got in his shop later. How's Clarence doing this morning?" I asked.

Gita sniffed again and handed me a steaming cup of coffee. "Took his medicine too easily. I don't like it. Looks like a gizzard stone."

Like chickens, basilisks ate rocks to help grind food in their gizzard. But basilisks weren't chickens. They weren't lizards either. They were something that our world didn't understand and had no tools to mend if broken. Once every few months, Clarence coughed up a pearl-like stone. I had a theory that it was polished in his gizzard, like a rock in a tumbler. But why he expelled only those few stones, I didn't know. They were kind of pretty—jet black and iridescent—and prized on the black market. I had a jar full of them, but so far neither Gita nor I could find anything magical about them.

To make things worse, when Clarence molted he gobbled up the feathers that fell out of his avian side and the skin that shed from his reptile side. This was an instinctual reaction to hide from prey in the wild, but it sometimes left him with an intestinal blockage. So, gizzard stone or bad molt? Either way, Gita's special hair-ball remedy eased the process. He usually fought us like a hellcat when we tried to administer the medicine. That he accepted it easily was not a good sign. Worry tugged at my heart, but then worry seemed a way of life these days. Worry for Clarence, worry for Gabe and Jacoby. And Mason.

Mason had been gone for five months. He left for France right after Pierre released Polina from the bloodstone, hoping to bring back a weapon that could defeat her. Every day that went by without hearing from him convinced me a little more that he was never coming home. My mind shied away from that thought. His absence was still an open wound and I wasn't ready to let it scar over yet.

Willow twined around my ankles, looking for a second breakfast. I picked her up and hugged her hard. She squirmed until I put her down, and I dumped a handful of kibble in her bowl even though it wasn't empty. Because I was a sucker for her kitty face.

"You spoil her." Gita frowned and wiped tears from her eyes.

"Yep." I didn't bother to argue. Gita would have done the same if I wasn't looking.

I checked on Clarence. He lay like a wet rag in his pen. There was nothing I could do for him. And by the One-eyed God, I was sick of saying that.

I needed a distraction.

BY LATE AFTERNOON, I'd cleaned all the critter habitats and vacuumed up the hay, sawdust and sand that never managed to stay inside the cages. My kitchen and bathroom sparkled and I'd started the laundry. None of it was enough to distract me. My thoughts relentlessly strayed to the people I loved and couldn't help. Angus. Jacoby. Clarence. Mason. There was not enough dirt in the world to squash my worry.

It was time for fresh air and a change of scenery.

"Hey, Errol, want to help me check the wards?" I asked.

The bodach stuck his head out of the ceramic house beside my bonsai tree.

"Fglfmbth." A distinct feeling of grumpy agreement splashed across my mind. Errol communicated with a peculiar mind-speak. Though his words were unintelligible, their meaning was always clear in my head.

Jacoby had landed in Pierre's machine to save Errol, and the bodach wouldn't forgive himself if Jacoby didn't wake up. After the attack, Errol had lost his unique ability to mind-speak. It had returned after a few weeks, but Errol was changed. His moods were darker, and I could often feel his anger and guilt like they were my own. A bit of sunshine would do us both good.

I scooped up Errol and headed outside to find Gabe digging a pit in the backyard. It was a beautiful May afternoon. The air held the promise of summer. Gabe had stripped to his jeans, and I took a moment to savor the sight of his sweat-slicked, rippled abs. Hey, a girl can look. It had been so long since I felt the touch of a man. A sudden deep and shocking longing for Mason hit me like a knife to the gut.

"Put your tongue back in your mouth," Emil whispered, coming up behind me. "It's a very unattractive look on a lady."

"As if you weren't having the same thoughts." I quirked an eyebrow at the vampire. I'd seen the way Emil's eyes tracked Gabe.

"But I'm no lady." He shook his head. "Besides, I have my bloodlust under control. No more kissing for me, remember?"

Emil had used the same spell from Queen Leighna that put my sword into a kind of stasis. The queen had warned that, like many fae spells, a kiss would break it. So, while Emil no longer thirsted for the taste of human blood, his love-life had taken a serious hit. If he had feelings for Gabe, that was probably a good thing.

"What are you guys whispering about?" Gabe stopped digging and leaned on the shovel. Wow. That pose belonged on the cover of a bodice-ripping novel.

"Just admiring the landscape," Emil said.

I dug an elbow into his ribs.

"How's the new pool coming?" I asked.

"I think it's deep enough. I'm just cleaning up the edges." Gabe pointed to a spade stuck in the wet earth and said to Emil, "You can get your hands dirty too."

Emil sighed like Gabe had asked him to hold up the world. "These are designer boots, and I won't even let you guess at the price of this shirt."

"So take them off," growled Gabe. "You came here to help, didn't you?"

"I suppose." Emil kicked off his boots and pulled off his shirt. Next to Gabe's bronze sheen, his skin gleamed alabaster white in the sun. And unlike Gabe's brawniness, he was lean and lithe with a runner's musculature.

"You're going to burn," I warned. "There are work clothes in the garage." Opji vampires avoided the sun. They wouldn't burst into flames like in the old movies, but their eyes were sensitive to light and they sunburned easily.

When he left, I pointed to the squamice dancing around Gabe's ankles.

"What's with the little brats?" They were the busiest critters I'd ever encountered. I had yet to catch them asleep, and they never seemed to stop moving.

"Aw, they're not so bad," Gabe said. "They just need a job. Like herding dogs."

The mice-lizards had proven that nothing was safe from their curiosity and their nimble little hands.

"So you found them a job digging ditches?"

Before Gabe could answer, the office widget vibrated in his back pocket.

"Valkyrie Pest Control. How may I help you?"

Gabe's sunny smiled disappeared, and he turned away to whisper into the widget.

"I told you not to call me on this line." Pause. "Yes, I left early. I said I would." Pause. "No, I can't get away for lunch. Not even for that." He saw me watching with raised eyebrows and stalked off around the side of the garage to finish the call in private.

Emil returned, wearing old coveralls and a straw hat.

"Which one was that?" I asked

"Marla. She won't last out the week. Too clingy."

"Gabe doesn't last a week with anyone these days," I mumbled. Not that I had anything against consensual sex among adults, even a lot of sex. But Gabe seemed a little manic about it lately, like he was trying to extinguish the memory of Dutch between the sheets.

"When you look like that…" Emil paused and smiled sadly. "Well, let's just say, when we go out, there's never a shortage of fine looking people who want to go home with Gabe."

Poor Emil. He had it bad.

I left the guys to their digging and walked the perimeter of my yard with Errol tagging along behind me. His small stature made it hard for him to keep up normally, but I moved slowly, checking the wards. If Polina was coming for us, I wanted to know my defenses were sound.

After Joran's attack, I'd boosted the wards. Anything bigger than a raccoon had to come through the front door. Breaking the boundary ward would send a magic shock wave that I would feel from anywhere. It wasn't perfect, but at least no one could ambush us. And I'd keyed all my mobile rescues to the new ward, so they could come and go, even Jacoby. Because someday, somehow, I'd wake him up.

Errol's keening was at least as good as mine, so as we walked, we both searched the ward for any soft spots, places where the anchors were coming loose.

"Mfggnth." *Here. You need to build it up right here.*

"You're right. This section needs boosting."

Errol had very little arcane skill, other than his ability to fry anything electrical when agitated. But he could detect even the tiniest grain of magic. And he could boost magic in others. He'd been instrumental in helping me unlock the green side to my power. Now he held up his walking twig and grumbled.

"kvthmt." *Need help?*

"No. I've got this. Why don't you walk the perimeter and let me know if you find any more holes. Oh! And look for four-leaf clovers. Gita needs them for Clarence's tincture."

I patched the ward, adding a touch of green magic to camouflage it. Errol returned and grunted his approval. I was pleased with myself. It had been a long haul to master my green magic. It was still untested in the field, but I felt confident that if I needed it, I could call on the power of any natural environment. I just hoped I wouldn't have to test it.

"Gthmbth." Errol held up a four-leaf clover. *There's more.*

"Show me."

He led me back toward the yard, to a patch of grass and clover growing beside the new pool. It was too early in the season for a really good crop, but I found a few more four-leafers. Instead of plucking them, I decided to try something new.

"Do you think I can force it to grow?"

Errol took off his ratty hat and scratched his bald head. "Hrthblt." *It's risky.*

"Maybe. But Gita needs them. She's convinced they will help Clarence."

He shrugged and I sat in the dirt to contemplate the problem. How could I convince the clovers to reproduce faster?

"What'cha doing?" Gabe had disappeared but now returned with a hose.

"I'm trying to grow clover. What are you doing? That hole won't hold water, you need to line it with something."

He scowled. "You think I don't know that? I want to loosen some rocks at the bottom. The earth is like clay, and I'm tired of digging."

"Okay. Just don't get me wet."

I left him to it and turned to the patch of clover. I could do this. I narrowed my focus to one four-leaf clover. The plant's tiny energy sang to me. I fed it a bit of magic and it responded by growing about an inch. But I didn't just want it to grow. I wanted it to replicate, to make a dozen more four-leafers. This was a much more delicate communication than I'd ever attempted. I sank into meditation. My mind filled with green life, blue water, yellow light. The loamy smell of spring rot and the spicy scent of earth baking under the summer sun.

These are the plant's memories! Memories of the species, so ingrained that every new shoot of clover had the same impressions from birth.

I don't know how long I sat ruminating on the eternal life of a clover, but I got no closer to convincing it to reproduce. After a while, I came back to myself and stretched. Only the afterglow of the setting sun remained. The yard had turned dark and cold. I'd been lost in the magic for hours, but it felt like minutes. At least, for those few hours, my thoughts had been free of worry for the first time in a while.

Gabe was gone. The pool was half full of muddy water, but I saw three large rocks piled at the edge. He'd pulled them out and I hadn't even noticed.

Errol had stayed with me. He dozed in the grass beside my foot. I nudged him.

"Hey, it didn't work. Let's go inside."

He snorted awake, and after getting his bearings, he pointed at the clover. "Mggbth." *Try again. I'll help.*

"Fine." I was already sitting in the dirt. "Let's do this."

I sank back into my focused stance. It was easier this time. The clovers welcomed me. I felt at home. I reached a hand to touch the tiny leaf. Errol grasped my finger, shooting his own power through me like a bolt of white-hot lightning.

Magic burned along my nerves and erupted from my pores. I jerked away, not wanting to hurt the plants, and magic erupted from me in a lashing torrent that sounded like a clap of thunder. The backlash knocked me back ten feet. I landed in a cold splash, right in the middle of Hunter's pond.

I sat up sputtering and dripping muddy water. Mr. Murray poked his head out the window to grump about the noise, saw the smoking grass, and retreated.

Errol laughed so hard, he rolled on the ground.

"Ha, ha." As I stepped from the pond, a clump of mud fell out of my hair. I wiped my face on a wet sleeve.

"You have a visitor," Gabe said, coming around the side of the garage. "And it looks like perfect timing. Did you bathe in the mud?"

My stomach filled with fluttery things. Could it be him?

I was sopping wet and covered in mud. This was exactly the moment Mason would choose to come back to me. And I didn't care how I looked. I would eat mud if it meant he was home.

I jumped out of the pond and ran toward the garage. And there, standing on the cracked pavement beside my dumpster was…

…Betsy Lacroix.

Her face looked harder than I remembered, like she'd aged ten years instead of just a few months. She'd cut her blond curls into spikes that accentuated her fae look.

"I can't deal with these anymore. You take them." She shoved a plastic bin at me.

Last fall, I'd tried to help Betsy find her sister Maeve, who'd gone missing. We'd found her, but not soon enough. Unfortunately, Gerard Golovin's alchemists had turned her into a golem-like creature, and when she tried to get back home, Hub officers killed her.

"What's in the box?" I asked as I pried it open.

"Don't!" Betsy slammed her hand on the lid. "It's those fifollet things. What did you call them? Will o'wisps? I tried to keep them for Maeve's sake, but I can't figure out what they eat. And if they escape, you'll never get them back in the box. Believe me. It took me two hours to move them from their cage."

"What am I supposed to do with them?" I shot a glance at Gabe, but he just shrugged.

"I don't know!" Betsy's voice rose. "That's what you do, isn't it? You deal with freaks." Then she got back in her car and took off, leaving me with the bin of will o'wisps.

I sighed, and peered through the translucent plastic.

"Any idea what these things eat?" I asked.

"On it," Gabe said as he flicked through pages on his widget. "Not much info here. Most citations seem to think they're a myth brought about by sightings of bio-luminescent swamp gas." He frowned. "I'll keep looking."

"Well, I'm going to clean up. Tomorrow, I'll go see Nesi. Maybe he'll have some answers." I tucked the box under my arm and headed inside.

Some days I wondered: if I live in a madhouse, does that make me crazy too?

A Glory of Will O'Wisps

May 5, 2081

Will o'wisps have gone by many names over the centuries: ghost light, feu follet, jack o'lantern, hobby lantern, hinkypunk, and my favorite, Ignis fatuus (Latin for "foolish flame").

People once believed these mysterious lights were lanterns held by hobgoblins or other fae creatures as they walked through woods or marshes, luring lost travelers to their doom (hence the name hobby lantern). Others believed the wisps were elemental spirits. A more modern view is that these eerie lights are a product of swamp gases being released. This hypothesis has some merit, since wisp sightings often happen at night.

I won't discount any of those theories entirely. It's quite possible that a lost traveler was once led astray (and probably eaten) by a hobgoblin. And maybe there are elemental spirits as small as fireflies. And swamp gas? Sure. I'll buy that.

But I can add to this discussion with my experience.

I now have in my possession a bunch of feu follets. Will o'wisps. Would that be a flock? A swarm? I'm going to call it a glory of will o'wisps because when they fly around, filling the night with light, my heart feels full.

Their magic doesn't taste elemental to me, though they are incorporeal, in that I can see right through them. But they are definitely a creature of some sort. They look like little floating, faceless pigs. My guess is that these creatures are not native to Terra but came through a crack in the veil during the wars.

They seem friendly enough so far. They're zippy and fun, but annoying when they swarm around your face. Like sprites without the teeth.

So, I bring you another critter conundrum. What do will o'wisps eat? I am at a loss. They show no interest in any corporeal food, which makes sense. How would they digest it? I've had them for about a week now and haven't seen them eat anything. I'm getting worried. All reasonable suggestions will be considered.

COMMENTS (6)

Could they eat swamp gas?
Cryptoman498 (May 5, 2081)

> Good answer! I'll see if I can find some swamp gas. Maybe in the Laval Flood Plains. Thanks!
> *Valkyrie367 (May 5, 2081)*

I have an old grimoire here that calls for one cup of "will o'wisp light." I don't know how you'd even capture that, but there is a handwritten notation in the margin to find it in a cemetery.
ThatAlchemyGuy (May 5, 2081)

If it is an elemental spirit, it would thrive in its element. Try fire, wind, water and earth. My guess would be fire.
cchedgewitch (May 6, 2081)

> Good thinking. I lit a candle for them, but they didn't seem interested. The shower was a bust too. There's earth in my apartment from all the plants, but they haven't taken an interest in that either. Wind? I guess I'll have to wait for a storm to try it.
> *Valkyrie367 (May 6, 2081)*

Stop filling the world with your lies. God is the only elemental spirit.
Truckinalong (May 7, 2081)

bbott's Agora sprawled across several acres of land in front of the old college in Sayntanne, only a few blocks from my place. The market had grown over the years from a few stalls of farm goods to shops of every kind, many specializing in the arcane arts. People traveled from the east end of the ward just for the experience of walking its winding lane ways.

I remembered how Jacoby loved to touch every item on display like a toddler hyped up on sugar. I let myself smile at that memory for a moment before tucking it away.

Jacoby would recover. I would make sure of it.

As I passed a stand of old oak trees with Penfield Hall looming behind them, other memories tugged at me. Mason and I stealing a few moments alone in the shadow of those trees. But Mason was gone, the gods only knew where. He could be dead. No. I pulled my thoughts away from that precipice.

"Hey, watch it!" A gnome growled as I nearly stepped on him.

"Sorry." I put the memories and worry on hold to pay attention to my surroundings.

The afternoon sun cast white light on the shacks that lined the path. People of every color, height and girth filled the lanes or stood behind tables piled high with produce, antiques, and handmade goods of all sorts. A family of shape shifters had moved in, selling caps, mitts and boots made from the fur of small animals. It would be dangerous work to hunt those in the Inbetween. But even in early May they did brisk business.

I passed by the witches who sold philters and other potions. An ogre sharpened knives on his grinding wheel. He was small for an ogre, but he stood head and shoulders above everyone else. And there was the usual assortment of fae, alchemists, godlings and humans browsing shoulder to shoulder.

I loved this place. It gave me faith that the founders of Montreal Ward had been right to work together and that we could continue living in harmony, despite the few rabble-rousers like Gerard Golovin.

Last year, Golovin, then the alchemist prime minister, had pushed a bill through parliament to build a new railroad that would reach Manhattan Ward. When construction proved too dangerous, he built a crew of golem-like creatures to do the heavy digging, just in case Terra showed her displeasure by collapsing the new tunnel. Unfortunately, Mason's old friend Pierre Garnier had created the golems using forbidden magic. He'd stolen the souls of dozens of fae to animate them. We'd stopped Pierre and recovered the illicit bloodstones, but Golovin's railroad project continued. In fact, they'd already met the Manhattan crew halfway between the two wards. In a few weeks they would launch the inaugural train from one ward to the other.

Something shimmered on the edge of my vision. I turned into the sun and squinted. Ghosts are hard to see in the daytime, which is why most hauntings happen at night. But they're always there. And for those of us who do see them, they can be distracting, like a smudge on your sunglasses that you just can't get rid of.

This ghost wove in and out of the crowd and around merchandise tables. Was it following me? Probably not. Since I'd put my sword to sleep, the local ghosts had left me alone. I was no longer the gateway to the other world that many of them craved.

I turned down a lane way and stopped, pretended to admire a stall full of dried gourds. A flicker of light at the edge of my vision told me the ghost had turned the corner too. Two more turns and I was certain it followed me. There was no point reaching for it with my keening. The amount of magic in the market made that sense useless.

I glanced back once more but couldn't spot the ghost. Then I ducked through the hanging cloth that marked the doorway to Nesi's shop.

"Ah! Just the princess I wanted to see." Nesi still believed I was royalty from another planet. He looked up from the massive book he'd been reading.

A jeweler's loupe was forgotten on his forehead and his one good eye focused on me with sharp intelligence. His other milky eye leaked tears down his face. He didn't bother to wipe them away, and I wasn't sure he even noticed.

"I might have news about the dervish," he said, closing the old book before I could see inside it. Nesi had an impressive library of occult books, but he was stingy with their contents. He'd scanned some of the lesser tomes and put them on the ley-web, but that was just a marketing ploy to get real magic users interested.

Other than the books, his shop was crammed with crystals, shrunken heads, bunches of dried herbs and cages filled with birds and other creatures.

"News like a cure?" I asked. Nesi had been searching for a remedy to Jacoby's condition since it happened. I'd all but lost hope that he would find something.

"A cure implies he's sick. He's not sick. He's lost."

"I'm not sure what that means."

Nesi tugged on one of the braids that dangled from his chin. "It means that when the dervish went nova, his spirit split away from his body. And he's having trouble finding his way back."

I shivered at the thought. Poor Jacoby!

"Is there anything you can do?"

He grunted. "Maybe. I'm looking into it." Then his face brightened when he saw the box I was holding. "Now what have you brought me today? Something to eat? Something to sell?"

"No. Just a couple of puzzles. And Gita wants some four-leaf clovers. Clarence is having a nasty molt. She wants to make a tincture."

"Is this enough?" He pulled a jar from a top shelf and handed it to me. It was full of dried clovers.

"Are they all four-leafers?"

Nesi's eyes narrowed. "You implying that I would cheat you?"

"No of course not. I'll take them all."

Then I laid the plastic box on his counter, careful not to disturb the baubles and crystals.

Nesi peered at the blue lights shimmering through the lid. Before I could stop him, he opened the box and the will o'wisps shot out. One flew right by my face in a flash of blue fire.

"I think they're will o'wisps," I said. "But up close, they look like tiny blue pigs on fire."

Nesi trapped one in his cupped hands and grunted. "They're sluggish. Shouldn't be able to catch one so easily."

"The girl I got them from inherited them from her dead sister. She doesn't know what to feed them. You think they're that weak?"

Nesi examined the tiny critter. "Tardigrade."

"What?"

"It looks more like a tardigrade or what some people call a water bear. Not a pig."

"I know what a tardigrade is," I said somewhat snappishly. Nesi liked to show off.

"Fascinating," he said. "I've never seen one up close. Though I suspected they were more than just swamp gas or fireflies."

"Any idea what they eat?"

"Not a clue." He pulled down another book and flipped through the stiff pages. "Only one brief mention of them here. Says they are frequently found in bogs—which we knew—and cemeteries. You could try releasing them into the Laval flood plains."

I considered that, but until I knew what they subsisted on, I didn't want to release them into some environment that could harm them or where they could do harm.

"Maybe I'll just pass by the cemetery later and see what happens."

Nesi nodded and pulled down a basket from a jumbled selection on a high shelf. It was tightly woven and shaped like a beehive. He removed the lid, turned it upside down and attached a string as a handle. When he held it up, the wisps settled inside like a cloud of sparks. He cupped the bottom of the basket with the lid.

"That should hold them better than a plastic box. They need air and freedom, but it's got a warding spell on it to keep them contained."

I thanked him and paid for the basket (and the spell), the clovers and a bag of crayfish for Hunter.

Outside, the sun was slanting toward night. I tugged my jacket around me to keep warm and scanned the market.

The ghost was nowhere in sight. Next stop: the cemetery.

approached the gates of Lakeview Eternal Gardens, though "gates" was an ambitious description. In reality, the wrought iron sign that once arched over the entrance was bent and rusted, with only "rdens" remaining to mark the spot. The cemetery had once been on the north side of the old highway, but that road had mostly crumbled into the water, I remembered biking here when I was a kid. A monument to fallen soldiers loomed at the top of the hill. It looked like a castle, and I'd pretended to be a princess battling invaders from inside my fortifications.

The old gate was stuck partially open by debris, and I squeezed through to stroll between the few remaining headstones, ignoring the loitering ghosts. The once immaculate pathways were cracked and bloated from flooding and cold winters. Most of the headstones were long gone, destroyed in the floods or looted for building material. It was a sorry sight.

The basket of wisps dangled from my arm, casting an eerie blue glow. I hoped, as the light faded, someone didn't mistake me for a hobgoblin.

Ahead and up the hill, the remains of the castle-like mausoleum were back lit by a blood-red sunset.

The wind whipped my hair, tugging it from my loose braids as I stared at my old playground. The castle's archway had collapsed, but the towers on either side remained. Standing among the ruins brought back vivid memories of a happy child playing princess warrior. I could see her bicycle dumped carelessly on the grass. She skipped under the archway, chanting stories she made up in her head, and she was blissfully unaware of the power that would manifest inside her in just a few more years. Or of the desperate turn her mother's illness would take, forcing them to flee to another world for a cure.

Had that really been me? Had I ever been that carefree?

While I tripped through memory lane, a gargoyle perched on the tower stretched his wings and stood.

If one thing proved how much I'd changed from that innocent girl, it was the fact that seeing a gargoyle come to life didn't even disturb me.

"Hello, Kyra." His grotesque face softened with a shy grin.

"Hi. It's Berto, right?"

He ducked his head in acknowledgment.

Berto was a lieutenant in Mason's Guardians, the vigilante gang that patrolled neighborhoods Hub was unwilling to police. I'd met him only a couple of times, but he was remarkable for his height. Most gargoyles were short in stature. Mason told me this was due to the difficulty of getting large chunks of marble in the old days. Berto had the usual gargoyle face—wide mouth, overhanging brow with a faint simian cast—but he was tall and lean.

He flexed his leathery wings, stretching them after his sleep. We were six weeks until the summer solstice and the days were getting longer.

"You must hate this time of year," I blurted, before my brain could filter my words.

Berto cocked his head. "Why do you say that?"

"I'm sorry. I just mean…the days are longer, and you're stuck in stone for so many more hours."

"It's not so bad." Berto looked up at the falling down mausoleum. "This is a nice spot to spend the day. There are squirrels and rabbits. And birds. They keep me company. I think I'd rather be stone than lose eight hours a night to the little death of sleep."

It was an interesting perspective I hadn't thought of before.

"If you'll excuse me, I'm on patrol soon." His legs tensed and wings flexed as he readied for flight.

"Berto?"

He relaxed and turned back to me.

I could barely say the words, but I couldn't *not* say them either.

"Have you heard from him?"

Berto's heavy brow lowered and he shook his head.

"Not since February." When he saw the look on my face, he stepped in and took my hand. My fingers disappeared inside his big, rough grip. "But I'm sure Captain Mason is fine. He'll be home soon with a wild tale of adventure. You take care until then." He patted my arm before launching into the sky.

I fought back irrational tears as I watched him disappear into the night. Then I turned to my task at hand.

What the hells am I doing here?

That thought kept repeating in my head. Not that graveyards bothered me. I'd spent most of the fall of '76 camped out here, battling an infestation of Baenas, two-headed mole-like creatures that could chew through wood and dirt. They ate through those to get to their favorite delicacy: decaying human bones. Yum. They were necrovores. Dead eaters.

Hub had paid me a pittance for that job, but it was my first work for ward officials and had led to many more lucrative gigs.

I hoped the will o'wisps didn't turn out to be necrovores too. The old bones didn't need their magic any longer, and they wouldn't begrudge giving a little to feed the wisps, but it was dirty work, reburying the dead.

Something was stirring up the wisps. They zipped around the inside of the basket and I was about to slip off the lid, when a ghost stepped out from behind the ruins of the fallen castle.

I jumped back. Usually, I let my keening scout unfamiliar territory, and I'd picked up the dozen or so remnants that hung around the old graves, but this one snuck up on me.

"How did you do that?" I asked.

She smirked and put one hand to her hip as she considered me. It was hard to tell the age of most ghosts; their diaphanous glow gave them nice clear complexions. This one had big eyes in a thin face. Dark glossy curls did nothing to soften the harsh lines of her nose and cheeks.

She leaned in and sniffed me, which was just silly because ghosts have no olfactory sense.

"You smell like a dryad. Don't tell me you can't hide yourself in the trees."

I had been practicing that kind of camouflage, but I wouldn't give away my secrets so easily.

I crossed my arms. "Why are you following me?" This had to be the same ghost I had spied at the market. I didn't like being followed, and I really didn't like dealing with nosy ghosts.

"I saw you in the lab with Queen Polina. You were there." Her accent was Eastern European. Polish, I thought. "And I know you saw us—the spooks. So I thought I'd follow you, see if we could…talk." She pursed her lips and looked away.

This happened a lot. Ghosts were drawn to people who could see them. But most ghosts were barely a memory of themselves, nothing more than a repeating gesture, like those hovering about their graves. But some ghosts had power, and they were more alive. Those ghosts, once they knew I could perceive them, were always desperate to chat. It was lonely, wandering the world with no one but the dead to talk to. Normally, I would make a quick excuse and be on my way, but this ghost stopped me in my tracks.

"*Queen* Polina?" No way. Mason's ex-wife was many things—witch, murderer, adulterer among them, but never a queen.

"That's what she made us call her. Those of us who survived her lust for magic, that is."

Now I understood. This ghost was one of the spirits that had been locked in the bloodstone with Polina. Mason lost the stone in the mid-twentieth century and during that time it gathered many more souls. In the aftermath of the explosion that freed Polina, thousands of souls spewed from the stone. I'd hoped they were dispersed and found their way to their proper afterlives.

"Are there more of you that remained on this plane?"

"A few dozen. Those that worship Polina. Even in our prison, they acted as her servants and minions. Now that they are free, they won't leave her."

"And you? You don't worship her?"

"Gods, no. She's a real…well, I'm too polite to say it, but it rhymes with witch." She grinned, and her form brightened as if humor somehow made her more corporeal for an instant.

"What's your name?" I asked.

"Naomi Balan." She held out her hand, then remembered I couldn't shake it. "Sorry. This being dead takes some getting used to. In the bloodstone it was different. We were all the same, so no one noticed we were dead, if that makes sense. But being back here…the world has changed so much, and yet so little. I forget that I can't touch things easily. And unless I make a real effort, no one can see me. Except you." She grinned. "That's why I followed you. You saw me at the market, I was sure of it. And see? I was right."

"So what…you want to just hang out?"

Naomi's face lit up. "That would be great."

I sighed. "I'm just here to figure out what these little beasts eat." I held up the basket. The wisps were spinning in a frenzy. "Once that's done, I'm going home. And you can't follow me there. Deal?"

"Deal."

I slipped the lid off the bottom of the basket. The fat little wisps zipped out and buzzed around my head. Their fiery blue shapes stood out in the fading light. They were pudgy and silly, like bumblebees.

"Go fetch or whatever you need to do," I said to one wisp that bobbed right in front of my head. It flew straight for Naomi. She squealed and slammed into me.

It was like being struck by a car. Sudden pain and breathlessness as she entered my body. Then I felt her stirring in my gut. Every nerve ending screamed about this impostor riding in my veins.

In a moment the feeling passed, but she was still lurking there, watching behind my eyes.

"Get out!" I shook my head and stomped my feet. No good. She was lodged in there. And then I saw why.

The wisps were bumbling about in the shadows when they sensed another loitering spook. The sweet little will o'wisps froze like rabbits caught in headlights. Then their blue light flared, casting a wan glow over the shuffling spirit. He was an old man, stooped and tired, but he lifted his chin and smiled.

I had only a moment to wonder who the poor soul was before the wisps attacked. I fell back in the dirt, landing hard on my hip as they plunged by me. They shimmered and bloated, as big as an apple, then bigger. The cute piggy snouts turned out not to be snouts at all. They opened into black maws with rows of shark-like teeth. The pack fell on the ghost, ethereal teeth sinking into his neck, arms and chest as they sucked the soul dry. Like a deflating balloon, the spook shriveled to nothing and disappeared with a sonic POP!

The will o'wisps turned to me. They hung in the night, and suddenly the piggy look wasn't so cute. They were monstrous.

Run! said the voice inside my head, but I recognized it as Naomi's, and I stood my ground until, one by one, the wisps shrank back to their normal size. They no longer danced, but bobbed like drunken slugs. I scooped them into the basket and jammed on the lid.

I hoped they didn't need to feed often because...ew!

"You're safe," I said. "Now get out of my head, or so help me, I'll find a priest and have you exorcised off this world."

The ghost clung to my mind like it was a life raft.

I sighed. Time for a little tough love. Sometimes, the dead were too scared or confused to accept death and they clung to any semblance of life. My Valkyrie training taught me how to deal with clingy spirits. I shoved Naomi from my mind with one big, psychic push.

"Hey!" She appeared beside me, her form agitated and sparking with white fire.

"Never do that again," I growled. Apart from being really creepy, possession by a ghost felt like pure violation, an assault on the core of my being where I kept all my little secrets, hurts and yearnings.

"I'm sorry! I panicked. What the hell are those things anyway?"

"They're your worst nightmare." I turned my back on her and stalked to my truck. "Go find someone else to haunt. I'm not interested."

For my birthday when I turned seven, my mother treated me to high tea at the Ritz. I felt like a princess with my fancy dress and white gloves. I brought my favorite doll in a matching dress and she had her own highchair at the table. Other mothers and girls with their dolls filled the remaining tables. We ate cucumber sandwiches with the crusts cut off and had clotted cream in our tea. It was all very posh, but I couldn't sit still like a well-mannered girl. I wanted to explore the beautiful garden patio decorated with white ribbons and flowers. A little bridge crossed a pond teeming with fat red fish. Mom had thrown out my ruined gloves later because I insisted on petting the fish.

The glow of that memory came back to me as I stepped into the lobby of the hotel. It was only slightly dampened by the scowl of the concierge who looked at my work shirt, boots and kit and hissed, "In the basement!" Apparently, work crews weren't supposed to come in through the front lobby. Well, la-dee-da.

"Come on, boys," I said to Gabe and Emil who trailed me, carrying a pet carrier, nets and other supplies. "This guy says the rats are in the basement."

"Keep your voice down!" The concierge's tone spiked, then he turned to the guest waiting behind me. "There are no rats, I assure you."

Maybe not. But a nest of cerastes was just as bad.

As we headed for the elevator, we passed the old patio garden. It hadn't changed much in seventy years. Wars may come and go, but the Ritz was eternal. I wondered if they still had fish in the pond. But a wedding reception was taking place in the garden and I couldn't go in. It was probably better that way. Remembering the fun times with my mom never turned out well. At least not since I burned the only bridge to Asgard, making sure I could never see her again.

We took the elevator down to the basement and came out in a long, dingy hall by the laundry room.

"What are we looking for again?" Emil asked.

"Snakes," snapped Gabe. "I told you that already."

I frowned. Gabe had been grumpy all morning. Granted, Emil could be annoying, but he'd been on his best behavior so far.

"Not just any snakes," I said. "Cerastes."

"What's so special about them?" Emil asked.

"Well, for starters, they have horns. Four pairs, to be precise."

"That sounds dangerous."

"Not really. Normally, they hide in sand and use the horns to lure in prey. They're not venomous."

"Sand? How did they get into the basement of a hotel?"

"I have no idea. Probably some idiot who had a couple as pets and let them go when they realized how much work they are. It happens."

"And now they've nested down here. How on earth are we going to find them?"

"That's where you two come in. And those two." I pointed to the cage in Gabe's hand. It carried the squamice, already kitted up to scout out the smallest nooks and crannies in the basement.

"Won't the snakes eat the little guys?" Emil said.

"Not unless they've mutated into some monstrous version of themselves," I said.

Emil looked confused.

"Cerastes are no bigger than garter snakes," I clarified. "They eat small toads and beetles. No way they could subdue a squamus. This will be a good test." When Gabe didn't respond, I poked him. "Don't you think so."

"Sure." He nodded. A few days ago, I couldn't shut him up about his new pet project. He'd spent hours training the squamice to wear the cameras and come on his commands. Where had all that enthusiasm gone?

"Hey, you okay?" I asked.

"Fine. Let's just get this done. It stinks in here."

"Well, the chill coming off you will freeze out any critters living down here." Emil poked him. "And oh, that scowl is very scary."

"Why don't you shut up for once?" Gabe's scowl deepened to a snarl.

"Boys, don't make me separate you, or I'll turn this car around right now," I said.

"Kyra, we're not in a car," Emil pointed out.

I crossed my arms and glared at them. "It felt like the thing to say when dealing with squabbling juveniles."

Gabe turned away to unload the squamice. He opened the cage and one little white face poked out, followed by one curious brown face. A tiny camera was attached to each head with bio-glue, making them look like robotic mice. They perked up, sniffing the air. Then their lizard back ends slithered out and, with a flick of their tails, they were gone.

Gabe fussed with his receiver until he got a good picture. I peered around his shoulder. The screen was split in two with their names on top of each. So far Sweat Pea and Niblet were running side by side, so the images were similar.

"It's almost too dark to see anything," Emil said. "Can't you adjust it?"

"I'm trying." In a moment, the screen lightened, and I could make out what looked like the backside of drywall. Bare wooden struts passed by every few seconds.

"They're inside the walls," I said.

"How do they know where to look for the snakes?" Emil peered over Gabe's other shoulder, resting a hand on his arm.

"They don't," Gabe said. "They're just running. But if they find anything, the tracker can lead us to the right spot."

The squamice stopped. Ahead of them, something moved.

"Make the picture clearer," Emil said.

"I can't!" Gabe's reply came through gritted teeth.

Niblet edged a bit closer. In the faint light, I could barely make out the mass of serpentine bodies, tangled like a ragged ball of yarn, shifting and squirming as they twined around each other.

"Those aren't garter snakes," Emil said. "Their huge!"

"You're just seeing them from the squamice perspective," Gabe said. "They're not that big."

A giant snake head snapped at the screen and it went black.

"Shit! Did that snake just eat him?" Emil grabbed Gabe's arm, but Gabe shook him off.

The second screen showed Sweat Pea running again.

"That was a hibernaculum," I said "The cerastes are mating. Did you get the location?"

"Yes." A deep line creased Gabe's brow. Then the other screen went blank too.

"Are they dead?" Emil said.

"No! Just the camera units. Look, their vital signs are good."

"Well, get them back on line!"

"I'm trying. It's not working!"

"Give me that!" Emil grabbed the control.

Gabe shoved him.

"Guys, stop it!" I snapped.

A loud crash came from above. Magic flared over my keening, and I recognized its flavor. It rumbled across me like the growl of a really pissed-off wolf. Shifters. A whole lot of shape-shifters had just changed shape all at once. That couldn't be good.

"You know where the nest is, right?" I said.

Gabe nodded.

"Good. Take the nets and go scoop up that hibernaculum. Don't worry, they'll be in a stupor if they're mating. Then find those squamice. That concierge won't thank me for getting rid of one infestation only to bring in more rodents.

"What are you going to do?" Emil asked. Another crash came from above and he winced.

I pointed to the ceiling. "I'm going to see who let the dogs out."

Emil squinted one eye at me. "You are so very strange."

The patio was in shambles. I skidded to a stop at the garden's entrance as a rose-covered trellis crashed to the floor. A slash of blood stained the big white bow nestled among the flowers. Beyond this barricade, a dozen wolves writhed in half-form, their features stuck somewhere between canine and human. Other wedding guests screamed, cried and tried to flee, but the door was blocked. One wolf went mad and clawed at a bridesmaid, tearing the bodice of her pink satin dress and scoring her chest with four bloody lacerations.

Oh, hells! I had nothing with me to stop crazed wolves.

I turned and ran for my truck. Five minutes later—too long!—I returned with a pressure sprayer, my home-made dart gun and my sword. I found the pathetic concierge cowering in the corner and shoved the spray tank at him.

"Fill that with water." He gaped at me with bulging eyes. "Now!" I grabbed his sleeve and propelled him toward the kitchens.

I climbed over the trellis barricade, one hand gripping my sword. Its magic was silent, but it was still sharp enough to cut off heads in a pinch.

Several wolves were still stuck in their change. I'd seen wolves shift before. It was always a painful, drawn-out horror, but this was taking too long. Something was wrong. Whatever had forced them to change was corrupting their magic.

Three bodies lay dead or dying in pools of blood. Another, dressed in a blood-stained bridal gown, was half hidden under the main table. Beside it, two wolves fought like rabid dogs, teeth gnashing, claws tearing chunks of fur and flesh off their opponents. Other half-wolf, half-human monstrosities tore apart centerpieces, shredded tablecloths, and smashed dishes in a frenzy of destruction.

Where the hells was that concierge?

A human bridesmaid ran at me, clutching the shreds of her dress. Her up-do had been raked askew, and a gash spilled blood down her face. She tried to grab hold of me like she was drowning. As much as I wanted to help her, I couldn't let her incapacitate me.

The concierge finally returned with my sprayer. Gabe and Emil were right behind him. They leapt over the barricade. I grabbed my spray tank and latched the bridesmaid onto Gabe.

"Move that trellis and get the guests out of here!" I shouted over the noise of breaking dishes and howling wolves. Gabe didn't argue. He hoisted the crying woman over the trellis, then put his back into moving the obstacle.

"You," I pointed at Emil, "grab a wolf."

He grinned.

The two fighting wolves had fallen into the pond and were splashing blood-tinged water all over the floor. As one lunged at the other, Emil plucked him from the pond like he was a wet puppy. Despite his slight frame, Emil was insanely strong.

The wolf turned on this new assailant and clawed him across the neck. Emil punched him in the face. The second wolf jumped on his back, biting the fleshy part of his shoulder.

I didn't worry about Emil. His wounds were already healing. Instead, I primed the pump and sprayed both wolves full in the face. The one on his back fell off, shrieking like a wounded hyena, clawing at his eyes even as he shifted back to human. The second wolf quickly followed him to the floor. In a moment, they were nothing more than pasty white, naked men curled in the fetal position, their bodies rippling with convulsions.

"What is that stuff?" Emil wiped blood from his chin.

"A little concoction of Gita's making. Mostly wolfsbane with some other potent herbs mixed in."

"Cool. Let's do this then." He grabbed another wolf as it ran by and I doused it.

Gabe had opened a small gap in the barricade and the human guests bunched there, panicking to get out. I could do nothing to help him.

Emil and I dropped four more wolves. Then a table exploded upward in a shower of wood splinters and china shards. In its place stood an eight-foot tall, severely pissed off grizzly bear.

The beast flexed its massive shoulders and roared, spraying spittle. The sound was loud enough to bruise eardrums.

I sprayed it in the face. The bear looked surprised, then dropped to all fours. It shook its ponderous head like a wrecking ball, smashing tables and chairs. But it didn't go down. Apparently, wolfsbane didn't affect bears.

I shoved the sprayer at Emil. "Finish the other wolves." He ran off, and I backed away from the bear, already priming the dart gun with a few pumps. It wasn't much bigger than a pistol, but it was all I had in the truck and it was pre-loaded with enough sedative to take down an ogre. I had no idea what it would do to an enraged bear-shifter.

Before I could pull the trigger, a massive paw swiped the gun from my hand, and I went flying into the pond. I scrambled away until my back hit the decorative bridge where I had once stood in my party dress to feed the fish.

The furious bear pounced, sending a splash of water into the air. Before it cleared, I ducked under the bridge, scrambling up, now dripping pond water as I unsheathed my sword with slippery fingers. I expected the bear to pause at the bridge, but it barreled through. Splinters of wood blasted me, and I fell on my ass, losing my sword. The bear reared up and roared, announcing its triumph. It dropped back to all fours, huge maw gaping as it lunged for my leg.

But instead, its teeth clamped down on a stone arm.

Attached to Mason.

He screamed a guttural oath and shoved his fist deep into the bear's throat.

Mason was home! I had never been so happy to see anyone in my life, but before I could process that fact, the bear roared again. Mason punched him in the face. A paw the size of a dinner plate swiped across Mason's chest. What seemed like a mere tap was a slap that sent Mason crashing over the ruins of the bridge.

I scrambled out of the water.

The gun! Where's the gun?

I found it under a pile of debris and jerked it up, released the safety and pulled the trigger. My shot took the bear high in the chest and lodged in thick fur. It only infuriated him even more. I struggled to reload as the bear raged. Mason appeared at my side.

"Hold him," I said. "I need just a second."

He didn't question me. He threw himself at the bear, lodging his stone arm between grizzly jaws. A shaggy arm wrapped around Mason and squeezed. He screamed. I jumped over a broken table, pushed the gun against the bear's chest and fired, hoping the dart pierced fur and flesh.

The bear dropped Mason, flailed for a moment, then toppled like a ton of rocks, landing halfway in the pond.

Mason looked green.

"Are you okay?" I asked. I wanted to grab him, touch him, hug him. But the pinched look on his face told me he was in pain.

"A couple of broken ribs," he said. "It's nothing."

"When…I mean…How are you here? Are you part of the wedding?" That was ridiculous, of course, but my brain couldn't accept that he stood before me in the slightly broken flesh.

He grinned.

"I was invited. The groom is an old friend of mine." He pointed to where the wolves, now in human form, were shakily getting to their feet. "But no, that's not why I'm here. I came looking for you. I could have waited for you to come home, but I've waited long enough, so I bribed Gita for your schedule."

His gaze was intense, roving across my face, my disheveled hair and torn work shirt.

I squinted at him. "What did you bribe her with?"

"Wouldn't you like to know? That was part of the deal. I can't tell you." He crossed his arms and then winced at the pain from his broken ribs.

I needed to get him out of there.

"You!" The shout came from the groom who had been kneeling by the bride in her bloody dress. With the debris cleared, the wound on her neck was clearly visible. "You did this!" The groom flew at Mason, fingers clasping to strangle him.

"Daniel, stand down." Mason fought off the man, even though his injuries must have been screaming. "I didn't do anything."

"It was you!" Two more wolves came to stand with their pack mate, but

Gabe pushed through them and together, he and I yanked the enraged groom off Mason.

"The champagne," Daniel panted with the effort to get the words out. Foam flecked his face and his eyes were red and wild. "The toast. It was a gift from you. From the Guardians."

Something in the champagne had forced the wolves to shift, or maybe it had spiked their fight-or-flight instinct, compelling the change and the madness.

"Get your hands on one of those bottles of champagne," I whispered to Gabe. He nodded and slipped away.

Mason and Daniel were now talking together in low voices. The other wolves, seeing their pack mate calm down, had turned away to help the wounded.

I tramped back into the pond and found my sword under the remains of the bridge. For over a hundred years that little bridge had survived recessions, fires, and wars. But a were-bear on tainted champagne had taken it out. I pulled the sword from the water and wiped it with a blood-free bit of table cloth. The blade would need a good oiling.

Mason found me and took both my hands in his. The warmth of his skin on mine enveloped all of me.

"I really want to be with you tonight," he said. "But I have to stay and take care of this."

"What happened?"

His gray eyes sparked with silver. "Someone spiked the champagne, then sent it as a gift from the Guardians. Daniel is an old friend. We help him when he needs extra hands for a job. So he never suspected this…assault."

"But he knows you didn't do it, right?"

"He does now. But the wolves are hyped up on fear and pain. I have to make sure things don't get out of hand. You go home and I'll find you later. As soon as I can."

He squeezed my hands. I turned to go, then stopped.

"Mason," I called, "did you find what you were looking for in France?"

He smiled and he was so gods-damned beautiful my heart hurt.

"Not what. Who."

10

Emil left us at the hotel. He needed to find a quick source of blood to replenish what he'd lost in the fight. At home, Gabe and I unloaded the truck. He'd rounded up the squamice in the hotel basement and they were dozing in their cage.

"What are we doing with these?" Gabe held up the plastic bin containing the squirming ball of horned snakes.

"I guess they'll go to Dorion Park," I said.

Gabe made a pained face and looked at his widget.

"Not you. I'll take them later. You have a date?"

"Yes. Can I use your shower? I'm already late."

"Sure." I could sit around in pond water for a little while longer. "Just don't use my exfoliating scrub, or I'll take it out of your wages."

"But it makes my cheeks so soft." Gabe strutted out with his hands clasped to his backside.

I found Gita in her closet, reading a new, precious paper copy of *Angela's Ashes* by the light of her widget. So that's what Mason bribed her with. Smart guy.

"Everyone all right?" I asked.

She gave me a mumbling, sniffling, "Yes," then stuck her nose back in her book. I shut the door.

Errol sat beside his bonsai tree, legs dangling over the edge of the pot. His face was fixed in a frown as he watched Jacoby. A thin stream of smoke rose from the pipe clenched between his teeth. How long had he been sitting like that? I really needed to get him out more.

"No change?"

"Htbrt." *None.* Errol's bloodshot eyes didn't leave Jacoby.

Gabe came out of my bathroom with his hair glistening wet. He looked very well put together in a black shirt and jeans that hugged his hips. You could hardly tell that he'd been catching vermin and fighting werewolves all evening.

"I'm heading out," he said.

"Use protection!" I called after him.

"Yes boss." He waved behind him as he left.

After my shower—in which I had to wash my hair twice to get out the fishy smell—I toweled off and threw on jeans and a clean shirt, thinking I could grab a quick bite before Mason arrived. I'd missed lunch, and it was well past dinner time. But in the living room, I found Mason standing over Jacoby's shrine with a kraken perched on his shoulder. Hunter twined one tentacle around a lock of Mason's hair—hair that was longer and curling a bit around his ears. The rest of him was exactly as I remembered—broad shoulders and strong arms that, in the quiet of the night, I could still feel wrapped around me. He wore a scruffy beard and it suited him. And when he turned his gray eyes on me, I felt that familiar tug of longing to get lost in them.

"I was hoping he'd be better by now," he said. Jacoby lay like a corpse. His thin, fuzzy chest rose and fell so slowly, it was barely perceptible.

"We're working on it," I said. "I had a specialty vet look at him, but he'd never even heard of a dervish before. Nesi's searching his old books too. But every day I see him like that…" My eyes felt hot with tears.

"Don't give up yet," Mason said. "We'll figure it out."

I leaned on him. "I'm so glad you're home."

"Me too."

I plucked Hunter off his shoulder, but his suckers were clamped on tight and he wouldn't let go. *I know exactly how you feel, little buddy.*

"I think Hunter's glad to see you too."

"He's not so bad. But…ow!" He pulled his hair from the tentacle's grip.

I had to bribe Hunter with fresh crayfish before he agreed to go back to his tank.

"Are we alone?" Mason asked.

I looked around at the dozens of eyes peering at us in the dim light.

"Well, Gabe's on a date, if that's what you mean. We're about as alone as we can get here."

"I'm glad to see Gabe got over Dutch." Mason tugged on my hand and I moved closer to him.

"Gabe gets over Dutch every week. Three or four times a week, actually."

Mason frowned, and I said. "I didn't mean that to sound so bitter. I'm just worried about him. He seems to be spinning off the rails."

He tugged me closer.

"You've had a lot to worry about the past few months. Jacoby, Gabe and Angus getting arrested. I didn't mean to be away for so long."

"But you found him? Or her?"

He nodded and brushed my wet hair away from my shoulder. "I brought back Polina's old teacher. I want you to come meet him."

"Now?"

"Yes, now. I have to go back, and I'm not ready to let you out of my sight yet."

He kissed me and it was like coming home. His mouth opened to taste me, his tongue gentle and hot. My legs went to water, and I leaned in, pressing my chest against his, my thigh against his, wanting to feel all of him at once. A moan escaped me, and he sank deeper into the kiss until we finally had to come up for air.

He grasped my hands at our sides and leaned his forehead against mine. "We'd better go now, or I'll take you right here with all your critters watching."

"Oh, their innocent eyes," I teased, but I relented and stepped away. "Let's go meet this famous teacher. But I'll follow in my truck. Do you mind if we drop off a ball of mating snakes in Dorion Park first?"

"You're not like other girls." He kissed me on the nose. "I've missed that."

"Good because I'm going to need a cheeseburger on the way too. And some fries."

We dumped the cerastes in the park a little after midnight, then ate fries sitting on a bench tucked into a corner of the garden behind Mason's house. He planned to have a late dinner in the early hours of the morning—gargoyles kept such weird hours—but I couldn't wait, so I'd compromised and left off the burger.

"When do I get to meet this mysterious mentor?" I said between munching.

"Yuki? Soon. I want to have you to myself a bit longer." He grinned. "There's ketchup on your cheek."

I licked grease and ketchup off my fingers then grabbed a napkin from the sack. He brushed my hand away and wiped my cheek with the tip of his finger.

"It's like watching the wild animals getting fed at the zoo. I probably shouldn't put my fingers near your mouth."

"Ha ha." I knew we should have bought something less messy.

"Gods, I missed you." He leaned in and kissed my cheek where the ketchup had been.

After devouring the fries, I tucked away the garbage.

"Let's walk a bit before waking Yuki," Mason said. "He's wiped out from the trip."

We held hands and wandered through the garden, heading toward the old cemetery. We found excuses to touch. He pulled me close to avoid a branch that had fallen across the path. When the wind picked up, I plucked a stray leaf from his sweater and smoothed down the fabric, feeling the solidness beneath it.

"Was the trip home really bad?" I asked.

"The crossing was hard. Constant damp and cold. We hit some foul weather too."

"Is Yuki…is he a gargoyle?" I traced the edge of his palm with my thumb.

"No. A sorcerer and…well, I'll let him explain if he wants to."

We stopped at a ring of patio stones. Raised garden beds lined either side and were sprinkled with spring growth. But the night was chill. Summer was still a month away. I shivered and Mason pulled me closer.

"Cold?"

"A little."

"Do you want to go back inside?"

I shook my head. It was better to be cold but alone with him than inside with Dutch, Angus and the other Guardians.

"Let's sit." He pointed to a bench tucked into the shadows at the far end of the garden and winced as we settled on it.

"You're still hurting!" I'd almost forgotten about his cracked ribs.

"It's nothing. I'll be fine come sunrise."

We sat and he pulled me close, surrounding me in the feel of his magic.

"Tell me about him. About Yuki. He was your teacher?"

Mason nodded and ran the tip of a finger along my jaw. It seemed neither of us could keep our hands to ourselves.

"My father was an artist and a progressive. When I turned my hand to stone the first time, he knew I had the old Grimaldi magic. He hired Yuki to teach me."

"Grimaldi? Polina uses that name."

"It's my old family name. Marquis Grimaldi. But I gave up my title and my name when I saw the way things were going before the French Revolution. By then, Polina and I had already faced off. I lived alone with my young daughter. We left everything behind and moved to Wales. I became an alchemist. And we were happy for a time. Without Yuki, none of that would be possible."

"Why?"

"Yuki was my teacher first, but when I married Polina, she demanded to learn magic too. Yuki was reluctant to teach her. He sensed something dark in her even then. But Polina insisted. She would learn with or without his help. He gave in because he feared what she might do on her own."

Mason twined his fingers in mine and raised them to his lips. He seemed lost in memory, but after a moment he continued.

"In the end, Polina surpassed me. My few tricks are nothing compared to the power she commands. Yuki tried to keep her in check, but the stronger she became…the more she craved magic. She was addicted. A magic junkie. And then she found the spell for immortality…true immortality, I mean. Not just longevity. A spell that would make her invulnerable to disease or injury. But she needed the blood of her only daughter to complete the rite. My daughter." He rubbed the nape of his neck and winced when the movement jarred his cracked ribs.

"Yuki learned of her intentions. Without him, I would have lost my Brigitte. As it was, I barely escaped that fight alive. Imprisoning Polina in the bloodstone was a last resort."

A brooding shadow fell over his magic as his mood turned dark.

"So tell me about your trip," I said, trying to lighten things up. "What are the French wards like? What are people wearing? What do they eat?"

He laughed at my sudden enthusiasm, but before he could answer, a movement caught my eye and a streak of red flitted through the shadows under the trees.

"Was that a fox?" I turned, looking for the creature.

"Probably." Mason tightened his grip on my hand.

The fox bounded from the bushes. It sat upright on its haunches, black nose testing the air. A thick red tail curled around delicate feet.

"It's beautiful!" I didn't want to move in case I scared it away. There was something decidedly canny about that fox.

Mason's mouth hardened into a thin line. The fox bounded over to us and twined around his ankles, its tail flicking playfully. I jumped up, already thinking about the weapons on hand.

"That's enough." Mason rose and tried to untangle his legs from the prancing fox. It nipped at his ankles.

"Nori! Stop pestering them." The Japanese-accented voice came from the shadows. I turned to see a small man with a long, white beard step from the trees beside the garden. He wore silky black pants that fell almost like a skirt and a white tunic over those. The man bowed and Mason nodded back as the fox continued to dance around his feet.

"Nori!" Mason's voice snapped like a whip.

The fox melted and reshaped into the form of a lithe young woman. Her long black hair partially covered her, but that only seemed to accentuate her nakedness. She leaned into Mason and gnashed her perfect white teeth at him.

"You're no fun. I just wanted to meet your friend." She smiled at me. She was beautiful in that petite, feminine way that I could never aspire to.

"Go put on some clothes," the old man said, "then you can meet her properly."

Nori pouted, then shifted back into a fox and bounded off.

I'd never seen anything like it. The shifters I knew were mostly wolves, and now one bear. When they changed forms, even without tainted champagne, it was a painful thing to watch that took several gruesome, bone-crunching minutes. Nori's shift had been fluid, like a whitecap flowing into another wave.

"That was amazing. What is she?"

Mason frowned. He wasn't impressed with her antics. "Shifter. Of the Kitsune clan."

"I apologize for my granddaughter." The old man bowed to me. "She is young and foolish. I am Yuki. Henry has told me much about you."

I doubted that. Mason wasn't the chatty type.

"Yuki, please call me Mason here," he said. "Only the court judges call me Henry now."

Yuki looked affronted. "I helped your father pick that name. To me you will always be Henry Grimaldi. Now how does an old man get dinner around here?"

Dinner was a thrown-together affair. Mason and Berto cleaned out the fridge, dumping casseroles, platters of meat and cheese, and half-eaten salads on the table. I helped Angus with plates and cutlery while Dutch opened bottles of wine. Yuki and Nori disappeared for several minutes, and when they returned, Nori's eyes were red-rimmed as if she'd been crying, but she held her chin high. Whatever scolding she'd endured, it didn't dull the fierce determination in her demeanor.

Before we sat, Nori went up to Mason and laid her open palm on his chest. My legs instinctively tightened under me, but I held back the urge to jump up and slap her hand away. She closed her eyes and leaned back as if waiting for a kiss.

Just what in the hells had been going on during that long boat ride across the Atlantic?

Then I keened the magic blossom from her. Mason jerked and winced. Finally, he removed her hand and squeezed it.

"Thank you. It feels better now."

"Why did you not tell me you were hurt? I would have healed you sooner." Her pretty pink mouth pursed.

I relaxed back in my chair. Nori was a healer. Interesting. It was rare enough magic that true healers were sought after everywhere.

She turned to find me watching and smiled, a little too self-satisfied for my liking.

For a moment no one spoke as wine glasses and plates were filled. Then Angus teased Berto for picking onions out of his salad and Nori complained that

Angus was hogging the bottle of wine. I was suddenly tossed back twenty years to dinners in Asgard with my mother, my grandfather and all my aunts, uncles and cousins around one enormous table. I blinked away the heat in my eyes.

"You okay?" Mason leaned over to whisper.

"I'm fine." I smiled and shoved a hunk of cheese in my mouth.

"Here Mason, you must try this." Nori, who sat on the other side of Mason, tugged on his sleeve and offered him a spoonful of something. "It's delicious." She tried to feed it to him. I caught Angus rolling his eyes and felt better about the anger the woman spiked in me.

"It's pâté," Mason said, pushing her hand away. "You're supposed to put it on bread."

Nori popped the bit of pâté in her mouth and moaned. "So good." No one should be able to look sexy speaking with a mouth full of duck liver, but she pulled it off. She ate the few bits of food on her plate just as daintily, like a little bird pecking at crumbs.

The fries had barely taken the edge off my appetite. I piled my plate with a sample of everything. Mason grinned at my obvious pleasure and tried to steal a pickle off my plate. I stabbed him with my fork.

"Ow!" he jerked his hand away.

"Pickles are sacred."

"I'll remember that," he said, shaking out his fingers.

"Oh! Poor you!" Nori smothered his hand in her tiny ones. "Let me fix that." But before she could bring the full weight of her magic to bear, Mason pulled away.

"It's fine. Just leave it."

Nori pouted.

Angus, who never ate much, watched us with an amused grin as he leaned back in the chair and sipped his wine. He winked at me. As soon as we were alone, he'd give me the rundown on this woman.

"So, Nori," I leaned forward to see her past Mason. "Where did you learn to be a healer?"

She shrugged with just the tiniest uplift of her shoulders. "It is just what I am. Like the fox. I did not learn to be a fox. I just am."

Interesting. Most shape shifters were made, not born. But I'd heard of heredity shifters, families that passed the ability down from one generation to the next. It seemed the kitsunes had that ability. Maybe that's why Nori's shift had been so effortless.

The talk soon turned to the problem on everyone's mind: Polina.

"She's holed up with Gerard at his estate on Buzzard Island," Angus said. "We've had the boys watching her for several weeks, but so far we can't get close enough to see anything important. She must have some kind of ward that we trip because every time we get within a kilometer of the place, she sends out guards to chase us off."

"Not a ward," I said. "Ghosts. You can't see them, but they patrol the walls."

"Ghosts?" Mason frowned.

"Spirits she somehow tied to her when she broke free of the bloodstone."

"How do you know this?" Yuki asked. He had eaten very little, and now he sat cross-legged in his chair sipping wine.

"Well, I've seen the ghosts from a distance," I said. "But I also met one at the cemetery a few days ago. She'd been following me. Seems she remembered me from the night at Pierre's lab."

"You can see ghosts?" Angus asked. "That's fabulous. We need you on our patrol. You can spot their numbers and track their schedule."

"I can do that," I said. It would feel good to be doing something. Anything.

"What about this ghost in the cemetery? She's not part of Polina's crew?" Mason asked.

"She says not. She has magic of her own. Enough to resist Polina."

"I'd like to talk to her. Ask her about her time…in there with Polina." His face was deceptively neutral, but I knew he harbored a deep guilt for creating the bloodstone. It was bad enough that he'd trapped one soul in it for hundreds of years, but he'd lost the stone during the twenty-first century, and for decades it had been used for dark experiments, gathering thousands of souls. Along with Polina, these had escaped the bloodstone the night Jacoby went nova. Most had dissipated into the ether, hopefully finding their way to the afterlife. Others, like Naomi, had stuck around for reasons only they could tell. Still others had been bound to Polina somehow, and now they served her.

"I can try to find the ghost again," I said. "But there's one thing about all this I don't understand." I pushed my empty plate away and Mason refilled my wineglass. "Why did Polina come back in her corporeal form, but not the rest of the ghosts?"

Everyone went silent, thinking, then all eyes turned to Yuki.

"I do not know," he said. "She has, perhaps, fashioned some dark rite that protected her while imprisoned in the stone. I cannot know until I see her and taste her magic."

"She'd need a pretty big power source to enact such a rite," Mason said. "Where would she get that inside a bloodstone?"

"The other spirits," I said. "Naomi—that's the one I met—she told me that Polina ate them. I wasn't sure what she meant."

Yuki nodded thoughtfully. "I must get close enough to test her."

"I can't see how. She doesn't seem to have any vulnerabilities," I said.

"She does," Yuki said. "All those who embrace the dark powers leave themselves with a weakness." The room was silent as we waited for him to continue. "Polina's magic is the magic of death. People believe that necromancy is fueled by the dead. That is not true. Necromancers harness the energy of a soul breaking away from its mortal body. It is a great explosion of power, but ephemeral in nature. And that is the root of its weakness. Life magic may not be so flashy, but it is constant, ever-flowing and resolute. An unstoppable force that can smother necromancy like a wet blanket over a fire."

Yuki sat back, sipping his wine. I considered his words and had many questions. Did that mean life magic—green magic—could stifle Polina's power? How?

"But if she's eating souls," Angus said, "she's on a whole new level of bad-assery. Seems to me those old rules might no longer apply."

Yuki inclined his head. "Perhaps this is so."

I decided to cut through all this esoteric talk. "So how do we kill her?"

"If she has a body, kill her like anyone else," Yuki said. "Cut off her head. Stab her in the heart. Slit her throat." I swear he had a little twinkle in his eye.

"Not necessarily in that order," Angus said.

"This will help." Yuki held up a pointed blade about six inches long with a bone handle. "This has been in my family for a very long time. My grandfather called it a witch-killer. Once it touches her blood, it will suck away all her magic."

"The trick will be getting close enough to use it," Mason said. "That's where Yuki comes in."

The old man nodded. "She was a mischievous student. Often, she forced me to shut down her magic when things went…how do you say…crooked."

"It's like a magic slap." Mason smiled and shook his head. "Used it on me once or twice too. Not fun. But it will freeze her abilities."

I put aside the image of a young, eager Mason learning the fine art of magic.

"Can you still do it?" I asked.

Yuki sat up even straighter in his chair. "I may be old, but fire burns in these bones. So yes, I can stop her cold. But it will last only a few minutes. You must be ready."

"I will be," Mason said. His eyes seemed to darken as he looked inward at other, less happy memories.

"No. Not you." Yuki snapped. "You know this, Henry."

"Don't start with that nonsense." Mason pushed back his chair.

Yuki glared. "I never speak nonsense. Do not forget, I knew your great-grandfather. He went mad from the Grimaldi curse."

Mason made a noise somewhere between a grunt and laugh, and said, "I need more wine, if you're going there." He stood up and headed for the wine cellar.

I turned to Angus. "Do you know about this curse?"

"Oh, aye. It's a right bugger, but easily avoided. If a Grimaldi man kills the woman he loves, he'll go mad as a hat."

"I saw it with my own eyes," Yuki said. "Henry's great-grandfather accidentally poisoned his wife with bad…how do you say?" He looked at Angus.

"Mushrooms." Angus's gnarled brow lowered. "The poor man didn't know his chanterelles from his death caps. Nearly killed them both, but after she died, he went mad anyway."

"That's bullshit," Mason said as he returned with two more bottles of wine. "Alphonse Grimaldi gave his wife syphilis. That's how she died. And it drove him crazy too. The mushrooms were just a cover."

"No." Yuki said. "Not a cover. I was there."

"Whatever." Mason's expression said he wanted to put an end to this conversation.

"And what of the others?" Yuki's turned from Mason to me, as if it was important that I believe him. "Other Grimaldis have suffered the same fate. Bertrand? Mad. Clement? Mad."

"Seems like Grimaldi men killed their women a lot," I muttered.

"Okay. Enough." Mason said. "True curse or not. I don't love Polina, so it doesn't matter."

"You did once," Yuki said. "Do you want to risk it?"

Angus rose from the table and rubbed his hands together. "It's time to grab the bull by the tail and look him in the eye. Berto and I have to patrol once more before dawn. We'll swing by Gerard's estate, but now that we know about the ghosties, we'll keep a good distance." Berto rose and nodded politely at each of us. Angus waved as they left. Without them, the table now seemed too intimate with just the four of us. Nori's gaze fixed on Mason's hands as he worked the corkscrew. With his sleeves rolled up, it was easy to see the muscles on his forearms bulge as he pulled the cork. I couldn't help thinking of those strong hands cupping my hips and those arms holding me…

I glanced up to find Nori staring at me with an odd expression— thoughtful, but in the way a predator looks when it finally figures out its prey.

"I should go too," I said, rising.

Mason left the bottle. "I'll walk you out."

He stopped me by the front door. "You could stay." He slipped a hand under my chin and stroked the soft spot under the line of my jaw. I leaned into it, just glad to feel him close again.

"Not tonight. You're hurt. I'm tired, and…"

From the dining room we could hear Yuki scold Nori in Japanese for some misdemeanor, and then the house fell silent. It felt expectant, like the big arguments of the night hadn't been resolved, only delayed.

"And we're not alone," Mason finished for me.

"Exactly."

He kissed me. It was soft and sweet—a promise of more good things to come.

"Tomorrow," he said.

"And you'll tell me all about your trip. I want to hear everything." He nodded, kissed me and closed the door as I headed to my truck. I was suddenly tired, like someone had pulled my plug and all my energy was swirling down the drain.

A white fox waited beside my truck. His black eyes and nose gleamed like onyx tucked into his snowy fur. Then he stretched. His fur morphed into a long beard, his delicate feet turned into the bare feet of an equally delicate man. Yuki stood before me, completely unabashed by his nakedness. Without his silks, he looked frail but proud.

"You must be the one to kill the witch," he said gravely. "Henry has always been blind to the power of things he does not believe. He will not see. It is not a curse or a prophecy. It is a defect that runs deeper. A family failing that lives in his DNA. If he kills Polina, he will go mad. It will destroy him. Promise you will do it."

What else could I say?

"I promise."

The witch-killer appeared in his hand as if he'd pulled it from thin air. It reeked of magic—something spicy and sweet with an undertone of sulfur.

"You must take this." He held it out, but I didn't reach for it. I'd had my share of magical blades. They always came with a price.

"I don't want it."

"You must!"

"Don't worry. I'll kill the witch when the time comes, but I'll do it my way."

Yuki tried to stare me down. I didn't blink. Finally, he bowed, shifted back to fox, and dashed into the shadows under the trees.

With the ruins of Lakeview Field of Honor Mausoleum at our backs, Mason, Angus and I surveilled the cemetery grounds that sloped toward the water. The wind had died with the sun. Nothing moved in the shadows except for a few sluggish ghosts hanging around their ancient graves.

"Anything?" Mason asked.

"Not yet." I brought the will o'wisps to feed, but didn't let them out of their basket, in case we found Naomi first. I didn't need her panicking and jumping inside me again. Just the thought of it gave me the heebie-jeebies.

"Maybe that's a blessing in a hand basket. I'm not sure I want advice from a spook anyhow." Angus scratched his chest and peered at the remains of the once beautiful garden pond that was now a marshy mess of new reeds poking through the winter rot.

"You think she moved on?" Mason asked. I assumed he didn't mean to the next town.

"I don't think so. She seemed pretty happy to be alive again."

"Even in that limited capacity?" Angus asked. "Seems sketchy."

Suddenly, Angus went flying, as if something shoved him from behind. His stunted wings flapped once, and he landed face-first among the reeds. He sat up sputtering pond water and mud. Limp grasses were tangled in his brambly hair.

Naomi appeared laughing so hard she doubled over. When she finally got control of herself, she said, "How's that for limited capacity?"

The surprise on Mason's face told me he could actually see Naomi. Angus spat out a wad of muck and Naomi burst into giggles again.

"You think that's funny, do you?" Angus scowled. He threw a clump of mud, but it went right through her and splatted on the ground at my feet."

"Ooh, I like this one. Where did you find him?" she asked me.

"Angus is a friend," I said. "And this is Mason."

She studied him. "You were there too. In the lab."

"I was." Mason nodded once. "We would like you to tell us what you know about Polina. But first, how is it we can see you?"

A sly look came over her face. "A magician should never reveal her secrets. Ruins the trick." She crossed her arms and glared at him.

"Fine. Keep your secrets, as long as you tell us Polina's."

Angus was trying to pull himself out of the weeds. Naomi floated around his head, twining her fingers in his hair. It would have been flirty if not for the whole ghost thing. Angus's eyes widened and his back straightened as she circled behind him, brushing ghostly fingers along his wings.

"Why should I," she finally asked. "What's it to you?"

"I put Polina in that bloodstone," Mason said.

"You!" Naomi shot into the air. The force of her anger made her glow brighter. "Were you working with that Nazi doctor?" A spectral wind that I couldn't feel tossed the hair about her head. "Did you put me in that godforsaken prison too?"

She zoomed toward Mason, the picture of a raging spirit. I stepped in front of her, shoving the basket of wisps between us.

"Keep those away from me!" Naomi said.

"Then calm down and listen to what he has to say." I had one hand on the basket's lid, ready to release the wisps.

"Fine." She shrank to her normal size. "What do you want to know?"

Mason held his hands up placatingly. "First, I didn't put you in the bloodstone. I created it, and for that I'm sorry. But I wouldn't send an innocent to such a fate." During World War Two, a Nazi doctor had found the bloodstone and used it in his heinous experiments, killing thousands of men, women and children and locking their souls inside the bloodstone. Years later, when Mason recovered the stone, he buried it, hoping it would be forgotten.

"Well, I wasn't exactly innocent, anyway." Naomi smirked.

I looked to Mason. He nodded and backed up, letting me take it from there.

"We need to know how Polina kept her corporeal form when all the other spirits locked in the stone didn't. And we need to know how many spirits she has in thrall. And anything else you can tell us."

"She calls them subjects. Not thralls. She can ride their mind, see what they see, hear what they hear. But there are only about twelve of those bastards left. I've been hunting them." Her feral grin made me wonder what those other ghosts had done to her inside the bloodstone. "And they must call her Queen. That's what she wants: to be queen, and not just of the few thousand souls locked in a magic box. Queen of everybody."

Even Queen Leighna didn't rule Montreal. She was only one arm of a triumvirate of ministers from the fae, human and alchemist tribes. The checks and balances of the triumvirate ensured every faction had a voice. It didn't sound like Polina had any intentions of sharing.

"Why are they loyal to her?" I asked. "What hold does she have over them?"

Naomi turned her big, dark eyes on me and smiled. "Fear."

"Fear of what? They're already dead."

"There are worse things than death." The ghost flew toward me and right through me. Her magic clashed with mine.

"I told you not to do that again."

Naomi hovered just out of reach and smirked.

"You think that's bad? You should feel what Polina can do to a soul. She eats them. But not before tearing apart their magic, bit by bit. The screams of those poor souls…it went on forever." Her color dimmed as if the memories threatened to smother her. "She's a monster. Polina will rip your world apart and eat its heart. Mark my words."

The night fell silent, except for the spring peepers in the pond.

Angus finally untangled himself from the muddy reeds. Naomi held out her hand to help him up, but when he tried to grasp it, his fingers went right through her.

She smiled shyly, "It takes a lot of energy to touch something. I can only do it once in a while. I'm sorry I pushed you." She was pretty in a creepy way. Tonight, she wore her hair braided with beads woven in the tresses. They would have jangled on a mortal person, and the silence of her movements added to the creepiness.

Angus smiled. "'Tis all right. I needed a bath anyway."

"You still do." Naomi plucked at a wet reed stuck to his shirt. Her fingers went right through it, but Angus shivered at the touch. Naomi's face screwed up as she concentrated on the reed. She reached for it again. This time, her fingers glowed. She grasped the offending stalk, plucked it from Angus's shirt and tossed it aside. Her face lit with a grin.

"Polina is much better at it," she said.

"Is that why she appears like a regular human?" I asked. Mason turned away, as if he couldn't look at the creature that had suffered because of his creation. But he was listening to every word.

"Oh, but she's not. She's just as insubstantial as the rest of us." Naomi twirled like a little girl wearing a tutu.

Now I was confused. "But I've seen her. She could hold things. And she slapped me. It sure felt corporeal."

Naomi stopped dancing. "I don't know how to explain it exactly. You have creatures in this new city who can change shape, right?"

I forgot that when she lived in this world, magic was almost nonexistent.

"You mean like shape-shifters? Werewolves?"

"No, the ones who wear their fake faces like masks. Some of them are such good masks even they forget they're wearing them. But I can see through to the real monsters underneath." She tapped the side of her nose with one finger.

"You mean glamor?"

"Yes. Polina is exceptionally good at glamor."

Was that even possible? Unlike Naomi, I couldn't see through most glamors, but I could always sense when a fae used one. Or at least I thought I could. I had sensed nothing of the sort with Polina. Or had I? I'd felt a protective ball of magic around her. I'd thought it was a ward, but what if it was an elaborate glamor instead? Could she fashion a glamor so physical it made an incorporeal being corporeal?

"So I spilled my guts to you," Naomi said. She was walking around Angus, studying him like he was a horse on the auction block. "Now you have to tell me what your plans are. Why are you so interested in Polina?"

"Well, Mason here…that is we…" Angus stuttered to a stop. Naomi's excessive attention made him uncomfortable.

"We're going to kill her," Mason said.

Naomi turned to him, like she'd forgotten he was even there.

"Brilliant. Can I help?"

My world shrank to a cocoon of warmth. A fire blazed in the hearth before us. I sat on a puffy couch in Mason's darkened living room, leaning into the well between his shoulder and chin. He kissed the top of my head, resting his lips against my hair for a long moment, as if he too didn't want this moment to end.

His house guests were asleep and the Guardians were on patrol. For once, we were alone. It was the calm before the storm. We both felt it. Angus's trial for murder would start in a month. Polina was on the loose, planning gods only knew what evil. My house seemed on the verge of big changes too, with Clarence and Jacoby both ill and Gabe…well, I still didn't know what was going on with Gabe, but his mood hadn't improved in the last week.

For tonight Mason and I decided to put aside all the crap in our lives and just be a couple. We'd earned it.

Mason unbraided my hair and ran his fingers through it.

"It's like silk." His voice was a deep rumble beside my ear. "I missed this."

"I don't think we've ever had the chance to just sit together, with nothing else on the agenda."

"You're right. Screw agendas. This is much better." He pulled back my hair and kissed me under my ear. Direct hit to my groin. His lips blazed a path across the sensitive skin, while his hands slipped under my shirt, looking for more skin.

I groaned and turned to him, searching for his mouth. His lips met mine, even as I tugged up his shirt to press my hand flat on his chest. The deep well of his magic tolled with every beat of his heart. It was the most familiar and the sexiest sound to me.

Mason undid the buttons on my shirt and covered this new bare flesh with kisses.

"I love your work shirts," he said. "But I love it even more that you wear these sexy bits underneath." He ran a finger under the strap of my bra, but made no attempt to remove it. Instead, he kissed a line around the lacy fringe of the cup while his fiery tongue sent arousing jolts through my core. This was quickly escalating, and in another moment I wouldn't care that we were in his living room and not the privacy of a bedroom.

Mason cupped my face in both hands. "You are so beautiful." His voice was husky with emotion. "While I was away, I kept a picture of you in my head, like a beacon showing me the way home. I didn't get a chance to say it before properly. But I love you, Kyra Greene."

"I love you too." It was amazing how easily those words came out. And once out, they became part of the magic in the air. My shirt fell away, and I straddled him to work on his clothing. The fire at my back was an extra layer of heat on my skin. He pulled me in, and our lips came together again. I couldn't get enough, wanted to taste every inch of him. I arched my back and his lips kissed and nipped a path down my throat to my chest.

The front door slammed open.

"Nori!" Angus shouted from the entrance. "Mason! Get Nori!" He staggered in, carrying someone over his shoulder.

I jumped up, grabbed my shirt and shoved my arms into it. There was no time for buttons. Whoever dangled limply over Angus's shoulder was in bad shape. Blood stained Angus's chest, arms and face. More dripped from the dangling arm of…Berto. The Guardian was unconscious.

Dutch appeared, pulling a robe around him. "Go wake Nori," Mason said. Dutch disappeared again into the section of the house with the guest bedrooms.

"Put him on the table." Mason pointed to the dining portion of the great room. I ran over to remove the few ornaments and candlesticks from the table. Angus laid Berto down, and then collapsed into a chair, clearly exhausted.

Berto was a mess. He'd been beaten up. The skin around his eyes was turning black and blue already. His nose was broken and blood covered his face, neck and chest.

"He's got at least two gunshot wounds," Angus said, and now I could spot those too. Blood oozed from his shoulder, but the worst was the hole in the right side of his chest that made a horrible, wet sucking noise. I tore off my shirt and wadded it into a ball, pressing it onto the wound.

"What happened?" Mason asked.

"Hub." Angus bit out the word like a curse. "Hub did this."

"Are you sure?"

"Sure as the rising sun."

"The others?"

"I don't know. Most got away, I think."

Nori arrived, followed by Yuki and Dutch, who carried a first aid kit. She glared at my semi-nakedness, but when she saw Berto bleeding out on the table, it was like a gear shifted in her brain, and she became all business. She wore a silky pink robe, and her hair was long and loose for sleeping. None of that seemed to bother her as she leaned over the bleeding body. Taking the wadded shirt from me, she peered at the wound. She was tiny and could barely see over Berto's chest, so she climbed onto the table.

"I'll need hot water and more bandages," she said. Blood already covered her sleeve. Dutch handed the first aid kit to Mason, and then ran to the kitchen. Mason pulled out bandages, laying them within Nori's reach.

"Do you need a surgical kit?" I asked. "I have one in my truck." I often had to stitch up critters on the job, and sometimes myself.

"No, the bullet went right through. Just stand back," she said. "I need room, and you're muddying the currents."

The rest of us moved back several paces. I didn't know what "currents" she was talking about, but a few seconds later, I understood.

Nori placed her hands on Berto's chest. I keened the magic gathering around her like a cloud. Then the cloud funneled down to her hands as if she sucked all that magic into the tips of her fingers. She prodded the wound. Berto convulsed on the table, and I thought he was going into cardiac arrest, but Nori hung on. Sweat beaded on her forehead as she worked, massaging the magic. I couldn't quite tell what she did, but the sucking wound began to close.

Dutch returned with a bowl of water and more towels cut into bandages. Nori didn't lift her eyes from Berto.

"Clean his other wounds so I can get a good look," she said curtly. Mason and Dutch each wet a cloth and began gently swabbing their brother's face, neck and shoulders.

Nori crouched on Berto's abdomen, hands pressed to the wound, eyes shut and forehead creased in a frown of concentration. I knew healers existed, but I'd never seen one save a life. She was amazing, and I suddenly had a newfound admiration for the woman. She was obviously much more than the vapid, flighty thing I had pegged her for.

Nori worked on Berto for over an hour. She sent her magic into him again and again, repairing tears and encouraging the blood and flesh to regenerate. Her hands shook from the effort. What was this healing costing her? Sweat drenched her as she concentrated all her energy on one last surge of healing. For a moment, her nose and eyes seemed to shift to fox, but it happened so fast, I wasn't sure if I imagined it.

"There." She slumped sideways. "I got it. Nasty little bleeder." She leaned back, wiping sweat off her forehead with the back of one hand, careless that she smeared blood across her face.

Berto's face was so pale, he looked like he'd already turned to stone.

"Dammit! He's not breathing." Nori laid her hands on his chest again. This time, I clearly felt the jolt of magic she sent into him—once, twice, and again. Berto bucked as if she shocked him.

Nori laid her cheek against his chest, listening. Her hair fanned out like a black silk scarf, trailing in the blood. Finally, she raised her head and smiled weakly.

"He'll be fine now. The wound on his shoulder will heal on its own. I need to rest." She sat up and swayed, nearly toppling off the table. Mason caught her. She looked up at him with tears of exhaustion streaking down her face, somehow more beautiful than ever.

"I'll put her to bed." Mason picked her up as if she weighed no more than a doll. Nori wrapped her arms around his neck and leaned her head on his shoulder in the exact spot I had been only hours ago.

"What in the hells happened?" Mason said as soon as he returned.

"They set us up," Angus growled. He'd downed three fingers of whisky and was nursing a second glass. "There was a riot in Carterville, or so we thought. Berto called it in at about…" He rubbed a hand over his face.

"At 11:10," Dutch said. I jumped in my chair. He was so quiet I'd forgotten he was there.

"Right. What he said." Angus used his glass to point at Dutch and sloshed whisky over his hand. "I wasn't too far, and I brought Paco with me. When I arrived, Berto was there with Drew, Freddie and a few others. They were right in the thick of things. The rioters were looting stores and throwing rocks. Berto got in the way and took a hit to the head. He went down. I saw him fall. But before I could get to him, he was dragged away by protesters."

"What were they protesting?" I asked.

Angus shrugged. "I have no idea. It didn't seem to matter at the time."

Dutch looked up from his widget where he'd been scrolling through the news feed. "It was a political rally, led by the Olympians. Was supposed to be peaceful. Organizers say they were hijacked by another group."

Certain godling factions in the city were pushing hard for a fourth political party to represent their interests.

"Aye. I saw them thugs. All dressed in black like some special task force, but without insignias. But here's the kicker. I recognized a few of them. They were Hub."

"Wait." Mason held up a hand. "You're saying Hub officers fought with protesters?"

"I'm saying they started the violence." Angus's brambly brow lowered and his lips set in a grim line.

"Why?" I asked.

"I don't know. But as soon as we arrived, blasters started firing. I'd like to know who tipped Berto off to the riot. Someone wanted Guardians in the thick of it."

We all looked to Berto, who now slept on the table. His breathing was regular and even, but his face still resembled a mashed eggplant. He just needed to survive until sunrise and the gargoyle magic would heal all his wounds.

Mason paced in front of the big window looking over the terrace. He stopped as a new thought occurred to him.

"The champagne from the wedding. It was laced with that new street drug," he said. Gabe had retrieved a bottle and Mason's alchemist friends tested it. This was the first I'd heard of the results.

Angus nodded. "Aye. They call it Spirit."

That was bad. Spirit was a hallucinogen, easy to overdose on for humans, and one of the few drugs that affected wolves. As I'd seen that day at the hotel, it brought on a primal madness that let their inner wolf out.

"It would be tough to buy enough of it on the street to dose an entire wedding," Mason said.

"Aye…" Angus rubbed his shirt that was crusted in Berto's blood as if it itched him. "You think they got it somewhere else?"

"Yes. Like in Hub evidence lockup."

This night was going from bad to worse.

Dutch held out his widget. "Says here that Guardians started the riot." He turned to Mason. "You'll probably be getting a call from Hub anytime now."

Mason's widget beeped with an incoming call. His face clouded with fury.

"Yes?" he answered. "No, I've been here all evening. I heard. No, I'm not coming into the city. You want to talk, come here." He disconnected.

"Call everyone in," he said. Dutch was already dialing. "I don't want anyone alone in the city tonight."

14

Built over a hundred years ago, the Olympic Stadium (also known as the "Big O") had seen better days. The once iconic tower had been sheared off when the ward first ignited. Half the roof had fallen in, and about once a year, voices in parliament called for it to be torn down. But inevitably some other emergency won the attention of the public, and so the fate of the stadium was in limbo. Now the donut-shaped building was home to various government offices, at least the parts deemed structurally sound.

And they had rats.

To be fair, the hysterical building manager I spoke with thought the infestation was the fae kind. He couldn't imagine that plain old rats could be so destructive. I knew better, but I'd promised to take a look. It wasn't often that I got called out for something so mundane, and I welcomed the easy ride.

I was preoccupied with the attack on the Guardians. Mason had spent the early hours of the morning answering questions from a Hub detective, while all the remaining Guardians waited out the scandal in the forest of Dorion Park. Mason didn't want Hub questioning them until he could figure out why they'd been targeted. Two Guardians were still missing. I hoped they were just hiding out in the city, waiting for nightfall so they could return home. It was a slim hope. They should have called in before sunrise.

First the shifter wedding fiasco with the Spirit-laced champagne ostensibly sent by the Guardians. Now a peaceful godling protest had turned violent. And again, someone was trying to pin the blame on Mason's crew. It didn't take a detective to figure out who. Polina was sticking to her word and destroying the things closest to Mason. We had to stop her before she hurt more innocent people.

But I still had a business to run and bills to pay. So, despite a nearly sleepless night, I was chasing rats this morning.

I stepped into an elevator and hit the down button. Today was a scouting mission to assess the problem. I'd warned the manager I didn't exterminate. And if I couldn't humanely trap the rodents, he'd have to hire another pest controller. The real problem was the building's structural damage. I wanted to find where the rats were getting in. There was no point fixing an infestation if more critters were going to move in next week.

The elevator let me out in a long, curving hallway filled with greenish light from old fixtures. I took out a flashlight so I could poke into corners, and moved along the hall, letting my magic spread before me as I searched for tiny rodent lives. They were all around. I sensed them in the walls, under my feet, over my head, running between the floors. I opened doors to find empty offices and storage closets. Shifting boxes on a shelf of forgotten office supplies, I found rat droppings.

Damn. This was bad. There was no way I could trap and re-home that many rats. Still, I was getting paid for this morning, so I thought I'd better make it worth the trip. A door to a sub-basement was nearly rusted shut. I had to work at it, but eventually it opened. Shining my thin light into the complete blackness, I debated going down those stairs.

I let out my keening. The basement was teeming with life, the magic of thousands of critters just going about their lives.

And then I felt it. I wasn't alone with the critters. Big magic—human in size and taste—came at me from behind. A cloth bag was yanked down over my head. I swung my flashlight like a cudgel and was rewarded with a grunt of pain, but my attacker pinned my arms and I dropped the light. I kicked out and screamed, knowing there was nobody nearby to hear me. He punched me in the stomach, and I fell, gasping. A hand pushed into the bag and covered my nose and mouth. I gulped in air, but got only the sickly sweet smell of sedative.

My head pounded. And my eyes didn't work. I blinked several times before realizing my vision was fine, but the room was completely dark. Not even a crack of light from a shaded window. I sat up. My stomach lurched, and I leaned over to vomit up bile. I hadn't eaten in…I had no idea how long I'd been out. My ribs hurt where a bruise blossomed upward from my attacker's punch. My fingers roamed from the bruise to my belt. Widget and weapons were gone.

Was my abductor nearby? He'd removed the bag on my head, and my hands weren't restrained. That meant he was confident I couldn't escape. We'd have to see about that.

I felt around in the dark. My fingers scraped against rough wood at my back. A wall? I inched along it. No. It was a crate, with a second one beside it. I stood, sending my keening out to get a better feel for the room. The air was dead and stale and…slightly fishy. That's when I realized the lurching wasn't just my stomach. We were moving. A nagging sound now became clear. The rumble of an engine. I was on a boat. A ship, by the feel of space around me.

What in the hells? Why would someone kidnap me and put me on a ship? I was a nobody. A small business owner and sometimes civil servant. Why go through all the bother?

An image of Polina's sneering face flashed across my mind.

I will take everything from him, even you.

Polina had done this. I was certain. It was all part of her plan to get revenge on Mason. She could have just killed me. Whoever she hired could have dumped my body in that sub-basement. But that wasn't Polina's style. Death was too easy. She wanted Mason to suffer with worry, to search for me…oh, Gods. Mason would be frantic. I didn't know how long I'd been missing, but I knew with all my heart he'd be looking. And with the Guardians' reputation under attack, he didn't need this distraction.

And that's exactly what I was. A distraction. While Mason spent all his time and resources searching for me, Polina and Gerard could be plotting a coup or raising a demon. Or eating babies for sport. The One-eyed God knew they were up to something. All winter they'd been quiet. Gerard pretended like his demotion from prime minister had been his choice, while he pushed the railroad farther into the Inbetween. And soon he'd greet the delegation from Manhattan. And with the Guardians out of the way and half of Hub on Gerard's payroll…

I had to get out of here—had to get back to Mason before my disappearance became the catalyst that took down our ward.

I inched along the crates, my fingers catching on splinters of wood, my balance awkward on the shifting floor. Finally, I came up against a metal wall, and a few feet to the right I found a door.

The handle wouldn't turn. It was locked.

"Hello? Is anyone out there?"

I banged on the door until my fists bruised and my voice cracked. I was thirsty, hungry and lost. Tears filled my eyes. I was going to die down here in the dark. How long did I have? I remembered the rule of threes for survival. A person could survive three weeks without food, three days without water, three hours without shelter, and three minutes without oxygen. My dry throat told me I was well into my three days without water.

I slapped the door with the flat of my hand and kicked it, screaming with frustration as much as fear.

A sound made me jump. I reached out and felt the handle turning.

"Hello? Get me out of here!"

The handle jerked and a beam of light broke the darkness. I threw a hand over my eyes to shield them from the sudden brightness.

"Eh? What're you doin' in here?" came a gruff voice.

As my eyes adjusted, I peered into the face of my rescuer.

I emerged from the cargo hold into bright sunlight to discover that my attacker had dumped me aboard a ship bound for Toronto along the St. Lawrence Seaway. My rescuer, Geoffrey, was a tall man with a craggy face and a white beard that stood out against his dark skin. After checking me over for injuries, he brought me before the captain to plead my case.

Captain Perth had little patience for a stowaway who would take up water and food rations with no return. When it became clear that I wasn't a willing participant in this crime, he waved me away and told the first mate to find me a bunk. He wouldn't turn the ship around for one passenger.

I wouldn't be dismissed so easily. "Captain. I demand that you call the Montreal coast guard and have them collect me. I'm a victim of a serious crime. Someone on your ship did this to me. Don't you think the authorities should investigate?"

His brilliant blue eyes were set in a weathered face topped by a wisp of red hair. He stared at me with a flinty expression, and I realized I had overstepped. I was a problem he didn't want to deal with. What if I just happened to fall overboard? Problem solved.

"I'll call the coast guard," he drawled. "But they won't come for you. And as soon as we make port, I want you off my ship."

"Please, have them contact the Guardians. At least let my family know where I am."

Perth nodded, but I didn't have high hopes that he would pass on the message.

The first mate found me a bunk. It was little more than a thin mattress on a shelf built into the bulkhead.

"Here." He handed me a worn wool blanket in that delightful hen-shit color that seemed to be the staple of military tack. "It's not much, but when everyone is home, it gets pretty steamy in here. You won't freeze."

He left me with instructions to see the quartermaster when I got hungry. I was alone in the crew quarters, a large below-deck space with a dozen bunks. There weren't enough beds for the entire crew, and I wondered if they shared. It made sense. At least a third of the crew would have to be on duty at any time. I sniffed the blanket the first mate had given me, and my already touchy stomach lurched. I needed air.

The ship was called *The Hecate*, not particularly auspicious. It was a monstrosity of gray steel with a hull and trim that had once been painted red, but was now faded and peeling. I stood at the stern rail to watch the sun rise behind us. Montreal lay in that direction, but we headed west. *The Hecate* was laden with trade goods for Toronto Ward. There would be no stopping until then. No one could explain how I'd ended up locked in the cargo hold. My attacker could still be on board or he might have dumped me in port. Either way, I watched all the crew suspiciously.

I'd been unconscious for nearly a day, and it felt a lot longer. Mason would be stone for the next fourteen hours. Had he gone to bed wracked with worry for me? Did he even know I was missing yet?

I wandered to the starboard side and found a spot tucked between crates of goods lashed to the deck to watch the land slide by. The boat had sailed six hours ago—six hours during which I slid farther and farther from home.

We rode the deep shipping channel, but the shore was only a few kilometers away. Did I dare try to swim? I could probably make it, even if the water was cold. But then what? The big ships powered by ley-line batteries didn't make great time against the current of the St. Lawrence, but we'd traveled far enough that getting home would mean spending several nights alone in the Inbetween. I shuddered at the thought.

A sea serpent surfaced beside the ship. Its massive purple head crested the waves, and it sent a spout of water into the air before it sank again. Its long body rolled by…and kept on rolling. By the gods! That thing had to be ten meters or longer.

Suddenly, the trip to Toronto seemed like a good option. I would have to suck it up and enjoy the ride.

"There you are." Geoffrey walked with that peculiar gait of someone who spent a life at sea. Of everyone on board, he was the only one I trusted. He'd heard my cries and let me out of the cargo hold. When he'd opened that hatch to find me, I'd nearly fainted in his arms.

He brought me a tin mug of coffee and a scone that was hard enough to break teeth. Geoffrey laughed when I tried to bite into it.

"Not like that. You've got to dunk it first."

I softened the pastry in my coffee and it wasn't so bad. Or maybe I was just starving.

"I'm sorry the captain won't take you home. If it were up to me…" He had a kind smile, and I tried to smile back, but my heart didn't believe it.

"It's okay."

"Hey!" Hank called from across the deck. The small, white guy with a needle-like nose was never more than a few steps behind Geoffrey. "We're in for a bit of weather in the next few hours."

I gritted my teeth. I hate that expression. We're always in for a bit of weather. "Weather" encompasses all the mutations of sky and wind. He meant a storm was coming, but I choked back my rebuke. Hank just bugged me.

Geoffrey grinned. "Yep. I can feel it in my big toe. Never fails to alert me to a change in the weather."

They were both right. The wind had picked up, and clouds muted the bright morning.

"Captain asked me to come find you," Hank said. "He heard from the coast guard. Said we were too far for them to send a…what did he call them? Oh, yeah. A collection team. That's right." He turned to me, jumping from foot to foot with nervous energy. "I guess that means you'll be sticking with us for a bit."

My heart sank.

Geoffrey laid a hand on my arm. "Don't you worry. We'll take care of you."

I wanted to hug the big, kind man, but I only nodded.

WE SPENT A rough day. The ship slowed as the storm picked up speed, and it wallowed in the channel. The constant swaying motion did nothing for my equilibrium. I refused Geoffrey's generous offer to share his rations at lunch because I wasn't sure I could keep them down.

I lay in one of the crew bunks and worried. How would I get home? Would the coast guard call Mason? Had Captain Perth even asked? Would the ship get stranded if blown off course? My mind circled around these questions, picking at each one but finding no answers.

I released my grip on the scratchy blanket. My knuckles ached. My head ached. My stomach churned. I had to have faith that these sailors knew their business. After all, they ran this trade route all the time. Surely they'd weathered storms before. I kept telling myself that as the day wore on.

I must have finally slept. I woke feeling wooly-headed and my bladder was about to burst. The ship seemed calmer. The storm had passed and the steady rumble of engines was reassuring. Several people slept in the bunks nearby, so I rose quietly and found the head.

There was no water to wash with, and I realized why Geoffrey and the others gave off a decidedly ripe smell. But now that my bladder was taken care of, thirst became my next priority. I headed up the ladder to find food and water.

In the galley, the ship's cook was busy cleaning up. She was a tiny, whip-thin woman with a ruddy face set in a permanent scowl.

"I'm sorry I missed dinner," I said.

"S'okay. Second watch just ate. Stew's in the pot." She pointed to a metal table. "Sit."

The stew was barely warm and consisted mostly of potatoes in a thick broth. I didn't care. I was ravenous. The cook also handed me a canteen.

"This is your water ration. It gets filled every morning. Only once. So don't waste it."

I nodded and, despite my thirst, I resisted the urge to gulp it.

After eating, I thanked the cook who waved me off without even looking, and I headed topside.

The moon was low over the horizon and the sky fully dark. The clouds had blown away to reveal a blanket of stars. Standing at the rail, I watched the Inbetween slip by. The shoreline was wild with densely packed trees.

Sometimes, an old structure appeared—the remains of a dock or a water tower leaning over the treetops—reminding me that once this land had been well populated.

There were still people out there—homesteaders who refused to live within the wards, bandits who roamed in packs, preying on the homesteaders and the few travelers who dared to move through the Inbetween. And hunters of wild animals or those who hunted humans, like the opji.

"We're coming up on Grandill." Hank came to stand beside me. "Sometimes them felons come right up to the edge of the water and watch the boats go by."

Grandill was the prison island where Montreal dumped its murderers, rapists and other criminals. Some were fae or shape-shifters who couldn't be kept in normal prisons. Grandill was warded much like Montreal, but its barrier was meant to keep people in rather than keep them out. As the small island came into view, I studied the shoreline, wondering if any of those convicts were watching us. They might dream about escaping on the boats they saw floating by, but they would never reach us.

Just last year Mason had almost lost his court case, and I feared he would be sent to this desolate spot. Angus's fate was still to be written. In another month, he'd be on trial for murder. I didn't believe he would get a fair hearing. If Polina had used Gerard's influence to start a riot, then they had pull within Hub. But then, the way things were going, I might not even see the trial. With no money and no connections in Toronto Ward, my only hope of getting home would be to sign on as a mercenary guard with a caravan traveling to Montreal. That could take months.

The night was too dark to make out anybody standing on the shore, but as the island slipped by, I felt eyes watching us from the gloom.

"My grandpa ended up on that island," Hank said. I turned to study his profile. His pointed nose twitched like a weasel scenting a nest of bunnies. His eyes were too close together, and thin brown hair capped his round head like a helmet. Something about him put me on edge. Geoffrey obviously tolerated him, but…I let my keening flit over his magic. It tasted sour, like nervous sweat, and it rang with sleigh-bell tinkles. That meant I was dealing with a fae. But I couldn't detect a glamor, and Hank seemed perfectly mundane.

"Your grandfather? Why?" I asked, more to be polite than out of curiosity.

Hank squinted at the water. "Locals say he killed and ate a bunch of kids, but I don't believe it. They were just prejudiced against our kind."

"Your kind?"

He puffed up his chest. "Fae. I'm one quarter Sidhe on my dad's side." I think he'd have worn a badge if he could.

"Where are you from?" He slid a sly look my way. It was impolite to ask a person's race. Asking "Where are you from," was an accepted way around this taboo. I could take it literally, and say, "From Montreal," or I could offer up a more detailed account of my background. Though my lineage wasn't a secret, recent events made me shy away from giving too much information.

And besides, Hank just made my keening itch. He might have been friends with my rescuer, but I didn't have to trust him. Critter wrangler rule number eight: beware of the sparkly lure. It's usually attached to a vicious hook.

"Montreal," I said. "Born and bred," which was technically true, but told him nothing about my lineage.

The hatch in the middle of the deck opened and a dozen guards surfaced. They spread out on both sides of the railing. Several stacks of metal cargo crates made good blinds, and they took up defensive positions around these, pointing primed blasters and crossbows at the shore.

"What's going on?" I asked.

Geoffrey answered as he followed the guards up on deck. "We're approaching the locks. Hank, get kitted up."

Hank nodded and scurried away. Geoffrey carried a crossbow over one shoulder and a blaster over the other. More sailors appeared from below and were all similarly armed. They spread out to fill in the gaps between guards.

"Are you expecting trouble?" I asked.

"Always." Geoffrey's amiable face was locked down in a serious frown. "Raiders roam this section. They would love to snare themselves a ship. Mostly we're too far offshore for them to tackle us. But going through the locks, we'll be vulnerable. You should go below decks until we're through."

"I can help," I said. "I'm better with a crossbow, but I can shoot a blaster too."

Geoffrey gave me an I-don't-buy-what-you're-selling look.

"Really, I can. If we get boarded, I'm also pretty good with a blade."

He considered me. "If we get boarded, it will all be over." He handed me the crossbow. "Civilians don't get guns."

C H A P T E R

16

When I was a child, we had little money. My mother still made things fun by creating special "Mommy and Kyra" days. We'd plan a grand adventure, pack a lunch, and head out to explore some new place. Other kids went to the movies, the mall or the amusement park. We went to the creek to catch crayfish or hiked in the woods.

On one of those special days, we visited the Beauharnois locks to watch the big ships pass. I remember jumping up and down with excitement when I spotted the first ship in the distance. It pulled into the narrow lock and the gate closed behind it. I ran back and forth along the fence, watching as the water rose, bringing the massive ship with it. The captain honked the foghorn for me, and I felt like I was a million feet tall. Later, we picnicked beside the impressive dam that created hydro electricity for a large chunk of the old Montreal. It was a simple day of joy found in sunshine and wonder—the purest way a child can experience the world.

As *The Hecate* slowed in its approach to the locks, I felt none of that joy. A heavy sense of foreboding hung in the air. The locks looked like a relic of another age. The chain-link fence that had once kept out an eager child was now bent and broken in several places with its gate rusted to a deep bronze color. As the ship slipped into this berth, I turned to view the old generating station in the harsh noon-day sun. The dam had been bombed during the Flood Wars, changing the landscape and creating new pathways for the St. Lawrence. Part of the power station still stood, though most of the building was a crumbled ruin. A delegation of Hub soldiers was stationed there to guard the locks. They had built a tower beside the station, and I could see guards on the viewing platform, guns ready as they scanned the horizon for trouble.

The ship came to a stop. The air was heavy with silence. Then the great engines started to grind as water pumped into the lock, and the ship began to rise.

Hank slipped up beside me. The side of his blaster glowed with a pulsing green light. He'd primed it to fire.

"This is the worst part. The waiting," he said. "Did you see that pile of rubble as we came in?" He pointed over his shoulder. "That used to be a tunnel under the canal. It was ruined during the war, and the canal had to be rerouted. Now raiders use it as a launching ground for their attacks. As long as we sit here, we're vulnerable."

We waited. The ship rose slowly, too slowly. The Beauharnois canal once comprised two locks that would lift ships over fifteen meters. The wars and the rising sea had destroyed the second lock, but we could still be stuck here for half an hour, like sitting ducks.

All hands on deck stood in silent vigil, eyes scanning the broken shoreline. My hand itched on the trigger of my crossbow.

A guard in the tower crumpled to the ground, out of sight. An alarm sounded and soldiers poured from the power station, while raiders scrambled out of the ruins. So many! There had to be a hundred of them, wielding bows, swords and old-fashioned projectile guns. They split in two. Half of them swarmed the guard tower despite the rain of blaster fire. The rest came for the ship. Sailors and guards fired, but the raiders were fearless. Even as their comrades fell under the constant blaster fire, they kept coming. They threw ropes with grappling hooks over the ship's rails and lobbed grenades that exploded with deafening concussions, filling the air with smoke. Guards fired into this melee while sailors raced to cut grappling ropes.

A hook clanged to the deck beside me and jerked taut against the rail. I ran to it, but my kidnapper had taken my belt kit. I had no knife to cut it away. A face appeared over the rail as if materializing through the smoke. He was scruffy with a black beard, long matted hair and wild eyes. He saw me and grinned. I broke his nose with the butt of my crossbow. He grunted and his eyes went wide as blood sprayed across his face. I thumped him on the head and he fell to the cement far below.

The ship continued to rise. I needed to cut that rope.

"I need help here!" I yelled. A blade hit the metal railing only inches from my chest and skittered across the deck, followed by a hail of arrows. I ducked behind a cargo crate.

Stupid, stupid. Yelling had only alerted the raiders to my location. The knife that had nearly ended me lay four feet from my hiding spot. I risked creeping out for it and was rewarded with gunfire pinging off the deck beside me.

"Kyra!" Geoffrey called from somewhere near the main hatch to the decks below. "I got you covered." He'd seen my dilemma about the grappling hook. He fired his blaster over my head, pinning down the raiders, and I lunged for the knife.

I used the momentum of my leap to slam against the rail and paused to take a breath. Geoffrey continued his barrage of blaster fire, but I had to stand to cut the rope and would be a clear target.

I gripped the knife in a hand slick with sweat.

Lets hope it's sharp.

I rose and swiped the blade across the rope. It barely made a mark.

Damn the gods!

I sank below the cover of the railing wall. Arrows flew over my head and clattered to the deck. Geoffrey had paused to conserve the battery pack in his blaster. I spied him peeking around the shaft of a deck crane and held up my hand, one finger raised to indicate I needed a minute before trying again.

It was times like these I missed my Valkyrie sword. Once that blade had been an extension of my arm and my magic. It would have sliced through the rope and the rail like they were butter. But then I'd been forced to put the bloodthirsty blade into stasis, and now it was at home in my umbrella stand.

My throat ached at the thought of home.

A shout from below told me more raiders were coming. I had to cut that rope. What if my magic wasn't just about my sword? What if…

I gripped the dull knife and willed magic into it. A jolt of power warmed the blade. I jumped up and severed the rope with one slice. A raider who'd been mid-climb screamed as he fell. Then came a splash as he hit water. I tried not to think of him being ground against the wharf by the massive ship.

The boat lurched. During the fight, the lock master had done his job. The gates were open, and we were on our way. The raiders yelled in frustration as their booty slipped away into the canal. In minutes we were out of range of their guns and bows.

A fire burned in the guard tower.

"Don't worry about them," Geoffrey said. "Now that those bastards failed, they'll slink back into the holes they came from."

"A dangerous job, living out here, cut off from all civilization." I was thinking of the soldiers who must battle raiders daily.

Geoffrey nodded. "You did well. Not your first fight, I take it?"

"Not really. My family often had trouble with giants raiding our borders." That got a raised eyebrow from Geoffrey, but I didn't elaborate. In truth, during my time in Asgard, I'd only fought in one skirmish against the giants. Shortly after, my grandfather signed a peace treaty with Gillingr II, King of the Jotunheim giants. So, the rest of my battles had been in the training yard against other Valkyries.

"I was trained to fight. But not aboard a ship." I looked around at the destruction. The marauders' grenades had done some damage. A cargo crate was blown open, spilling its contents across the deck. Several wounded sailors were being attended to by the ship's cook.

"I don't know about you, but I always need a drink after a fight," Geoffrey said. "I've got a little hooch secreted away in my bunk. Want a splash?"

"No, thanks." My stomach hadn't settled yet. I didn't need the extra turmoil of alcohol. Instead, I asked the cook for a sharpener and found an out-of-the-way spot on deck to hone my new knife.

Only four guards were left on watch as we sailed free of the canal. The ship was quiet as everyone rested, getting ready for whatever the Inbetween decided to throw at us next.

The afternoon sun warmed me, and while I worked on the blade, my mind went over the battle. Something nagged at me. I turned the knife over in my hands, looking for nicks, while I struggled to free the impression that lingered in my subconscious.

The blade. It had nearly gutted me. And it landed on the deck by my feet. Neither of those should have been possible. Not if a raider threw it.

I stood, my heart thudding, and returned to the rail where I had cut away the rope. Overhead, a flag whipped in the breeze. The flagpole had deflected the knife. I searched, running my fingers over the old metal surface.

There. A silver mark shone against the rust. A clear scoring where the blade hit the inner side of the pole. Someone on deck had thrown the blade.

The back of my neck prickled, and a voice hissed from behind me.

"Frankly, I thought you'd figure it out sooner."

Hank.

Before I could react, he bent and drove a shoulder into my stomach. The air whooshed out of my lungs as he lifted and tossed me over the rail.

My scream cut off as I hit water and plunged down into the cold, murky depths.

By the time I fought my way to the surface, the ship was far out of my reach and growing smaller as it continued its journey westward.

17

ven in May, the St. Lawrence River was brutally cold. I wouldn't last long as it sapped the heat from my body. Hanging in the water, I turned in a circle, debating my options. The north shore was the best choice for getting home. If I could reach it, I'd have about fifty kilometers of the Inbetween to travel—fifty kilometers of unpredictable weather, traps of wild magic, deadly beasts and marauders to contend with. The south shore was marginally closer, but if I went that way, I'd add twenty-five kilometers to my trip.

Part of me wanted to give up and let the cold take me under. Hypothermia was a kind way to go. Just like going to sleep. Already my legs and arms felt leaden. The current pulled me east, back toward the prison island. A wave splashed my face, and the icy water burned my throat and sinuses. I flailed and coughed, and suddenly, drowning didn't seem like such a peaceful thing.

I swam northward.

The Flood Wars had reshaped this seaway as the river cut a new path and chunks of mainland plunged into the water, creating hundreds of tiny islands. One such island appeared to my right. The current would drag me alongside it, but my ultimate goal had to be the shore.

My boots weighed me down, but I didn't dare discard them. The only thing worse than trekking through the Inbetween would be doing it barefoot. I wasn't a strong swimmer, but I was fit and rested. My strokes cut through the water, and after ten minutes of swimming the shore seemed no closer. Stroke after stroke. The exercise did nothing to warm me and cold settled in my core. I tried not to think about the things lurking in the dark depths below my flailing feet.

Suddenly, a black body popped up in front of me. A cormorant had been diving for fish and surfaced close enough that I could touch him. He seemed as startled to see me as I was to see him. Water rolled off his glossy feathers. He cocked his head to study me, and my eyes were drawn to the wicked hook on the end of his beak. He must have decided I was no threat because he turned his back to survey the waves.

A second bird landed beside him, and then a third. Did they know something I didn't? Dozens more cormorants arrived, and the water churned as a school of river perch surrounded me. Once, cormorants had been nearly wiped out by pollutants like DDT. Then when they made a comeback, fishermen raised angry shouts that they were invading the waterways and should be culled with controlled hunts.

As I watched this thriving flock—the beauty of their sleek, black bodies, the poise of their dives—I thought, *good for them*. Maybe Terra had been right to slap down the humans who were willing to destroy such amazing creatures.

Then something bumped against my boots. I jerked my feet up to my chest, hoping it was just another diving bird.

An arching purple body crested the surface. The serpent rolled through the topmost waves, at least ten meters long. A second later, a huge maw opened under the school of fish, catching perch and birds in one gulp before sinking again. The cormorants squawked and took flight, leaving me alone in the beast's wake.

My mind went numb with cold and fear. I put everything I had into swimming for the island, all thoughts of making the shore now forgotten. I had to get out of the water. Behind me the birds continued to circle and scream their frustration, as they dared not land. A splash told me the sea serpent had surfaced again to feed. I turned and a hysterical cry escaped me as I watched the beast crest and dive. Its open mouth had to be a meter across and filled with hundreds of teeth.

I couldn't feel my arms as they pulled me through the waves.

I prayed to the One-eyed God.

Just one more stroke.

And one more.

And another.

Dear all-father, give me strength for one more.

And the god answered me. My boots hit rock, and soon I was climbing onto shore. I lay on the pebbly sand gasping for air until the sun's warmth finally touched my frozen skin. In the middle of the channel, the cormorants returned to feeding, and all was quiet. I never wanted to go back in the water again.

I forced myself to stand. Wet clothes stuck to my skin and my feet squished inside my boots. The canteen and knife still hung on my belt, and I thanked the One-eyed God for his generosity.

I walked the perimeter of the island in less than twenty minutes. It was mostly bare rock with a few optimistic saplings growing in the inhospitable soil. On the north side, I gazed over the water at my ultimate destination. It was twice the distance I'd already swum.

Anything could be in that water. More sea serpents or creatures I couldn't imagine. Even if I made it unmolested, I'd be swimming for hours only to contend with the dangers on land as soon as I made shore.

I couldn't do it. I had nothing left to give. I sank to the ground without even the energy to cry.

I DON'T KNOW how long I stayed there. The shivering finally brought me back to myself. My clothes had dried in the wind, but the sun was edging toward night and I needed to find shelter.

A dam of driftwood and debris was caught against a pile of boulders on the east side of the island. I removed some bleached-white sticks to build a campfire and arranged the rest in a lean-to against the rocks. I thought about calling to the bit of green life on the rocky spit of land to cover my shelter in leaves and vines, but I had no strength for it.

Part of the Valkyrie training was surviving in the wild, alone and with no resources. It was the last test before a novice could be named Valkyrie. I think my Aunt Dana enjoyed dropping me in the forest hundreds of kilometers outside Asgard with only my knife and my sword. I'm sure she hoped I would never return. But I had—no thanks to my wilderness skills. A young giant named Huyn had been traveling from his home in Jotunheim to meet with my grandfather. He found me trying to start a fire with nothing but my will and my magic and took pity on me. We traveled together for days, separating just outside the gates of Asgard, so Dana would think I returned by my own merits.

Later, I discovered that Huyn was a prince of the giants, youngest son to the king. These were the early days of the Aesir-Jotun treaty, and relations between our peoples were rocky. But throughout his diplomatic visit, Huyn never once gave away my secret, and Dana grudgingly awarded me the right to ride with the Valkyries.

Now, as I shivered in the growing dusk, I wished that Huyn had never saved me. Maybe then I would have learned the art of starting a fire. I broke wood into tinder and packed dried reeds around that. I focused my mind on one tip of one reed, willing it to spark.

After several long minutes without success, I sat back, feeling faint from the exertion. I needed a catalyst or a conduit, something to focus my energy.

The knife. I had heated it once to cut through the rope. Maybe I could use it to kindle the fire.

I held the blade's tip against the reed and pushed. The familiar jolt of power shot through my palm. The steel warmed, but not enough to spark a fire. I tried again and again until the hilt of the knife grew hot. I took off a damp sock, wrapped the hilt and tried again.

Smoke rose from the reed in a thin stream. I pushed magic once more. The reed blackened. A second reed caught from the first, then a stick. Soon I had a small, anemic fire. I fed it stick after stick until I was sure a sudden breeze wouldn't put it out.

I sat back and rewarded my efforts with a sip of water from the canteen. My rations, given to me that morning from the cook, were already half gone. I'd have to be careful, or I'd be drinking river water soon.

I dozed, waking to the sound of an engine. I hadn't been sleeping long. The sun was still a blood-red ball peeking over the horizon. I jumped up and ran to the shore. Two boats sped upriver. They had the look of Hub militia, ugly but functional silver boats with enormous outboard engines. I often saw these patrolling the ward around Montreal. A soldier stood fore and aft in each boat. They wore the black and gray mottled uniforms of the militia and scanned the north shore with binoculars.

What was Hub doing this far from the ward?

It didn't matter. I screamed and jumped up and down, waving my arms. If only the sky had been darker, they might have seen my fire. As it was, they sped by without even glancing my way, intent on the thick trees along the shore.

I crouched on the rocks, my arms clasped around my knees, and watched them retreat westward.

If they were patrolling, they would be back. I resolved that next time they would see me. So I set about gathering more firewood to build a beacon that no one would miss.

By morning, I had given up on the militia returning. I brooded until the sun rose high over my tiny island. My options were limited, but I had options. I could continue to wait for a passing ship to find me. There was a fifty-fifty chance they would be heading in the right direction. But would they see me? My pile of driftwood fuel was dwindling fast. So was my water, even though I been strict about rationing it.

I could build a raft and let it take me downstream. If I could navigate the current, I'd find help back at the locks. The soldiers there had contact with Montreal. Even if I missed the locks, I would eventually float home. It was a good plan, except that I had no rope or tools and precious little deadwood to build with.

I would have to swim for shore. If I made it, the trip through the Inbetween would be brutal. I'd have to scrounge for food and water along the way. If I didn't become food first.

I stood on the northern edge of the island, staring toward shore. A brisk breeze blew against the current, rippling the surface of the river. The water was slate gray and deep enough for a ship to pass. Deep enough for sea monsters. The world outside the wards didn't play by the old rules anymore. Creatures that were once myth and legend had sniffed out cracks in the universe and returned to Earth. Along with those sea serpents, there could be krakens or prehistoric sharks. Nothing was off the table.

And yet…I couldn't stay on the island forever.

Sunset found me sipping the last of my water and shivering. I was tired and hunger made me weak. I vowed that as soon as the sun rose, I'd make the plunge and swim for shore.

As the sky darkened, I built up my fire and hunkered down in my pathetic shelter, trying to ignore the emptiness that gnawed at my stomach. I tossed another stick into the flames. My fingers were cold and clumsy. Sparks cascaded upward. I followed their flight with my gaze and marveled at the rich tapestry of stars.

An old Aesir myth told of the world tree, Yggdrasil, that stretched across the sky. Its roots extended all the way to Earth. Looking up now, I could see the stars forming the branches of the great ash tree. They were so close; I felt like I could walk that road home. But I was still sound enough to realize that hunger was making me giddy. The stars were just stars. I wouldn't find the road to Asgard up the trunk of a celestial tree.

No, the road to Asgard was closed to this world because of bad decisions I'd made after my first love used my blade to kill himself.

Bad decisions. Could I ever get away from them? I ground my teeth thinking about my poor choices in recent months. People I trusted who betrayed me. Opportunities I lost because I was too afraid to make my feelings known…

Thunder rumbled in the distance. I glanced up at the clear sky. Not thunder. An engine.

A boat!

I dumped the last handful of sticks on my fire and willed it to burn high. The shoreline was only a few feet away, but I ran right to its edge, yelling and waving my arms.

The roar grew louder as the boat passed by the south side of the island. *Damn the gods!* From that angle, there would be less chance to see my fire. I ran to my camp and yanked a burning brand from the flames, then dashed back to shore, waving the stick with its red glowing tip.

The engine faded. They were already past the island, heading west.

"No!" The word caught in my dry throat.

You have to see me!

As the boat rounded the next bend in the river, I dropped my arm. The stick sparked as it hit the sand and went out. I was alone in the dark. Again.

And then the sound flared again. They were coming back by the north side. The powerful engine dropped into low gear and soon a boat idled toward me. It was a small vessel, not much more than a dinghy, but standing in the stern, steering with one hand, was Mason.

He had never looked more beautiful.

The boat ran onto the rocky shore. Mason jumped out and gathered me in his arms.

The kiss lasted until my legs trembled, and I sagged against him. He lifted me easily, one hand under my knees and the other around my shoulders, and carried me back to the fire. My head leaned against his collarbone. I could hear the slow, steady beat of his heart—his magic pulsing through his veins—and I realized that part of me had believed I would never see him again.

I started to shake.

"My god, Kyra. You're freezing."

My teeth were chattering and the night sky spun. But those were symptoms of dehydration and hunger rather than cold.

"You found me. I can't believe you found me."

He crouched to put me down.

"No. Don't." I needed his arms around me. They were my only lifeline.

"Just for a minute. I have blankets in the boat and water."

I made a mewling noise for him not to leave. I was too far past thirst to recognize how it was affecting me.

A few moments later he returned with a canteen.

"Don't drink too fast," he warned, then wrapped me in a silver emergency sheet and handed me a bag of trail mix. "It's all I have. Take a few bites until you know how it goes."

I nibbled on nuts, sunflower seeds and raisins while he stoked the fire.

"No more wood," I mumbled. "Burned it all, trying to make a beacon." My words were barely coherent. I sipped from the canteen again.

"Doesn't matter. I've got something better."

"I'm so tired."

"I know. But I'm here now. I'll take care of you."

"You mean I don't have to swim with the sea monsters?"

"Only if you want to." He didn't even question my crazed ramblings. Gods, I loved that man.

In a few minutes, Mason had set up a tent and tucked me inside it. The walls arched up to a domed roof and the whole thing was made of jelly-like material that glowed faintly yellow.

And it was warm.

"You alchemists have the best gadgets," I slurred, barely able to keep my eyes open.

"You're safe now. Just sleep."

And I did.

I WOKE WITH my face pressed against the wall of the tent. I was desperately thirsty, but so comfy in my silver sheet that I didn't want to get up. Thirst won out, and I turned to find Mason watching me with an intense gaze and an inscrutable expression. As soon as I sat up, he handed me the canteen. I drank deep, feeling more like myself. The shakes were gone. I was hungry, but not starving. And I was blessedly warm.

"What time is it?"

"About two hours before dawn."

I didn't ask how Mason knew this. Gargoyles were attuned to the sun that turned them to stone every day.

"We won't make it home before then," I said, and Mason shook his head.

"You could drive the boat, but I'd rather wait until nightfall. Whoever put you on that ship might watch for your return. And there are other things in the water that could cause trouble."

"You can say it. There are sea monsters. I won't shriek and faint."

"I never thought you would. But I'd rather be awake when we face monsters and murderers on the way home. I can't be much help during the day."

He was right. Traveling by night would be better. I'd already lost three days. One more wouldn't hurt.

"How did you find me?"

His expression darkened, and I'm not ashamed to say that it looked sexy as hell on him.

"Nori."

"What? Nori?" All thoughts of running my fingers through his hair faded. "How does she have anything to do with this?"

"She has a childish crush on me."

No shit, Sherlock. Only I didn't agree with the childish part. There was nothing innocent about Nori. If she acted like a child, it was only so that others underestimated her. But I'd seen the steel at her core when she healed Berto. She was a strong, capable woman who liked to act the child when it suited her.

"And how does that translate into me being kidnapped?"

"Seems she has some hacking skills. She broke into your widget to get your work schedule."

"It's not like it was a big secret."

"She told Polina where you'd be. That last job at the stadium."

Well, damn.

"Is she working for Polina?"

"I don't think so." He ran a hand through his hair and I realized how worn out he looked. He was pale, and the crinkles at the edges of his eyes seemed deeper. "She wanted you out of the way. Gerard is hosting a gala next week to launch the railroad. Nori wants to go. With me."

I laughed. I'd been so worried about an attack from Polina—thought of all the ways that would come, warded my house, warned my friends—and the spite of a jealous girl undid me in the end.

Mason bowed his head to hide his embarrassed smile.

"Anyway, Yuki got her to admit her crime, and she found out where they took you. I contacted the coast guard, and they said you were on board, but they had a distress call from the ship, saying you fell overboard."

He took my face in his hands, cupping my chin and running fingers through my tangled hair.

"I thought I'd never see you again, and it nearly drove me mad. I could almost believe Yuki's stories about the old Grimaldi curse."

"I was pushed," I said. "Polina's man stayed on board. Probably to make sure I took the whole trip to Toronto. Or to kill me if I made trouble."

"She wanted to hurt me." His hand tightened on my shoulder.

"Yes, but she also wanted this." I pointed to him and me and the tent. "She wanted you distracted, running all over looking for me. Something big is about to go down. I can feel it like a black cloud hanging over us. Gerard and Polina are about to make their move. They want you and the Guardians out of the way."

He studied me, not agreeing or disagreeing.

"Think about it. So far, she's had one Guardian arrested and me kidnapped. She also made certain that if the Guardians make any move to stop her, their authority will be thrown into question. All those are strikes against you, sure. But they're also strikes against Montreal. Other than Hub, the Guardians are the only peacekeepers in town. And I suspect that Gerard has key Hub officials on his payroll."

I'd had a lot of time to think this through. Mason was silent. His eyes watched my lips as I spoke.

"You don't believe a word of it," I said.

"I believe it." His voice was husky, almost a whisper. "But right now I have more pressing needs." His hand gripped my waist and pulled me toward him.

"You can't be serious. Now? I'm a mess. I think there's seaweed in my hair."

"I could dunk you in the river to clean you up," he said, but he was already kissing my neck. "But it's so cold. And I like the steamy places on you best. Like this spot." His lips traced a line to the soft skin on my throat. "And this one." His fingers found the button of my shirt, opened it and slipped inside. His lips followed his fingers, kissing and biting the edge of my breast.

"Such a shame to lose all this heat to the cold, cold water."

"And there are sea monsters." I gasped as his mouth closed over my nipple, and then I forgot the sea monsters, witches and cold water as he slid beneath the silver sheet with me.

C H A P T E R

19

ason left the tent before dawn to sit on the beach. He didn't want me to sleep beside his stone form. I drank more water and ate the dwindling trail mix, then snuggled down in the warm tent and slept.

I woke feeling better, if grungy. The fire had gone out, but the day was warm even as the sun set. I sat beside Mason with my knees curled to my chest and waited. A few minutes later, I keened the change in his magic, and he came alive. He stretched and worked a kink from his neck.

"I hate that you have to see me like that." He wouldn't look at me.

"I don't. It's part of who you are." I ducked under his outstretched arm and cuddled against his chest. He surrounded me with his arms and his familiar magic.

"I kind of wish we could stay here for another few days." He hugged me closer. "If it wasn't for the mad witch plotting her revenge against me, we could."

"And water. We're going to run out soon."

"And that." He sighed, and we rose to pack up the tent.

"When this is over, we could go away for a few days," he said. "Just the two of us. Somewhere no one will find us."

I smiled. "I'd like that."

We returned home that evening, landing at Perrot Island and giving the boat into the hands of an alchemist who was already waiting for us.

"Thanks, Amy," Mason said. "You can bill me for the battery usage." The deckhand nodded and tied off the boat. The alchemists shared resources on Perrot Island, including cars, boats and horses. Normally, they were used for travel into the Inbetween to collect samples for research, but alchemists could also use them for personal outings as long as the expense came out of their private funds.

"Do you want me to take you straight home?" Mason asked. "My place is closer. We could get some proper food into you."

I did want to go home, but I wasn't ready to leave the glow of affection that seemed to surround us since last night.

"Your place is fine, but I need to call Gabe."

Perrot Island was technically outside Montreal, but the Apex stone that fueled the ward sat on a tower on the island. That meant networks were back in play. Mason handed me his widget, and I made the call.

"Kyra!" Gabe's voice was frantic. "Angus called last night to say they found you, but then we heard nothing more."

I heard Emil in the background. *Is she all right? Does she need us to come get her?"*

I smiled. It sounded like the boys had spent a frantic day worrying about me.

"I'm okay," I said. "A little tired, dirty and hungry. Mason is here with me." I paused, needing to ask, but not really wanting the answer. "How is… how are things?"

"Everyone here is fine," Gabe said. "No change."

So Jacoby was alive, but still lost.

"Clarence?"

"He drank a bit of water this morning and ate some ground beef out of my hand. He looks a little rough around the edges, but I think he's coming out of it."

"Good." One less thing to worry about. "We're going to get something to eat, and I'll be home later. Are you heading out?"

"I guess so. I wanted to hear from you first. It was a good excuse to avoid going out with Emil. He wants to go to some vampire goth club. It sounds bloody awful, pardon the pun."

"You wouldn't know fun if it bit you on the…" Emil's voice cut off, and it sounded like Gabe dropped the phone.

"Sorry about that," he said. "Emil needed to be reminded that he's an ass."

"You boys play nice until I get home," I said. "Go out. Have fun. When you've faced real vampires, drinking wine with fake ones shouldn't be that hard."

"You're right. I'll see you tomorrow. And Kyra?"

"Yes?"

"I'm glad you're okay."

I smiled and handed the widget back to Mason.

"All good at critter central?" he asked.

"Yes. Now take me someplace with real food and a hot shower."

As it turned out, the shower and dinner had to wait. When we pulled up to Mason's place, Yuki stood on the balcony overlooking the drive. He met us at the door.

"Where is everyone?" Mason asked.

"Mr. Dutch is out for the evening. Mr. Angus is patrolling, and Mr. Berto rests in his room." Yuki's hands were clasped in front of him, hidden by his long white tunic. He didn't move out of our way to let us inside.

"And Nori?" Mason asked.

"My granddaughter is locked in the guest bedroom awaiting your judgment."

"*My* judgment?" Mason cocked an eyebrow.

"Yes, Henry. Our families have been allies for hundreds of years. Her actions have shamed us. I offer her life in compensation. I only waited to fulfill the punishment until you returned, to ask if you could grant her death by the blade, rather than a criminal's hanging."

"Death!" I interrupted "You can't be serious."

Yuki's serene gaze fell on me. "You of all people should know how serious this is." He turned back to Mason, awaiting his judgment.

Mason frowned. "I will have to think on it. Please let us get settled. Kyra had a long trip. I'll tell you my decision shortly."

Yuki bowed and left us in the foyer.

I rounded on Mason. "You can't kill a girl for one mistake?"

"Her actions nearly cost you your life," Mason said. "And it was no mistake. She went to Polina's agent deliberately, knowing what it could mean."

I paced in the great room, my thoughts in a turmoil. She was just a girl. A spoiled, spiteful girl, but young and stupid too. She should get the chance to grow out of it.

From somewhere in the house came the sound of glass breaking, like someone had thrown a dish against a wall, then muffled sobbing. Nori had heard we were home.

"What if I can find a better punishment ?" I said, not really believing that I was about to help the person who'd set the wheels for my abduction in motion.

Mason's eyes were hooded. "It would have to be something Yuki considered worthy compensation or his honor will be slighted."

Screw old men and their honor.

"I'll make Nori pay for her crime my way, and you old boys will just have to deal with it. Now point me toward a hot shower."

20

The following evening, Nori, Yuki, Mason, and I gathered around Clarence's cage right after sundown. Gabe hunkered down by his computer in a sullen mood. My office felt cramped with all the bodies packed inside it. Yuki gazed serenely from one cage to another. Nori looked like she wanted to be anywhere else but here.

"This is what you want me to heal?" Her mouth curled in disdain as she stared down at the basilisk. Clarence ruffled his wings and peered up with glassy eyes. "I am not an animal doctor." She crossed her arms and backed away from the cage.

"Well, you are tonight," I said. "That's my price. You do your best to heal my family. Though Clarence here, isn't the worst of them. I think he's coming out of whatever ails him."

Nori looked like she'd rather eat broken glass than touch the chicken-lizard, but she screwed up her courage and laid a hand across his head.

Clarence cooed, and Nori's expression softened.

After a moment, she said, "He's not sick. He's changing. You would call it…" She turned to Mason and spoke a word in French.

"Molting," he said.

"Yes, molting…but something more." Her fingers trailed over feathers.

"He's molted before," I said, "but it's never taken this much out of him. I'm worried he has a gizzard stone or something."

Nori closed her eyes and concentrated again.

"Or something. Definitely." She opened her eyes. "The…um…what is it again?"

"A basilisk," I said.

"He is stuck."

I wasn't sure what that meant, still thinking of the gizzard stone.

"Can you help him?"

"Yes, but let me see the other patient first. I have only so much energy. I wish to prioritize."

Before I could show her into the apartment, something skittered across the floor. Nori screamed and jumped backward, crashing into Mason.

Sweet Pea and Niblet zoomed around our feet and climbed a chair leg to get to the desk. They stood on their back lizard quarters with front paws extended, waiting for a treat.

"Sorry," I said, handing each squamus a cookie. "My assistant has been training them to come back at this hour, so we don't have to chase them around every night."

"It works too." Gabe scooped up the squamice and dumped them into a terrarium that had a solid locking mechanism.

"Do you have any normal creatures here at all?" Yuki asked.

"I have a couple of rats. Do you want to see those?"

The old man shook his head.

Inside my apartment, Nori was clearly rattled by all the critters staring out from their cages and terrariums. She made sure not to get too close to any of them, though Kur still managed to swipe at her with his little blue hand. Nori squealed. Gabe, who followed us in from the office, rolled his eyes. His affable mood from yesterday gone again, and a scowl was fixed to his face. His gorgeous brown eyes were rimmed in red as if he hadn't slept, and his usually impeccable appearance was scruffy: three-day beard, shirt untucked and wrinkled, hair untamed. I was starting to worry that he had picked up a drug habit. In the age of magic, Montreal could produce some spectacular drugs that were both entertaining and highly addictive.

I brought Nori to the shrine of Jacoby. In the middle of a ring of fresh flowers and dried herbs, his skinny body lay limply on a bed of cushions with the bear backpack tucked in the crook of his arm. The fringe of gray fur around his eyes was drooping and greasy. Gita tried to bathe him every couple of days, but there was only so much she could do.

Nori screamed, pulling me away from my worry. Hunter had slunk out of his tank—thrilled to have company—and locked his tentacles around Nori's ankle. Gita poked her head out of her closet, shrieked right back at Nori, then slammed the door again. Her muffled sobs continued from within.

"What the hell is that?" Nori's voice lost its sultry purr and vaulted towards hysteria.

"Banshee." I pointed to the cupboard. "Pygmy kraken." I pointed at Hunter, who gazed up at Nori with big watery eyes.

"Sorry." I swallowed a laugh as I pried the suckers off her designer boots. Hunter looked very pleased with himself as I dropped him back in the tank.

"You behave," I whispered.

Nori was shaken, but she wouldn't give up that easily. My price for her crime was healing. She might not be happy about it, but the alternative was to be handed over to her Grandfather's questionable mercy.

"This is unacceptable." Yuki pointed one grizzled finger at Jacoby. "The punishment must fit the crime. Healing some…some pets will leave our family in debt to you."

"Jacoby is not a pet," I said. "Neither is Clarence. They are family. Healing them would mean more to me than my own life. So yes, it's a fair exchange." I turned to Nori. "The only question is, can Nori heal them?"

"I will try."

"You need to do better than that or the deal is off." I crossed my arms over my chest and tried to look fierce. In truth, I would let the kitsune go whether she healed them or not. But she didn't need to know that.

Nori studied me for a moment, then sighed. "You must move all this mess out of the way." She pointed to the flowers and herbs. "Then I will need a candle, unused. White if you have it. And a cushion to sit on. And quiet. You should all go away for a while."

Mason and I cleared the herbs and flowers. Gabe returned in a few minutes with the candle and set it in a holder beside Jacoby. I grabbed the stuffed bear to get it out of the way.

Errol watched all this commotion from his perch beside the bonsai tree. But so far, he'd made no comment. I walked over to him and crouched to whisper.

"I think she's for real, but tell me if you feel anything unusual."

"Grthbtlt." *I will.*

Errol's keening was even more sensitive than mine. If Nori tried anything funny, he would call her on it.

Mason had moved Jacoby to the floor. He looked so tiny and pathetic lying there. Nori sat cross-legged on a cushion by his head. The candle burned to her right, creating a soft yellow ring around them.

Nori's lip curled when she laid her hands on Jacoby's fur. But she was a healer and a professional. She soon got over her disgust.

I keened a surge of magic. Jacoby's frail chest jerked, and the candle flame flickered. Then a ring of energy circled Nori and Jacoby, like the candlelight had created a ward around them. Instinctively, I stepped forward to break down this barrier, but Mason held me back.

"It's okay," he said. "I've seen this before. She's trying to protect us if something goes wrong."

Errol stood up and watched intently. He didn't like it either.

"She's worried about us?" I looked around at all my rescues who would be within blast range if things went sour.

Nori opened her eyes and shushed me, then sank into meditation. Her hands left Jacoby's head and hovered over his chest and stomach, circling as if she searched his inner core. Then she moved back to his head, resting her hands gently on his temples.

Minutes passed. I clutched the bear to my chest, my fingers squeezing its already depleted stuffing. Jacoby had found the toy in Cyril's apartment. His face had lit with pure joy when he claimed it. I noticed a tear in the inner seam of one leg and remembered the time Jacoby had shyly asked me to sew up another tear. That was the day he told me he named himself after Papa Jacoby's cookies. Before us, he'd never had a family, never had toys or anyone to give him a name. My fingers worried at the small tear, and I vowed that whatever happened tonight, I'd stitch up the bear that meant so much to him. And if he died, I'd bury it with him, so he would always have family nearby.

Nori remained unmoving for nearly an hour, while I paced, and then the candle suddenly went out. She sagged sideways.

"Water," she croaked. I ran to the kitchen and returned with a glass. She gulped it down in one breath.

"Is he better?" Gabe asked.

Nori shook her head, but I didn't need her confirmation. Jacoby's magic signature hadn't changed at all.

"He's not sick," she said. "He's gone."

"What do you mean gone?" Mason asked.

"I mean that his spirit has come untethered from his body. He must find his way back."

Nesi had said something similar—that Jacoby's spirit was lost, and his body didn't know it yet.

"What if I tried?" I said. Mason reached for my hand, but I pulled away. "What if I went inside him like you did? Maybe he would find his way to me?"

Nori shook her head. "It's too dangerous. Without training, your essence would fly apart in an instant."

"So train me."

"Kyra don't." Mason could hear the desperation in my voice. I would fling myself into the void for one of my rescues, and he knew it.

"You think it is that easy?" Nori snapped. "I have trained for years to become a healer. It is not something I can teach in a day or even in a month, and…"

She looked down at Jacoby but didn't say what we were all thinking. He didn't have a month.

"I boosted his immune system and fed him some of my magic. It will keep him alive a little longer. I can do nothing more." Nori looked exhausted now. The skin around her nose and eyes seemed stretched too tight, and her normally glossy black hair was lank and dull, falling around a moon-white face.

Yuki bowed to me. "I am sorry for your loss. We shall come back tomorrow to heal your chicken."

"I'll take you home," Mason said, but I laid a hand on his arm.

"Can you stay? I have something important we need to discuss. Gabe can drive them." I turned to Gabe. "Do you mind? I know you have a date." Gabe always had a date, but this was important. He grumbled something about overtime pay and left with Yuki and Nori.

Mason saw them to the car while I picked up Jacoby and laid him back on his pillow. I smoothed the fur around his eyes and squeezed his little hand.

"I'm sorry, buddy. I tried."

I pulled myself together and waited for Mason in the office. As soon as he returned, I handed him the teddy bear.

"Are we playing dolls? Because I prefer action figures." He raised one eyebrow at me.

"Just hold it." I loosened the stitching around the hole in the bear's leg. After fishing around in the stuffing, I pulled out a small, portable computer drive.

"What's this." Mason asked.

"I don't know, but Jacoby found this bear in Cyril's apartment after he was killed. So I think we'd better find out."

While my antique computer booted up, I made coffee. It was too late in the evening for me, but Mason had only been awake for a few hours. It was still morning to him. I turned to find Hunter wrapped around his ankle. The kraken held out a tentacle. Mason tapped it with one finger. Then he turned to me and grinned, sending a wave of heat right to my girl parts. He was sexy, kind, and he could handle my critters too.

"Okay, spill." I put a steaming coffee mug in front of him. "What's the real deal. You're actually a serial-killer trying to fit in with normal folks, right? Or, let me guess. You're wearing a glamor. You don't really look like…this." I twirled my hand to take in his dark hair, always just a little mussed, silver eyes that flashed with amusement and shoulders that somehow seemed strong and slim at the same time.

Mason eyed me with a slight quirk to his lips. "You didn't get any sleep last night, did you?"

I flopped down in the chair beside him. "It's just been a long time since I've, you know. Been with a man. Most of them run screaming at the sight of my apartment with its assorted tentacles, scales and fur."

"He's kind of cute." Mason gave Hunter another fist bump. "If you can ignore the wet socks, I don't mind him hanging around." I was never sure how much human speech Hunter understood, but he definitely responded to Mason's voice and curled around his shoe.

We turned our attention to the computer. I stuck the drive into the port and after the old machine thought about it for a minute, the screen filled with schematics.

"What in the hells is that?" I asked.

"I don't know." Mason scrolled through the pages. "But I suspect this is the reason Cyril was murdered."

"That's a rail car." I stopped him at a page that showed plans for a new type of train car. Except for the notation about the heavy security, the exterior of the car looked like any other, but the interior was split into dozens of cells just big enough to hold a man.

The next page showed the compartments filled with automatons eerily similar to the gencrew Gerard had used to construct his railroad—the golem-like creatures animated with the stolen souls of the fae. Mason kept scrolling to another design schematic. This one showed the golems decked out in full armor. The sketch detailed built-in weapons including blasters, blades and nebulizers that could quickly disperse gases in enclosed spaces.

"Oh gods." I could feel the blood pool in my feet.

Ever since I'd faced Gerard's hybrid golem-gargoyle creature in Betsy Lacroix's backyard, I'd been having nightmares about it. Now Gerard was bringing those nightmares to life.

"He's building an army," I said. "These aren't just workers. They're soldiers."

"How many can that car hold?" Mason did a quick count, then swore in French. "Over fifty. With just a couple of cars, he could have his army."

Mason and I stared in frank disbelief at the screen. I thought of the golem I'd faced. It had been unrelenting, super strong and difficult to kill. It took several bullets and knife wounds without falling. An army of golems would be unstoppable.

"What is he planning to do with them?" I asked. Queen Leighna and the fae court were the obvious targets. Gerard wouldn't forgive her for ousting him from the triumvirate council last year. But then, why did he need the custom train car?

I scrolled a bit further and found the answer.

When Gerard first proposed the railroad that would dig deep into the Inbetween, many conservatives (Leighna included) rejected the idea, arguing that Terra would never let them build such an aggressive construct. But Gerard wore down their arguments, touting the benefits of trading with another ward. Mansys, a Manhattan company, would build from their end and meet GenPort in the middle, sharing the expenses and the profits. But from these emails, it looked like Gerard didn't want to share. He planned to take over the entire enterprise. The language in the emails was cagey. They never named their target or outlined their plans fully, but coupled with the schematics, their meaning was clear.

They were planning an invasion of Manhattan.

"This thumb drive came from Lorraine Reed. Look, her name is cc'd on all these emails."

Lorraine Reed and I had an intimate relationship in that I'd fallen on top of her corpse in an alley. At the time, I was investigating Cyril's possible murder. I knew they'd been friends, but until now I couldn't be sure of the connection to Gerard.

"She was working for GenPort." Mason's expression was grim. "It looks like she spooked and ran. Probably gave this to Cyril for safekeeping and they tracked her to him."

I tried to look at the big picture, but it wouldn't come into focus.

"These emails were sent before Polina returned," I said, "but do you think she's helping him now?"

"Or pretending to. She'll work with him as long as his plans further hers."

But what exactly were those plans?

Mason ran a hand over his face. "If Gerard pulls this off, he'll start a war between Montreal and Manhattan."

We sat in silence, staring at the horror on the screen.

"So what do we do now?" I asked.

"We call Leighna." He was already pulling out his widget. I grabbed Hunter off his shoe so he could stand and pace around the apartment while he waited on hold. Finally, he thanked someone on the other end of the line and disconnected.

"Leighna is at a retreat. She'll call back when she returns."

That could be days.

"We need to find out when he plans to strike," I said.

Mason still paced. He'd messed his hair as he ran his hand through it while on hold.

"The gala is in two days," he said.

Gerard had gone all out to celebrate the launch of the first rail line to join two wards. On Thursday night, all of Montreal's elite would dress up and gather at the newly built train station to christen the GenPort train. The following morning, the train would leave with a delegation from Montreal, including Gerard. They would meet the train coming from Manhattan at the midpoint in the Inbetween, somewhere near Lake George. After a ceremonial joining which would be broadcast back to both wards, the amalgamated train would continue on to Manhattan. Two days later, the delegations would return to Montreal to sign the treaty that would enable trade between our great cities. It was an audacious week-long event full of pomp and ceremony.

"He won't strike at the gala," I said. "It's too public."

"Agreed. He'll attack in the middle of the Inbetween. No one will ever know what happened."

Manhattan would expect to greet the delegations with a big celebration, and Gerard would launch his armored golems on them.

"We have to be at that gala," I said.

"I've already got us tickets."

Right. Yuki thought it would be a good place to test Polina's magic. I wasn't sure if I agreed. But Leighna would be there too. If we hadn't heard from her by then, we could beg a few minutes of her time at the gala.

"I guess I'd better find a dress to wear." I frowned, but a light of mischief gleamed in Mason's eyes.

"Didn't I tell you? It's a themed event. Wild West. To honor the first railroads that crossed this land hundreds of years ago. You'll have to dress up like a tavern wench."

I laughed. "It will be worth it to see you in chaps and a cowboy hat."

He grabbed me and pulled me in for a kiss.

"You'd like that, would you?"

"Definitely, especially if you wore chaps and nothing else."

"Hmmm." He planted another kiss on my chest where my shirt opened in a V.

"And would you wear one of those leather bustiers that tie up in front like this?" He cupped my breasts, one in each hand, pushing them together.

"I could…" My mind blurred as his tongue found the cleavage between my pumped up breasts.

A squawk came from the office, sharp and full of distress. We turned to the door as the sound multiplied to a scream of pain and the crash of a cage falling over.

Clarence!

CRITTER MYSTERY: WHAT'S IN THE EGG?

June 1, 2077

I found this little egg lying under a bush today. It's probably a dud pushed out of a nest by its parents, but I brought it home just in case. I'm keeping it warm and hoping. We'll give it a few weeks to see if it hatches. It's robin's egg blue, but nearly as big as a chicken egg with spotting in a pale rust color. Any guesses to what might be inside? The winner will receive a virtual Valkyrie Bestiary badge and bragging rights. My vote is in the comments.

Egg Update (June 25, 2077):

It moved! There's definitely something alive in there! I thought it might finally be pipping, but I don't see any cracks in the shell. It's just a wiggler. Get your votes in now to guess the mystery creature inside.

Egg Update (July 12, 2077):

Pipping has begun! The countdown is on. A crack appeared. No visible beak yet, but lots of movement. This is so exciting! I canceled all my jobs today just so I could sit home and watch an egg hatch. Updates to follow.

Egg Update (July 13, 2077):

And the winner is…MartaB, who guessed basilisk. Part snake, part chicken, 100% cute. I named him Clarence. I'm assuming it's a he. Anyone know how to sex a basilisk? Or what they eat? So far I've tried fruit, milk, and fresh beef. He finally ate a bit of pureed meat after it sat in his cage for a few hours.

I'm guessing some kind of songbird.
Valkyrie367 (June 1, 2077)

> Did you find it near a marsh? Red-winged blackbirds have blue eggs.
> *Chickadidi (June 1, 2077)*

>> Not a marsh, but a small pond nearby.
>> *Valkyrie367 (June 1, 2077)*

Snowy egret.
Passerby388 (June 1, 2077)

Dodo?
Myearl (June 1, 2077)

> I'd like to say those are extinct, but these days, all bets are off.
> *Valkyrie367 (June 2, 2077)*

Bless you for rescuing this tiny soul. My guess is a mockingbird.
cchedgewitch (June 3, 2077)

Who cares whats inside? Fry up that bugger. On second thought never mind its too bitty to make a good omelet
Homesteader898 (June 4, 2077)

I'm changing my vote. I think there's some kind of lizard inside. Incubation has taken too long for a bird.
Valkyrie367 (June 29, 2077)

> Basilisk?
> *MartaB (June 29, 2077)*

>> Dont b stupid everyone knows basilisks are big snakes not chickens didnt u read the books?
>> *Pothead666 (July 13, 2077)*

>> Don't believe everything you read. But you should read more. Seriously, go read.
>> *Valkyrie367 (June 29, 2077)*

CHAPTER

22

fter interrupting our little tête-à-tête, Clarence took a turn for the worse. Mason offered to stay, to help me nurse him through it, but I knew he had important work to do, if we were going to stop Gerard and Polina. So I'd sent him away and spent a restless night in my office chair, catching only a few minutes of sleep with my head on the desk.

I woke often to Clarence's coughing fits that caught him like a seizure. Each fit left him weaker until he couldn't even hold up his head. Gita stayed with me through the worst of it. We could only get water into him, one teaspoon at a time, and we were lucky if he didn't vomit it right back up.

When sunlight streamed through the office's front window, Emil woke me from a sound sleep.

"You been here all night?" he asked.

I stared at him with blurry eyes. "Clarence." I pointed to the basilisk's pen, not able to form proper sentences yet.

"Is Gabe in?" Emil asked.

I looked around the office, then at my widget. It was after nine. Gabe was late. Gita was curled up under his desk, asleep.

"He should be here soon. Why?"

"No reason." Emil leaned against Gabe's desk. "Just that he took off on me last night, and I want to be sure he's okay."

Clarence let out a sound somewhere between a cough and a retch, and I was instantly alert. His eyes bugged out of his head and his beak flapped open. Nothing came out. Gita woke and sat up, banging her head on the underside of Gabe's desk. We both ran to Clarence's pen where he flopped around like a fish out of water.

I wondered if Nori was rested enough to try another healing. She'd said he was stuck, whatever that meant, but it was looking more like a blocked gizzard.

Basilisk stones had to come out one end or the other. It was a natural process that Clarence usually accomplished with ease, but something was terribly wrong. The stone had to be blocking his digestive tract. And he'd gone too long without eating. If he didn't pass it soon, he wouldn't survive another day of these seizures.

"Gita, we have to try your remedy now," I said. Gita had been steeping four-leaf clovers in banshee tears for weeks. She'd promised it would be a surefire cure for Clarence and maybe even Jacoby.

Gita looked at me with watery eyes and sniffled. "Tisn't potent 'nough. It needs to steep for 'nother week."

"Clarence doesn't have a week. He doesn't have an hour!" I shouted and waved my arms.

"Hey! It's okay." Emil grabbed my wrists and hugged me. I stood rigidly in his embrace, not because I felt uncomfortable with the physical contact, but because if I let my guard down, I would dissolve into a puddle of tears. And that wouldn't help Clarence.

As if to emphasize my point, Clarence's frail body seized again, and he went limp. He opened one glassy eye, but it didn't seem to see us. His chest heaved in a breath, paused, and heaved again. So slow.

"Gita, now!"

The banshee ran for my bedroom, where the tincture sat by the window to age in the sunlight.

She returned with the small glass bottle of crushed four-leaf clovers and banshee tears. I pulled the cork and dribbled the murky green liquid into Clarence's beak. It dribble right out again. I handed the bottle to Gita.

"You pour. Emil prop him upright."

"I got him." Emil lifted Clarence from his pen and laid him across his lap. I opened his beak and Gita poured a drop of liquid.

"Come on, buddy." I stroked his throat, happy when he swallowed.

Gita poured again. Clarence coughed it back in my face, covering me in green goo.

"More," I said.

Gabe arrived to find us all gathered around the green-smeared basilisk. His eyes told me what I didn't want to know. This looked really bad.

When the vial was empty, I took Clarence from Emil and rocked him in my office chair. His breath came in short, agonizing bursts.

I remembered when he was born. I'd found an egg on one of my job sites, abandoned under an old truck. I tucked it into my jacket pocket to keep it warm and took it home to incubate it, not really believing it was still viable. Several weeks later, it hatched and a gangly little body emerged—half bird, half lizard. To say I was gobsmacked would be an understatement. Once his baby feathers dried, they were fluffy and yellow. His serpent tail had a pretty green sheen. He was so tiny, he fit in the palm of my hand as he devoured spoonfuls of pureed raw meat.

Clarence was one of my first rescues, and he would be the hardest to say goodbye to.

"What do we do now?" I asked Gita.

"Now we wait." She reached for Clarence. "Let me walk him in the sunshine. A little movement will help."

And that was why I loved my banshee. Gita hated the sun. She spent most of her days in her coat-closet nest or our windowless kitchen. But for Clarence, she would brave the rays of the morning sun. I let her take him and Gabe trailed after, always her protector.

Emil sat on the corner of my desk.

"That's an interesting look."

I glanced down at my goo-smeared t-shirt and jeans that I hadn't changed since yesterday.

"It's tie-dyed, retro style." He frowned, not getting it. "You know, peace out? Sex, drugs and rock 'n roll?" He shook his head. Sometimes I forgot how much older I was. I'd grown up in the early millennium, when 1970s tie-dye and bell-bottom pants made a brief comeback. Cell phones were still a novelty, and Terra was just a big rock that humans could plunder.

"Never mind." I wiped a hand across my face and realized I'd been crying.

I cleared my throat and said, "What happened with you and Gabe last night? He seems in an even pissier mood than usual."

Emil slumped in Gabe's chair.

"I don't know. He was fine until some girl came up to him at the club. She whispered in his ear, and he left without even saying goodbye."

"Who was she?"

He shrugged. "Never saw her before. But she seemed to know him."

Please, Gabe, keep it together a little longer. I didn't need another problem in my life, and replacing Gabe as my assistant would be a big problem. Not to mention that I was worried for him. He'd become more than my employee. He was a friend.

"I think it's time we had a little intervention with Gabe. Find out what's going on."

Emil nodded in agreement, but before he could answer, Gabe ran through the door with Clarence in his arms. Gita rushed in behind them, wringing her hands.

"Something's happening." Gabe swept everything off my desk and laid Clarence on it. His body shuddered with convulsions again.

My ears popped as magic bloomed. This wasn't a basilisk stone. He was changing.

Clarence's stubby wings flexed, their span lopsided as the bones ruptured, morphed and re-knit into a new, broader configuration. His body followed suit. The belly narrowed and elongated. His front lizard legs shrank into nothing and his tail grew long and whip-like. Orange-gold cock feathers fell out and new ones blossomed in their place in a dazzling rainbow hue, from crimson at his head to deep indigo at the base of his tail. His wings were pearlescent white and wider than an eagle's. The comb on his head stood straight up and became a bony ridge above a wicked curving beak.

Only his eyes remained the same. In the quiet shock after this incredible metamorphosis, they settled on me with a deep gaze. He shook like a dog, settling into his new size. Then he slowly blinked once and lowered his head. I reached a tentative hand to scratch his bony brow ridge, and he leaned into my touch. Somehow, this amazing creature was still my Clarence. He was whole. He was alive. And he was massive.

Basilisks were metamorphs. Who knew? This was one for the blog.

We all stood in silence staring at the new, bigger, shinier, more deadly basilisk, and it struck me; I'd seen these creatures before—in the Inbetween when I traveled with Angus and Mason. We'd seen an entire flock nesting in a tree and I'd marveled at their beauty.

Clarence seemed nonplussed by his transformation. But when Gita bent to pick up his discarded feathers, he swatted her hand away with his tail. Then he hopped off the desk and ate the feathers. I watched in horror and fascination. The sound of feather shafts breaking was too similar to the sound of breaking bones. Clarence paused his cannibalistic feast and grabbed one of the large feathers that had once crested his head. He presented it to Gita in his hooked beak. She took the feather, clutched it to her chest and then ran to her closet. The door slammed on her muffled sobs.

Clarence plucked another feather off the floor and laid it in my hand.

"Thank you." I rubbed the golden feather with my thumb. "I will treasure it always." And I would because I was still going to lose him. This new and improved basilisk with his eight-foot wingspan couldn't stay in my little apartment forever.

C H A P T E R

23

"You need a dress." Gabe gave me his best disapproving look. I'd been avoiding the subject. The gala was that evening and I still didn't have a dress. Instead, I dug deep into my bookkeeping, telling myself that, gala or no, I had to take care of business. That way, I could show up in street clothes and not feel guilty.

"You're procrastinating on purpose," he said.

"I'm not wearing a dress."

"Oh, yes, you are." He crossed his arms and leaned back in his chair. "It's a themed event. Not only are you going to wear a dress, it's going to be fabulous."

"You are such a bully."

My lunch sat on my desk, but I was too tired to eat. Clarence perched on the filing cabinet. His impressive wings trailed halfway to the floor, and he dozed with his beak tucked into his feathers.

After his transformation, I'd let him out in the backyard, assuming he'd take to the skies and fly away. He soared so high he became a speck against the clouds. An hour later, I heard a knock on the patio door, and there was Clarence in all his new glory. He tramped inside and made himself comfortable on the back of the sofa, overlooking Jacoby's shrine.

This morning had been the same. He woke with the sun, flew off (to hunt, I assumed) and returned around midmorning to sleep.

It felt cruel to keep him locked up in my small apartment, but he didn't seem inclined to leave. I would have to do something about his accommodations as soon as this new crisis was over.

Mason still hadn't heard from Queen Leighna. I tried not to worry about Polina's influence and the taint she'd put on the Guardians. Surely Leighna knew Mason and I well enough not to believe those lies? But last fall, after the explosion in Pierre's lab, she refused to go after Polina. She believed the witch was a victim of the bloodstone like the rest of us—and a victim of Mason by extension. Had Polina spread her lies to the fae court? Was Leighna already compromised?

Doubt lingered in my gut like a bad burrito.

The only way to find out the truth would be to attend the gala and confront Leighna.

And so we were back to the problem of the dress. I hated shopping at the best of times. Shopping for a dress—even a costume dress—was up there on my least favorite things to do list, right next to a colonoscopy.

"You'll thank me for bullying you, when you see what I arranged," Gabe said.

I groaned. "What have you done." Gabe had a terrific sense of style, but if he'd picked out a dress for me, it would be too scandalous to wear in public.

A car pulled into our lot and parked by the office window.

"And here she is now." Gabe's smile was much too self-satisfied.

A young woman stepped from the car. She was petite and slim, with a rich brown complexion and waves of black hair held back by a glittery headband. She saw us through the window and grinned. Her smile was so much like Gabe's that they had to be related.

She came in carrying a fat garment bag.

"Kyra, this is my sister, Sashi," Gabe said.

"Nice to meet you," I said.

"Gabey, I've got two more boxes in the car," Sashi said. "Can you get them?"

"Gabey?" I laughed, and he gave me the stink eye.

"Rhymes with baby," Sashi said. "And he is the baby of the family. Isn't he just so sweet?" She had to stand on tiptoes to pinch his cheek. Gabe slapped her hand away and went out to fetch the boxes.

"Hard to imagine him as a baby," I said.

"Oh, he was impossibly cute. We all spoiled him." Then she put down the bag and sized me up. "So you need a dress, I hear. Something retro."

"Uh, yeah. Twentieth-century western wear to be exact."

"Good thing we just closed a revival of 'The Best Little Whorehouse in Texas.' I've got dresses that will make your man drop his guns."

"Um, yay?" What the hells was going on?

Gabe returned and set the boxes on his desk.

"Sashi is a costume designer for the Cohen theater downtown." He grinned. "Since you wouldn't go to the dresses, I brought the dresses to you."

"So what look are you going for?" Sashi began pulling out dresses and laying them across my desk. "Virgin lady? Tavern wench? Painted harlot? Cancan?"

"So many to choose from," I mumbled. "However will I decide?"

Sashi eyed me up and down and held a frilly green dress up to my face.

"With your coloring, green would be good, but this one is too froufrou for you."

Gabe leaned against the wall, ankles crossed and hands in his pockets. He wore a big grin.

"You're enjoying this way too much," I said.

"I am." He lifted his widget and snapped a picture as Sashi held up a skimpy red dress.

"No, that's not it either. You're tall. We should take advantage of that."

"Sure." I didn't think I was particularly tall, but since she was barely five-foot, I towered over her.

In the end, we agreed on a tight-fitting pantsuit in satiny black with thin bronze stripes at six-inch intervals. It blended nicely into a maroon and gold lace-up bodice with a white peasant shirt underneath. A long black duster and a cowboy hat completed the ensemble.

"You have cowboy boots, by chance?" Sashi asked. It turned out I did. An old pair of brown suede boots with bronze stitching that brought out the accents in the pants and bodice.

"Too bad they're not high heel," Sashi frowned when I slipped them on. "But they'll do."

"Who has high-heeled cowboy boots?" I asked.

"Sweetie, I work in theater. Even the bedroom slippers have heels."

She adjusted my hat and stood back beaming. "Perfect."

She'd brought a folding full-length mirror in her kit and I admired my new look. It was sassy and kind of sexy. I liked it. The best part was that I could glamor my sword to look like an old shotgun.

"It's not very authentic," I said. I was pretty sure cowgirls hadn't dressed in silky pantsuits and lace-up bodices.

"Who cares?" Sashi pinned the bodice to make a few adjustments. "It's the spirit of the thing that matters. You're going to knock 'em dead."

"That's the plan."

Gabe went to make coffee while Sashi finished trimming the bodice to better fit me.

"How's he doing?" she whispered once he'd left the office.

"Okay, I guess. Why?"

She pulled a pin out of her mouth. "He didn't tell you?"

"Tell me what?"

"I didn't tell you that my sister is a busybody who pokes her nose where it doesn't belong," Gabe said from the doorway.

Sashi put one hand on her hip and her eyes flashed. "So sue me if I care about my little brother."

"You can care," he snapped back. "You can also butt out."

"What's going on?" I asked, breaking into the sibling squabble.

"Our older brother was in a car accident." Sashi's natural exuberance faded a bit.

"Oh! I'm so sorry. When?"

"Three weeks ago."

Now I turned on Gabe. "Why didn't you tell me?"

He shrugged. "I just didn't."

I glared at him until he looked away, ashamed.

This is what happens to the strong silent types. They eventually forget how to process emotions.

I turned to Sashi. "Is he all right?"

"No. He's in a coma. Doctors don't expect him to recover."

"That must be hard on your family."

"It would be a lot easier if Gabe would do as he's told and come back to run the family business."

"Why me?" he asked. "I have two very capable sisters."

"And we both have real jobs." Sashi turned to me. "No offense."

"None taken." I still wasn't sure why Gabe took a mediocre job as an office assistant.

"Dad needs you. It's what you trained for." Sashi continued to tuck and pin my bodice. This was clearly an old family argument, and not one likely to be resolved today.

"I'd rather put a bullet in my head," Gabe said flatly.

"If you don't come home soon, you'll put a bullet in Dad's head."

"What exactly is the family business?"

"We're assassins," Gabe said with a straight face. "Just kidding. Dad runs a conglomerate that has many divisions—construction, security, but mostly banking and insurance. It's painfully boring. Can you imagine me sitting at a desk all day?"

I glanced pointedly at his desk.

"This is different. I help with hands-on stuff. Like that fight with the werewolves. Or the golem."

"You fought werewolves?" Sashi asked. "I'm telling Mom."

"If your old job was so boring, why does the trunk of your car have more weapons than a SWAT van?" I asked.

Gabe dropped into his chair as if exhausted. "Dad is also the head of our clan." He paused as if not wanting to continue. "The Saivites."

Holy, One-eyed Father.

"You're from *that* Devi family?"

"Yep. And on that note, coffee's ready." He headed for the kitchen, leaving a cloud of unanswered questions in his place.

The descendants of Shiva, the Saivites, were the most vocal of the godlings petitioning the Montreal triumvirate for better representation. Right now, only three parties could claim seats on the council: humans, fae and alchemists. Everyone else—the shifters, the godlings, the witches—had to vote along those lines. The shifters and witches didn't have enough power to make a difference. But there were a lot of godlings in town, myself included. The only reason they hadn't forced the issue yet was because the two biggest pantheons—the Olympians and the Saivites—hated each other. If they ever put aside their differences, they would have the votes to sanction a fourth political party, but no one was holding their breath. The two pantheons had been waging war against each other for decades—actual war that frequently ended in gunfire. Now the weapons in Gabe's car made sense. And so did his crappy mood for the past few weeks.

"That's the real reason Dad wants him to come home. It's not just about reuniting the godlings. There's fighting within our own community. Our brother, Aadesh, was the party leader. He got everyone to sit down at the table. Now, with him gone." She shrugged. "Who knows?"

"And your Dad thinks that Gabe can step into his shoes?"

"Aadesh was training him to take a leadership role before he left. There was a big fight between them. Neither would tell me what it was about." She glared at Gabe, who wouldn't meet her eye. "That was a year ago."

About the time Gabe came to work for me.

Sashi finished the alterations and packed up her gear. She hugged Gabe fiercely before turning to me.

"Maybe you could talk some sense into him?"

"I can try." Though my heart wouldn't be in it. I didn't want to lose Gabe as my assistant.

She hugged me too and left. I felt like a whirlwind had blown through the office.

"You look nice," Gabe said.

I squinted at him, and he shifted from foot to foot.

"Did you think I wouldn't understand? That I wouldn't give you time off to go see your brother?" The idea that he didn't trust me made me angry. Really angry. We'd worked side-by-side for a year. I relied on him to have my back on the job. I let him into my apartment.

I let him into my life.

And now I found out he'd been hurting for weeks and didn't tell me.

Gabe's handsome face was expressionless, but his jawline bulged from his gritted teeth.

My anger fled as quickly as it flared. I reached for his hand, but he pulled away.

"Help your family," I said. "They need you."

"You don't know what you're talking about."

"So enlighten me."

"I hurt him." His voice was barely above a whisper, and he wouldn't look at me. "I was so stupid." He sank into his chair and covered his face with his hands. When he looked up, his eyes were full of pain. "They tried to have kids for years. Aadesh and his wife. But they couldn't. She blamed him. And one night she slipped into my room. Gods, I was only sixteen. I should have said no."

He sat for a long moment, unmoving. My heart went out to him. Sixteen! That was child abuse in my book.

"I thought no one knew. I had almost convinced myself that it never happened. Then Aadesh found out. He wanted a paternity test for Sai…my nephew. I refused to be any part of it. Sai is Aadesh's son, no matter what any test says. We argued. It got violent. I left. End of story."

That was clearly not the end.

I weighed my words.

"These past few weeks, you've been distracted." He opened his mouth to protest, but I held up my hand. "I'm not scolding. Just trying to understand. Your brother's accident brought all this old history to a head. You need to deal with this now. I don't want to lose you as my assistant. The One-eyed God knows, I need you. But so does your family. And we both know there is no real future for you here. I'll never be able to pay you what you're worth."

"It's not about the money!" He exploded from his chair to pace the room. "I feel like I'm making a difference here, with people. With the animals. I can't go back to face a job I hate."

We both heard the unspoken truth. He couldn't go back to face his dying brother and her wife and son.

"I'm done with this." He grabbed his jacket from the back of his chair and stormed out. A moment later, I heard a squeal of tires as he pushed his little silver bullet to speed out of the parking lot.

CHAPTER

24

The gala was being held in the new train station, a vaulted building with architecture reminiscent of the early twentieth century. The walls and floors were fashioned out of faux marble, so shiny and posh you couldn't tell it was fake even up close. Everything gleamed, including the brassy metal light fixtures and handrails on the stairs leading down to the train lines. During the day, windows in high arches would fill it with natural light. Tonight extra sconces of soft yellow gleams lit the massive room that would become the station's main hub.

It was a space designed to impress, to cater to the elites who would pay the hefty fares to travel between two wards for the first time in over fifty years. Gerard touted the rail line as a boon to the citizens of Montreal, but the average person could never afford a ticket to ride. Would the train bring other kinds of prosperity to Montreal? That remained to be seen.

Gerard Golovin stood at the head of the greeting line like a king. He wore a black suit with a string tie, a ridiculous ten-gallon hat and a big gold star on his jacket, proclaiming him sheriff for the evening. Polina stood at his side, dressed in a formal gown of a deep wine color that should have clashed with her complexion and red hair, but somehow didn't. The tight bodice accentuated her tiny waist and pushed up her considerable bosom. She looked gorgeous, ripe like a tomato heated on the vine. I comforted my jealous side by noting that the ample skirts would restrict her in a fight. I was pretty sure I could take her. But if it came down to a fight, Polina's strength wouldn't be physical. Her magic would outclass mine any day.

We got into the long line of new arrivals waiting to greet the hosts.

Mason swore in old French beside me. He hadn't liked the idea of dressing up anymore than I had, and he downplayed it by wearing black jeans, an old black cowboy hat, battered boots and a duster that almost matched mine. I had a feeling his clothes weren't a costume, but something he'd actually worn once upon a time. The look just fit him somehow.

"What's the matter?" I asked.

"This is ridiculous. Polina is already acting like royalty and we're her fawning subjects. I haven't stood in a line like this since my father presented me at court to Louis XVI."

"How do you know it's not Gerard who wanted this? Did you see the size of that star on his chest? It's a pretty clear statement about who's in charge."

Mason's mouth set in a grim line, and he gazed at the power couple from under the brim of his hat. Wow, he could pull off a good brooding. He must have made one hell of a cowboy. I felt a twinge of regret that I had missed so much of his past.

"Polina's in charge. Always. Gerard might think he's calling the shots, but Polina will be manipulating him in a hundred tiny ways."

As we moved up in line, I could see that Polina held a thin leather leash in one gloved hand. And something was tugging on it. When we were still two couples back, she frowned and kicked out. I heard a yelp, and then Polina turned her glowing smile on the next guests.

"She brought her hound," I said. "I don't believe it."

"What's wrong with that?" Mason asked, but the couple ahead was already moving away and we were suddenly face-to-face with Polina and Gerard.

"Mason." Gerard didn't extend a hand in greeting.

"Golovin." Mason gave as much back. Gerard nodded at me, clearly not remembering my name and not wanting to engage with us longer than necessary. Polina had other ideas.

"Henry, darling. So glad you could come. And don't you look marvelous as a cowboy. Almost makes a girl want to learn to ride bareback."

Gerard frowned and his nostrils flared. Mason was right. She had him on a tight leash. That thought brought me back to the hound, and while Mason and Polina lobbed thinly veiled insults at each other, I bent to pet the creature.

Princess really was the ugliest dog I'd ever seen. She was brown with patches of thin white fur that showed her pink skin. Her bat ears were pointed, though one drooped, and her bulging eyes were slightly crossed. It was like Polina had deliberately created the most unappealing persona for her pet.

And it was definitely a persona because I keened the enormous magic hidden beneath it. This was a hell hound masquerading as a chihuahua. I had to give it to Polina, it was a terrific glamor, unlike anything I'd felt before. Most glamors were only a skin-deep disguise. To my keening, they felt like smoke encircling the wearer, and if I looked hard enough, I could sometimes spy the reality underneath.

Princess's glamor was more than superficial. It was like the beast sat in the middle of a ball of magic that warped reality around her. I couldn't penetrate it with a simple probe, and I wasn't certain that an all-out attack would break it either. One day I would like to try, but this wasn't the time.

Hell hounds were dangerous and unpredictable. I suspected that a large part of Princess's glamor was magic that restrained her better than the rhinestone studded leash.

"Hey girl." I fished a dehydrated liver treat from my pocket. These had been Clarence's favorites before he transformed, and I'd brought them precisely for this opportunity. Princess lunged for the treat and gobbled it down. I held out a second treat, but Polina jerked her away so hard, she choked. Then the hound growled, a deep rumbling sound at odds with her tiny stature.

"None of that!" Polina shouted. Then, when she saw the startled looks of the other guests, she smiled. "My poor Princess has a delicate stomach. Please don't feed her."

I stood up straight and smiled. "Of course." The best way to gain a hell hound's loyalty was to feed it.

"Well, this must be Kelly Greene," Polina said, as if we hadn't met before. As if she hadn't crushed my fingers under her boot or threatened me in the halls of Hub, promising to kill everyone I loved.

"My name is Kyra," I said. "And I'm sorry, I seem to have forgotten yours. Pansy, was it?"

Polina turned a shade of red that matched her dress.

Gerard cleared her throat. "This is my…fiancé, Polina Grimaldi. She orchestrated this entire event."

Fiancé? Interesting.

"Oh, I'm sure she did." I gave him my sweetest smile.

"Why Mason, you have such charitable tastes in escorts. Tell me, does she turn into a pumpkin at midnight?"

I leaned in and whispered, "You're mixing up the story. That can happen when you spend hundreds of years locked in a box. You should remember that Cinderella turned out just fine. But the stories never end well for the wicked witch."

Polina glared. Her green eyes flashed with fire. I was sure with a little more goading, I could get her to hit me with real fire. Part of me wanted her to lash out. My keening was wrapping around her, tasting her magic. Just one suggestion of power from her and I would be able to suss out how she was doing it—how could an incorporeal ghost create such a lifelike glamor?

So go on, Polina. Give me your best shot.

"She's not the only guest I brought," Mason said. Polina jerked her gaze away from me and went pale.

Yuki had been hiding in plain sight, something he seemed to excel at. He'd chosen to forego the western theme, but he still looked exotic in his white tunic, black silk pants and long white beard.

"Polina." He bowed to her.

"You!" The word burst from her. "You should be dead."

"So should you, my child. And so should Henry be. But here we are." He held his hands open in a placating gesture.

Gerard slipped his hand under Polina's elbow. "Come, my darling, we mustn't keep the other guests waiting." Polina shot him a black look, then smiled brightly.

"Of course, it was so nice to see you again, Master Yuki."

Yuki bowed and Polina turned to the next couple in line, but I could keen the dark energy swirling around her like a swarm of wasps.

"Now what do we do?" I asked as Mason led us to a table of refreshments. He took two glasses of wine from a passing server and handed one to me.

"Now we wait. Polina won't be able to resist confronting Yuki."

The old master declined the wine. He folded his hands into his tunic and stood with an air of serenity about him that I couldn't manage after an hour of meditation.

I scouted the crowd. The costumes ranged from elaborate to simple. A few people wore regular street clothes. One outfit caught my eye. A tall dark woman wore a cancan skirt with long ruffles in the back that tapered so short in the front, it barely covered the important bits. She paired it with a tight black bodice, a feather boa and a fan of peacock feathers in her hair. When she turned to catch my eye, I was shocked to see Merrow.

She nodded at me, then looked pointedly to the ladies' room.

"Hold this. I'll be right back." I handed my glass to Mason and wended through the crowd of dazzling guests towards the restroom. Inside, it was as plush as any five-star hotel. An attendant waited to give out hand towels. Assorted amenities were clustered in baskets on the counter. Toilet stalls lined the back of the room and the rest was given over to dainty couches where ladies rested from the exhausting job of being pretty.

Merrow stood by the sink, arranging the peacock feathers in her hair.

"Do you need a pad?" I said as I slipped up beside her. "Here, I've got one. Don't you hate it when your period sneaks up on you?" I didn't even know if the fae had menstrual periods.

Merrow scowled, but she took the proffered sanitary pad. Her eyes widened for the briefest instant when her thumb closed over the memory stick. It was a copy. I'd left the original at home.

"Thank you," she said and pocketed the pad and stick before heading to the toilet stalls. I followed her, making sure that none of the ladies reclining on the couches were interested in our exchange.

"You have to stop that train from leaving Montreal," I whispered. "Look at that memory drive. It's all there. Everything you need to arrest him." I refrained from saying Gerard's name in his own house. Call me paranoid, but he could have bugged the bathrooms.

"This rail line is the key to a major treaty with Manhattan," Merrow hissed. "Even Leighna agrees with it. We won't stop it just because of some grudge you and your boyfriend have." She turned away from me, but I stopped her.

"How many gencrew did you recover from the rail site?"

After we discovered that Gerard had been harvesting fae souls to fuel his golem work crew, Hub was supposed to confiscate all the gencrew. But I had my doubts. Hub's antagonism toward the Guardians proved that someone was paying them off.

Merrow balked at the question. She wasn't one to spill secrets. Then she sighed. "Ten."

"He has hundreds more," I said. "And he plans to deploy them soon. Get that information to Leighna tonight."

Merrow hesitated. Her lips pressed into a thin, noncommittal line, but she nodded and headed into the stall.

It was the best I could hope for.

It was standing room only in the train station. Servers dressed as tavern wenches and old-timey barmen circulated with drinks. The receiving line dwindled to a few stragglers, and then Gerard and Polina circulated through the crowd. There was a whiff of expectation in the air.

The lights dimmed and Gerard stepped onto a raised stage. A spotlight illuminated him starkly, and for the first time, I noticed how haggard he looked. His eyes were set in dark, puffy circles and the skin on his jowls hung loosely as if he'd lost too much weight too quickly.

"My honored guests." His voice boomed from speakers high on the stone columns that supported the ornate roof. "Welcome to Montreal Station, the most important building this ward will see for the next generation."

A spattering of applause followed that introduction. Someone whistled. Gerard was already sweating under the lights, and his face had an unhealthy orange glow.

"Before we get started with our presentation, I want to thank the wonderful woman who put this incredible evening together. Polina Grimaldi." He swept his arm wide, and a spotlight shone down on Polina standing off to the side of the stage. She smiled and blew a kiss at Gerard. He leaned back on his heels, puffing out his chest, like her kiss had somehow empowered him.

"Or I should say, Polina Golovin, since I am honored to announce that this beautiful woman consented to be my wife."

Crowds love a good romance and this one was no different. Gerard waited for the catcalls and cheering to subside.

"We were quietly married this morning and when we return from Manhattan, we invite you all to come celebrate with us at a reception."

Well that explained Gerard's hesitant introduction. He hadn't wanted to give away the big surprise.

I glanced at Mason. He brooded under his cowboy hat. I knew he didn't harbor any lingering feelings for Polina, but like me, he was probably wondering how this new union played into Polina's end game.

"And now I'd like to introduce the delegation from Manhattan led by my friend and colleague, Kester Williams."

A screen lit up behind Gerard showing a group of official looking people standing in front of a Mansys banner. At the center of the group stood a tall, bald black man. His skin seemed stretched too tightly over his prominent cheek bones, giving him a skeletal look when he smiled into the camera.

"Good evening, Montreal," Kester said. "On behalf of Mansys and the citizens of New Manhattan, I want to say that we all look forward to meeting our friends and cousins in Montreal." He held up two flags on little wooden sticks—the white star of Manhattan against a background of blue and red stripes and the red fleur-de-lis against white that represented Montreal. Then the camera panned to the crowd at the Manhattan end, where disco lights showed people dancing and saluting with drinks in their hands. It looked like we were at the wrong party.

"I know Kester Williams," Mason said. "He's a friend."

"You do?" It was rare to have friends outside your ward these days. I had a few contacts through the ley-line web and my blog. But I wouldn't call them friends.

"I worked with him before the wars," he said.

Interesting. Mason doled out so little information from his past. I studied Kester more closely as he spoke eloquently about the joining of our two wards. Without the benefit of my keening, I had no idea what kind of creature he might be. But he wasn't entirely human—not if he worked with Mason fifty years ago. He barely looked over forty now.

Gerard claimed the microphone again and saluted the Manhattan delegation before they signed off.

"And now I'd like to turn your attention to the amazing work that Mansys and GenPort crews have done to bring the dream of a united rail system to life." The screen switched to show the glowing gem on an Apex tower. The image panned out to a trail of towers that followed the new rail line into the Inbetween.

Gerard picked up the narration. "Until today, travel through the lost country between wards has been dangerous, expensive and time-consuming." That was an understatement. Traveling through the Inbetween meant facing vampires, marauders, wolves, dragons, and other assorted beasts that thought humans were a crunchy treat.

"But thanks to the GenPort and Mansys cooperative efforts, travel between Manhattan and Montreal will not only be safe, it will be comfortable and even, dare I say it, luxurious. Tomorrow my wife and I will join a delegation representing the fine citizens of Montreal. At 9:00 a.m. we embark on a historic journey. At exactly 6:17 tomorrow evening, our two trains will *kiss*." The screen behind him showed an animation of two trains gently bumping heads below an Apex tower. "Proving that once again, man is master of this world and humanity will rise above its limitations."

This brought a thunder of applause along with some booing. He ignored the dissenters and went on to highlight the technology, from the chain of Apex stones forming a protective ward all the way to Manhattan, to the sleek design of the new hover trains.

"These trains will be so quiet, they won't even disturb the birds in the trees as they pass by," he said.

"You look great, by the way," Mason whispered in my ear, pulling my attention away from the presentation. "Cowgirl is definitely your style." His hand slipped inside my duster and around my waist. Fingers crept under the edge of the bodice, looking for bare skin.

"Sorry," I said. "It's a body suit thing. No easy access."

His dark eyes flashed with amusement. "That's okay. I like a challenge. I'd like to see you in that body suit. And nothing else."

"I think I can arrange that." His fingers were hot through the silky material at my back.

On the stage, Gerard continued to outline the safety measures put in place to ensure the trains made the trip without disruption. The crowd was silent, so the voice that came out of the darkness seemed unusually loud.

"Is it true that the ward will shut down when the new system powers up?"

All eyes turned to the northwest corner of the room, where one bold reporter dared to interrupt Gerard's speech. Security guards were already pushing through the crowd toward him. People moved away, giving the guards clear access. They grabbed the reporter by the arms and pulled him away. A murmur of uneasy protest filled the room.

Reading the crowd, Gerard smiled and told the guards to stand down. The reporter yanked his arms from their grip and faced the stage with defiance.

"This wasn't meant to be a press conference," Gerard said smoothly, "but I don't mind answering that question, if only to put the rumors to rest. When the two trains join at Junction Point, the ward will be down for mere minutes." More murmurs filled the room. Gerard spoke over them. "Hub has made all arrangements to close the bridges and patrol the island from the water during that time."

The reporter lobbed another bomb. "Does that mean Manhattan will have access to our ward? What if they decide to shut it down?"

Cries of agreement rose from the crowd. Gerard raised a hand to quiet them. When they ignored him, he spoke over the rising din.

"Each ward will be kept separate, with a buffer between them at Junction Point. The plan is not to create one ward, but two wards united by common goals…"

"He's losing them," Mason said. All signs of flirtation were erased from his expression, and he dropped his hand from my waist. The crowd was indeed getting restless.

During the presentation, Polina stood off to the side with only the reflected glow of the spotlight on her.

She was watching us.

Her eyes met mine and held my gaze for a moment. Then she looked at Mason and smiled before heading into the shadows behind the stage.

"It's time," Mason said.

I stalled him with one hand on his arm. "She wants us to follow her."

"Of course she does."

"So it's a trap." I crossed my arms, not moving.

"It's only a trap if we don't know it." He saw the resolution on my face and sighed. "Look, all we have to do is get Yuki close enough to test her magic. But given the chance? A knife to the heart will work on her just like any other person."

I wasn't sure about that, but I said, "With all these witnesses? You'll be arrested for murder before her body cools."

His expression darkened. "I won't do anything stupid. Promise. Let's see what she has to say." I looked into his deep, gray eyes and he nodded.

Yuki tugged on my sleeve as I turned to follow Mason.

"Remember your promise," he hissed, holding out his witch-killer blade.

I suddenly had a bad feeling. This was quickly escalating from information gathering to assassination.

"No one is getting killed tonight. Scouting mission only. Remember?"

Yuki frowned and hid the blade. "But when the time comes…"

"I'll remember my promise."

We found Polina near the back exit, standing in the middle of an interior garden set aside to welcome passengers as they debarked the train. Her ugly little dog sat as far away from her mistress as the leash would allow, but she was alert, watching Polina for instructions. The garden was empty now, as everyone had gathered to watch the presentation. Gerard still droned on about his fancy rail cars in the background.

Yuki found a spot of ground beside a flowering bush and knelt. His white robe billowed around him as he closed his eyes and began to meditate. He needed five minutes to weave the spell that would capture a bit of Polina's magic. Only then would we know exactly how she had tethered her body to this mortal plane. We had to keep her talking until then.

Polina paced around the small garden. I keened the magic trailing behind her.

"She's spinning some kind of spell," I said to Mason and he nodded. His eyes never left Polina as she circled, looking us up and down with a faint sneer on her face. I could feel Mason's magic tightening around him too.

"You promised not to do anything stupid," I reminded him.

"Stupid is in the eye of the beholder," he said. Well, that wasn't reassuring. I hadn't told him about my promise to Yuki, and I'd felt guilty about that, until I saw the murderous intent in his eyes.

Polina needed to die. I understood that. Her soul was as black as tar. Naomi's stories about Polina torturing and eating souls still haunted my dreams. And she'd been willing to sacrifice her daughter for a chance to extend her own life. I was ready to kill the witch, but not here. Not with a room full of spectators and Hub security. She wasn't worth throwing our lives away. I would kill her, but at a time and place of my choosing. Preferably somewhere I could get messy about it.

Unless Mason forced the issue.

Yuki was adamant that killing Polina would send Mason over the edge of madness. I wasn't willing to risk the chance of losing him.

Polina moved around the garden, passing by Yuki who was still kneeling.

"Princess, guard!" Polina snapped her fingers.

The dog leaped, landed on Yuki's chest and knocked him flat. Yuki's head smacked the paving stones with a sickening thud. A chihuahua shouldn't have been able to hit with such force. But then, Princess wasn't a chihuahua. The hound sat on Yuki's chest to guard her mistress's prey, but there was no need. The old master was unconscious.

"You didn't think I would let him play his old tricks on me, did you?" Polina's snarl turned her pretty face into something corrupt. And did she just grow a foot? She was suddenly taller and glowing with an inner light. She loomed over us like an avenging angel.

I dropped the glamor on my sword. Mason's left arm went to stone and his right gripped a knife low in a fighter's stance.

My feet froze. I tried to move them but couldn't. My heart thudded in my chest and I caught a whiff of the spell she'd been weaving. It reeked of fear.

"It's a panic spell." My voice stuttered.

Mason grunted. "I know. Don't let her get to you."

But it was too late. The magic clawed past my defenses, covering me in a cloak of terror. A vivid flash of my last encounter with the witch tore through my mind. The bones on my left hand still ached from when she ground them into the cement. If Emil hadn't intervened, she'd have killed me. Easily. She could kill us now and witnesses be damned.

Polina laughed. And then she screamed.

"Help! Help! Oh, help me!" She smiled and deflated, losing her avenging angel look. Security guards came running, and she turned to them, her expression drawn with fear. She fell into one guard's arms and pointed at us.

"They tried to kill me!"

Within minutes, Mason and I were disarmed, handcuffed and led out to a van waiting to take us to a holding cell at Hub station.

A van sat in the parking lot behind the train station like it had been waiting for us. We'd been foolish to think that we could confront Polina and take her measure—foolish enough to believe we were safe in a room full of spectators. Polina's counterstrike proved that she was ready to put her plans in motion. I had no doubt there would be war. I just didn't know where the home front would be. Here or in Manhattan?

Merrow was on her way to Leighna's with the specs for Gerard's little train from hell. The Ice Queen would have to act. Hopefully she would get us released from custody first, if Gerard didn't have all of Hub on his payroll already.

That wish looked grim when a Hub officer—a round-faced man with a red, bulbous nose—shoved Mason into the back of the van and said, "Aren't you that Guardian guy?"

Mason ignored him.

"Hey, Ronny, doesn't he look like that Guardian captain?" he said to his partner, who was roughly attaching my handcuffs to a chain bolted into the floor of the van.

"Yeah, that's him." Officer Ronny yanked unnecessarily hard on the chain, jerking my hands forward. I didn't give him the satisfaction of wincing when pain shot through my wrists.

The first officer—let's call him pig-face—leaned in and spat on Mason.

"Your gargoyles killed some good officers at that protest last week. I hope they lock you up for a long time."

Mason didn't react to the spit dripping down his cheek. He stared back and said, "There was another man with us, older, and wearing a white robe. His name is Yuki. I need to know if he's okay."

"You should be more concerned with your own health right now." Pig-face locked Mason's chain in place. He backed out of the van, his smirking face illuminated by the overhead light before he slammed the door, leaving us in near darkness. In a moment, the van started to roll.

Mason wiped his face on his sleeve. "Are you okay?" he asked when he saw me rubbing my wrists.

"Yeah, they were trying to show they had their big-boy pants on."

He reached for my hand, but because of the chains bolted to the floor, our fingers couldn't touch. Instead, I nudged his foot with mine. I needed the contact. He smiled sadly and played footsie with me.

"Do you think Leighna can intervene for us?" I asked.

"Depends on what happens next," he said. "If that memory drive is enough to convince Leighna that Gerard poses a real threat to the ward, she'll have to act. But the info on that disk is dated from before Polina arrived. There's no proof that she's involved."

"So even if Leighna arrests Gerard, Polina will go free. Again"

"Yes, but if things go to hell, Leighna can use that as cover to get us out."

Mason's eyes were dark under his hooded brow. The only light came from small console lights along the benches.

"If things go to hell, we'll be low on Leighna's list of priorities," I said.

"Agreed."

"So what do we do."

"We escape." He held up his left arm. In the dim light, I could see that he'd turned it to stone. "We have only one chance, when they let us out of this van, but before they bring us inside. We'll have to be ready."

I nodded. Running from the law wasn't a life I wanted, but we had bigger problems.

"Do you think these officers are on Gerard's payroll?" I asked.

"Maybe. It doesn't matter. Polina has turned every Hub officer against us."

The van slowed to a stop.

Mason frowned. "That's not right. We haven't been driving long enough to reach Hub Station yet."

Without windows, we couldn't see our destination. The lock cranked and the back doors opened. Pig-face held a blaster trained on us while Ronny unlocked our chains, leaving us handcuffed.

"Now get out," Pig-face said. I scooted along the bench and jumped down to the gravel road. Ronny grabbed my arm, in case I had any ideas about running.

Mason stared down the officer. "We're not going to Hub Station, are we?"

"Oh, we'll get there eventually," Pig-face said. "But first we want to teach you a few manners, let you know what happens to those who get cops killed."

Mason waited another moment, then stood up. He kept his head bent as he exited the van and moved slowly enough that Pig-face got impatient. He yanked on the short chain between Mason's wrists. Mason stumbled, nearly knocking both of them over.

At that same moment, I said, "Ouch! Something blew into my eye." Instinctively, Ronny leaned in to see, and I head butted him. His blood sprayed across my face, but he swore and jumped back. I saw stars in my eyes.

Damn, that hurt more than I expected.

Mason used the distraction to thump Pig-face on the head with his stone arm. The cop dropped like a bag of dirt. Ronny was screaming and trying to hold his face together. I kneed him in the groin, then kicked him in the jaw when he doubled over in pain. Mason had already found the keys on Pig-face and had unlocked his cuffs. He cuffed Ronny's hands behind him, even though he wasn't getting up any time soon. He took off his bandanna and stuffed it in Ronny's mouth to gag him. By then, I'd uncuffed myself and bound Pig-face too.

"Let's get them into the van," Mason said. "We'll ditch it somewhere private. They'll make enough noise to draw attention eventually, but we'll be long gone by then. You drive." He tossed me the keys and we jumped into the front of the van.

"Where are we anyway?" I asked. Our widgets were among our personal effects in a bin on the floor by Mason's feet. I was glad to see my sword propped between the seats. Mason took out his widget and showed me the map.

"Looks like we're in the north end. Keep going that way, we'll ditch the van in the flood plains." He was already dialing Dutch to come pick us up.

We didn't have to drive far to find the edge of the flood plains. The road ended abruptly. I left the van in gear, and we jumped out to let it roll downhill until its front end lodged in the swamp. I turned to look down the dark abandoned road behind us. The night was moonless, with no cloud cover to reflect the city lights. I heard a raucous cry from above.

Clarence landed gracefully in a tree nearby. The branch dipped under his weight.

"How did he find us?" I asked. Clarence cocked his head as if to say, "Humans ask the dumbest questions."

"He's bonded to you," Mason said. "You've had him since he was an egg, right?"

"Yeah, but this is uncanny."

"More uncanny than a banshee living in your closet or having a dervish lost in limbo parked in your living room?" He raised one eyebrow. He'd ditched the cowboy hat, but he couldn't lose that roguishness.

"Point taken." Clarence watched us with that calm, direct gaze of a bird of prey.

"We should start walking." Mason had pulled a Hub blaster from the front seat of the van along with our personal effects. He now tossed me my sword. "Dutch will meet us, but the sooner we get home, the sooner we can make plans."

"But we're going to confront Gerard and Polina, right? I mean we have no other choice, do we?"

"Nope. We're all out of choices now."

We started walking, and I was glad my cowboy boots didn't have heels.

Clarence followed us, hopping from tree to tree until Dutch found us on the deserted road. Then he soared high above the car, just under the ward limit. The ward was keyed to small animals. Anything with magic smaller than a raccoon could get through. It didn't impact most birds or fish, but Clarence was bigger than an eagle. I wasn't sure if the ward would let him pass. Ruby and Ollie had done it, but dragons were special. Ruby proved that she could find doorways between worlds. There were many cracks in the veil, something that routinely aggravated the alchemists in charge of protecting the ward. But I had no idea if Clarence could find these cracks. He was often gone for long hours at a time, but I worried anyway. If he hit the ward, it could fry him like barbecue chicken.

I watched him through the window in the back seat of the car as we drove. Mason saw my concern and squeezed my hand. I let out a sigh when we reached Sayntanne. Clarence landed on the garage and stayed outside as we headed in to pack supplies.

"Do you think he'll alert us to any incoming dangers?" Mason asked.

"I think so." Since his transformation, Clarence's gaze had turned wise. "If he was smart enough to find us, he knows something is up."

Dutch waited outside too, standing beside the car, with the blaster within easy reach in the front seat.

"I just need to gather a few things." I couldn't believe how reasonable I sounded. We were planning to attack two of the most prominent citizens in

Montreal, with no sanction from Hub or even the queen's backing. We were out on a limb. And any assault we made would only bring it crashing down. It didn't seem to matter anymore.

"Do you have more weapons?" Mason asked. "We won't have time to stop at my place."

We'd already discussed it in the car. From here, we'd head right over to Buzzard Island where Gerard and Polina would be basking in the glow of their triumphant gala, and preparing for tomorrow's coup. If we were lucky, we'd get there before anyone realized our Hub van had gone missing.

I showed him the weapons locker in the garage and said, "Take what you want."

As I left him to it, I noted that Gabe had cleared out his things. The spare cot was bare. No clothes were left hanging around. In the office, his desk was tidy as usual, giving me no clue if he would be coming back. My heart hurt at the thought of the pain he was going through, but it was a problem for another day.

I changed out of the silky body suit and duster into something more practical. I liked the cowboy boots, but my regular boots had steel toes and could do a lot more damage in a fight. Then I headed to the kitchen and filled my backpack with the special sausages Gita had prepared for me. I'd been sneaking onto Gerard's property for months to feed that hell hound. I hoped that if we faced Princess again, the sausages would give her pause, even a couple of seconds could be the difference between life and having our throats ripped out.

I also added the usual supplies—water, extra knives, assorted herbs. A light peeked out from under Gita's door. A waft of brine hit me when I opened it. She was reading by the glow of her widget. I'd found a stash of rare paper books on a recent job. Gita had read them all already and was now working through her favorites a second time. She'd tucked Clarence's feather into the pages as a bookmark. "Practical Magic" wasn't a particularly sad book, if I recalled, but tears streaked her face.

"I'm going to spend the night at Mason's," I said. She sniffled and waved me away. I hesitated. I didn't want to alarm her with a big goodbye, but I felt like I had to say something.

"If I'm not back in the morning, you'll take care of everyone?"

She lowered the book and gazed at me. Her hair hung like gray seaweed around her pale, wrinkled face. Her eyes were so deep-set, they were lost in shadow.

She sniffed. "Don't get killed." Then she went back to reading.

I closed the door to find Mason frowning at his widget.

"Change of plans," he said. "And we need to leave now."

We hopped in the backseat of Mason's car. Clarence was perched on the flickering street lamp and he followed us as Dutch maneuvered around potholes and got on Highway 20 West, the route to Gallop Bridge.

Mason tried to contact Queen Leighna, but there was no answer. That worried me. Someone was always available at the Winter Court.

"Something big is going down," I said. Mason nodded. Before we left my place, he'd shown me a press briefing shot in front of the train station. Because of an impending storm, the launch for the meetup between GenPort and Mansys had been moved up. The train was leaving tonight, in less than two hours.

"Do you really believe there's a storm?" I asked.

"There's always a storm in the Inbetween," Mason said. "The wards protect against those, just like they do in the city."

"So there's another reason for the revised schedule."

Mason nodded. "This confirms that Polina is calling the shots. We spooked her, showing up with Yuki, and she moved up her plans."

"She took up Gerard's idea to start a war with Manhattan? I just don't see the end game."

"Chaos." Mason looked grim. "Polina creates enough chaos that she can sweep in and pick up the pieces. It gets her what she always wants. Power and the adoration of a people."

"So she's using Gerard. You think she put some kind of spell on him?"

"It's possible." Mason ran a hand through the hair at the back of his neck, making it stick up every which way. "She did a job on Pierre. But she can manipulate Gerard without magic."

"I guess it doesn't really matter. He's been in this from the beginning. Those were his plans on the memory drive, created long before Polina was in the mix."

"Yes, but Polina has a way of escalating things. When all this is over, remind me to tell you the stories of what she did to a village in France when she set herself up as a Queen there." He shook his head and looked down. I grabbed his hand in mine, grateful for the warmth of his skin. I just hoped that when this was over, we'd be alive to tell stories.

We'd briefly considered stopping the train before it left Montreal, but security at the station would be high and we were now fugitives. It was only a matter of time before every Hub cop in town was looking for us. Our only hope was to intercept it in the Inbetween before it connected with the Manhattan train.

We stopped at the ward gate on the bridge. The alchemist guard on duty knew Dutch.

"Don't shoot the bird," Dutch pointed to Clarence who flew in circles above the car. "He's with us."

The guard nodded and waved us through.

"They haven't found the missing van yet or realized that we escaped," Mason said. "Or we'd have been detained."

Yes, the One-eyed God was looking out for us tonight.

A PIT STOP at Mason's proved fruitful because Oscar was there, going over Angus's strategy for his hearing.

"You weren't at the gala," Mason said.

"Nah." Oscar dismissed the gala with a wave of his hand. "Funny how my invitation must have been lost. Gerard hasn't forgiven me yet for taking his old job." When Leighna forced Gerard to resign as Prime Minister of the Alchemy Party, Oscar, his deputy minister, stepped in to fill the position until elections could be held.

"You didn't miss much," Mason said. "A lot of bragging and posturing."

"I caught some of that on the video feed. Heard there was also some kind of scuffle near the end of the ceremony." He raised one eyebrow. "You wouldn't know anything about that, would you?"

"Polina accused us of trying to kill her," I said.

"And did you?"

"About a thousand times," Mason said. "But only in my head. It was a set up. She had a Hub van waiting to take us away."

We quickly filled them in on the events of the evening.

"Damnation and roses, but I hate that woman." Angus pounded the arm of the sofa he was sitting on. Interestingly, Naomi was also hanging around. Ever since they'd met in the cemetery, she and Angus had become buddy-buddy. She now pretended to sit on the edge of the couch beside him. It was a bit disconcerting to see the weave of fabric right through her.

"She's got you running around like a wingless chicken just like in the old days," Angus said.

"Maybe so, but we have more running to do," Mason said. "Into the Inbetween. We've got to stop that train."

Oscar had listened to our tale with interest. He took off his glasses and cleaned them. It seemed like a habit that helped him think. "And you say, Leighna is out of touch?"

I nodded. "We can try again, but we left several messages already."

"That news worries me at least as much as the idea that Gerard might kill the entire Manhattan delegation. While you're gone, I'll call in some favors in the Triumvirate Council and see if I can get answers."

"I think you should stay here." Mason laid a hand on Oscar's arm. "I don't think it's safe for you inside the ward right now." As the interim leader of the Alchemist Party, Oscar was effectively the third Prime Minister of Montreal. If Leighna was already missing, it could signal an attack on the entire council.

Oscar nodded. "That may be wise. Now how do you plan to stop that train? You'll need some serious fire power."

"I've got just the thing." Angus said with a grin. "I put them in the old barn, in case, you know, ka-boom." He made an exploding motion with his hands. That wasn't ominous at all. He grinned and headed outside with Naomi trailing along behind him.

"What is he talking about?" I asked.

"You'll see." Mason's expression was grim.

"While we wait, I'd like to examine the schematics on that thumb drive. Maybe I'll find a weakness in the train's security. Something you can exploit to shut it down without killing everyone aboard."

"That would be great, but how will you get that info to us?" I asked. "Once we're in the Inbetween, our widgets won't work."

Oscar's round face transformed when he smiled. He still looked like he was part gnome, but a young, rascally gnome.

"Ever since I heard Gerard's wild plan to join the wards and create, 'the longest defensive ward in history…'" He did a passable imitation of Gerard's arrogant manner. "I've been working on tech that will allow widgets to piggyback on the rail line's ward, extending their reach by hundreds of miles. Here." He handed me a widget. It was smaller than mine and fit in my belt pocket. "That already has the new program loaded. And my number is on speed dial."

I gave him the memory drive from Cyril's apartment in return. He plugged it into his computer and started scanning the pages.

Angus returned carrying a crate. Gently, he set it on the table. Instead of a crowbar, he slipped one of his woody fingers under the lid and pried it off. It was easy to forget how strong Angus was.

Inside, nestled in wood shavings, was another small gray box. I recognized that material. It was the null metal that Joran's crew had used to nullify dragon magic. Mason had fashioned a bracelet from it that I kept in my belt pouch for emergencies. It helped to keep my keening from being overloaded with magic. They must have taken the rest of the dragon collars to line this box.

Angus opened it. Inside were two shiny globes.

I slammed down my wards to protect me from the magic that leaked out of these abominations.

"The flash bombs," I said. "You went back for them!"

Last fall, Mason and I helped Hub clean up a breached ley-line. A snooker manifested from the breach and spawned. While chasing down one of its babies, we were almost blown up by a crate of these bombs. They were nasty things that exploded with magic so potent they could tear apart a building.

"We went back into that warehouse, though it was mostly demolished," Angus said. "These were the only two we could find. Kept 'em for a rainy day."

I couldn't bring myself to touch them. Even with my reinforced wards, the magic coming off them felt black and oily.

Angus handed the box to Mason. "One should do the trick, but best to have a backup, you know, like a continence plan."

"You mean a contingency plan?" Naomi said, eyeing Angus doubtfully.

"If you like."

Mason shut the box. "That solves one problem. Now transportation." He looked at the clock on the wall. Like most of the decor in Mason's house, it was an understated piece of art—a black granite circle with old-school analog hands. "We have eleven hours before those trains 'kiss.' The car will get us there in time if we aren't obstructed."

I remembered our last trip to the Inbetween. It was wild country with weather that could turn from blistering heat to blizzard in an instant. And the few drivable roads would be patrolled by marauders.

"Horses would be better," I said.

"Too slow," Mason said.

"I've just the solution." Oscar beamed. "I brought it here to show off. An alchemist can get a little too proud of his inventions, you know." He said this to me in an aside, like it was a secret. "Come, I'll show you."

On the driveway, hidden around the side of the house, sat a machine that looked like a skinny snowmobile, except it had no skis. Oscar powered it on with the touch of a button. The machine rose up and idled quietly about a foot off the ground. It was a hover bike.

Mason grinned. "Will it carry both of us?"

"Easily." Oscar showed him the basic controls, then handed us two helmets that had been strapped to the back. "There are microphones and speakers in each to communicate while you ride."

"You're just like Q from those old movies." I laughed. "First the widgets, now the sexy spy-mobile."

"Q who?" Oscar said, but Mason grinned. He got it.

"Now we just need to plot a route to arrive in time and in one piece," Mason said.

Gerard and Polina would be aboard that train, playing the role of influential newlyweds. Whatever they were planning, we would stop them. And this time, there would be no train station full of witnesses.

What happens in the Inbetween stays in the Inbetween.

Without fossil fuels, Gerard powered his rail system with electricity, like the old subway trains before the war, except this one ran on energy derived from ley-lines. It was amazing technology but slow, with an average speed of only forty kilometers per hour. The rail line also skirted east of Lake Champlain to avoid the Adirondack berserkers. That would add a hundred kilometers to its trip—a bit of good fortune for us, since we'd be leaving from the west end of the island.

We planned to head due south through the mountains, hoping our faster transport would mean the berserkers couldn't catch us. They were a tribe of mountain men that resembled the legendary Sasquatch. I suspected they were neither human nor Sasquatch, but an alien species that came through the cracks in the veil during the Flood Wars. They were violent, super strong and numerous in the foothills of the Adirondack mountains. And they thought human meat was a delicacy. So, yay for that.

"How fast can this thing go?" Mason inspected the hover bike with a childish gleam in his eye.

"Top speed of two-hundred kilometers an hour." Oscar tucked his hands in his pockets and leaned back on his heels, clearly proud of his invention. And with good reason. "Of course, you'll never hit those speeds in the mountains. But if you can get through to the old highway 87, you'll make it in time."

"How's it going to manage if we hit a spot of magic?" I asked. In the Inbetween, you could stumble across pools of magic that could swallow you like quicksand—magic that destroyed tech. It's why travelers preferred horses in the Inbetween. And why crossbows and swords would always be better choices than guns.

"I thought of that too." Oscar pointed to a green button between the handlebars. "There's a built-in fail-safe. First touch of magic and the whole thing shuts down. You reset it here."

I looked at my widget. It was after midnight.

"They're leaving now," I said. In a little over nine hours, the trains were scheduled to "kiss" and seal the wards just south of Lake George. I could see that Mason did the same calculation in his head, and he swore, something that always sounded sexier in old French.

"What's the matter?"

"We'll get there well after sunrise." He paced around the hover cycle. "Maybe I shouldn't go." He looked to Oscar, who held up his hands in retreat.

"Don't look at me. I'm an ideas guy. If I faced a berserker, I'd piss my pants right before it tore off my head."

Mason scowled and continued pacing. I knew exactly what he was thinking. The curse that turned him to stone every morning ate at his confidence. It was the reason he held back from so many things like running for Prime Minister of the Alchemists, even though he was the most qualified man for the job. It was also the reason he'd stayed away from me for two long years. And now he beat himself up for not being able to keep me safe in the Inbetween or to help me stop Gerard and Polina.

Because I was going, with or without him, and he knew it.

I reached for his arm to stop him. "You just have to get me there. Get me through the mountains. And if all goes well, we'll be at Lake George in five hours. Before sunrise. By then, Oscar will have a solid plan to blow up that gods-cursed train and all those golems aboard. Right?"

Oscar nodded. "That's the plan."

Mason met my gaze and I could see shame warring with fear for my safety in his eyes.

"Let's do this then." He pulled me in for a quick kiss.

THE BIKE HAD one small storage compartment under the passenger seat. We packed the flash bombs, water and dry rations for the trip. I didn't like riding with that kind of firepower right under my butt, but what choice did I have?

The first few miles through Dorion Park were the roughest as Mason got a feel for the sensitive controls. I'm sure I didn't help. I had my legs clamped so tight around him they cramped. My head felt big and heavy in the helmet, and I wore leather work gloves and a thicker jacket that Mason had provided against the cold. All of this equipment left me feeling like I was suspended in a cocoon that was hurtling through the night. I laid my head on his back and tried to breathe.

"You okay?" His voice came through the speaker in my helmet.

"I once saw a biker whose shirt back was printed with 'If you can read this, my wife fell off.' I thought it was hilarious at the time. Now? Not so much."

"Well, if you hang on any tighter, I'm going to lose the feeling in my hips." I could hear laughter in his tone. I relaxed the death grip of my legs, but he squeezed my thigh with one hand. "Don't. I like it."

"How fast are we going?"

"About forty."

"It feels a lot faster."

"You're not going to be sick on me, are you?"

Considering how many times he'd seen me puking my guts out, it was a fair question.

"Don't worry about me. Go as fast as you need."

Even at this speed, we'd beat the train to Lake George, but the sun was our first enemy. I wasn't sure I could drive this bike, and I certainly didn't want to do it alone in a berserker infested forest. We needed to get as close to Junction Point as possible before sunrise.

Mason started to sing softly in French. I didn't recognize the song and only understood the gist of it—a story about a little ship that gets lost on its maiden voyage and the sailors turn to cannibalism until the Virgin Mary intervenes. I had to hand it to the French. They had the best lullabies. I don't know why he chose that song, but his voice was soft and intimate in my ear, soothing like warm cocoa on a cold day and the purr of your favorite cat all in one. I relaxed a bit as the trees whipped by us in a constant blur. Once in a while, the bike lurched as the ground rose or Mason wrenched it upward to avoid an obstacle.

We increased our speed as he became more confident controlling the bike. He'd warned me to follow his lead and not pull away when he leaned into a turn. Soon our bodies moved as one. With my legs clamped around him, the hum of the motor settling deep into my core and his velvety voice in my ear…well, it was a little exciting. If we weren't pressed for time to prevent a war, I'd have told him to stop that bike and make love to me right there on the cold ground. Instead we drove on through the night, heading southeast, hoping to catch the 187 before anything nastier found us.

While crossing one large open field, I spied Clarence tracking us from above and the sight boosted my spirits.

We rode for over an hour at top speed. Mason gave up singing and only the faint hum of the engine broke the quiet. As the terrain grew rockier and the trees denser, we had to slow down. Eventually, we came to a creek, and drove along the banks until we found a spot clear of brambles where we could cross. We stopped to rest for a moment, sipping water from our canteens. It felt good to stretch my legs after sitting in that cramped position for so long. The bike's electric motor was quiet enough that the sound of a twig snapping made us sit up and scan the underbrush. It was impossible to see into the shadows beneath the trees, and my imagination ran wild, thinking of all the creatures hiding there. We were well into the foothills now, and even before Terra reclaimed this land, it had been a haven for wildlife.

A massive body stole along the edge of the stream. Its eyes caught our headlight and glowed. It opened a huge mouth and spat a hiss in our direction, before bending to take a drink.

"What in the hells is that?" Mason asked.

"Mountain lion, I think." They used to be plentiful in this area, but the big cat looked somehow wrong to me. The joints of its legs were off, more ursine than feline. But before I could examine it further, the beast jerked its head up, sniffed the air, and bolted back into the darkness.

"Second rule of critter wrangling," I muttered.

"What's that?"

"When scary things run away, something scarier is coming."

Suddenly, I could feel eyes watching us from the forest.

"Get on," Mason said, already jamming on his helmet. In seconds we were moving again, zooming over the water as we followed the river's winding path.

At least it was free of the foliage that had been slowing us down. When the river switched back westward, we turned into the trees. With the mountains to our right, we looked for a path that would take us east to the highway.

We didn't get far.

The ground dipped into a culvert filled with shimmering fog. At least to me, it shimmered. Mason couldn't see the pool of latent magic, and even as I shouted for him to go around, he drove right into it.

The bike stalled. Magic swirled at our feet, like dozens of tiny hands trying to pull me off the bike.

"It's a hot spot," I said, and Mason grunted his agreement as he fiddled with the controls.

During the Flood Wars, thousands of flash bombs—like the ones now tucked into the bike's trunk—were dropped on the land as governments rose and fell. They breached ley-lines, increasing the rapid return of magic to our world. And they destroyed all tech in their vicinity, killing some people, and mutating others. Some Alchemists theorized that these bombs were the genesis of the Inbetween. Others believed that the ley-lines had already flooded the world, making such weaponry a possibility. It was a chicken or the egg kind of argument that might never be explained.

We spent a tense minute sitting exposed while Mason hit the reset button and tried to restart the engine. Nothing. The bike was dead. The skin on my neck prickled. Someone was watching us. Clarence cawed from above, and I silently hoped that he would stay there.

"We have to push it out of here," Mason said, "and fast." He held out his left arm. It had already gone to stone. He gave me a dark look. He was fighting the change.

Dear gods, if he turned to stone, I would never move him out of the hot spot. He'd be stuck here, unable to escape the magic, and I'd be alone, on foot in berserker country.

I jumped off the bike and ran ten meters into the forest. The magic clung to me, trying to pull me back in.

"Here!" I called. "This is the edge."

I ran back to help him move the bike, which weighed about a hundred kilos. Mason jammed his stone arm under the chassis and we lifted, shuffled a few paces and put it down. Again, lift, shuffle, rest. Ten precious minutes later, we crossed the threshold, leaving the pool of magic behind.

Mason took a deep, steadying breath. I hugged him and his arms—both pliable human flesh—circled me. Our helmets bumped, reminding us that we had no time for comfort.

Free of the magic, the bike flared to life, but as we started forward, I spotted dark shapes flanking us in the trees.

"Something's out there," I said, too loud in the quiet of our helmets.

"I see them."

He shifted gears, and we sped forward, narrowly missing a tree trunk as he maneuvered through the dense underbrush. There was no path here. Branches slapped me. The bike bucked as Mason jerked it around a moss-covered boulder that suddenly appeared out of the night. The creatures ran through the trees with us. We slowed because of the constant obstructions, but they were fast enough to keep up.

"Mason!" I shouted as the shadow figures appeared right in our path. He redirected, lurching the bike left so hard, I nearly lost my grip. It was a desperate battle between speed and caution. Twice, the massive, hairy creatures blocked our way, and we had to divert.

They're herding us!

Mason veered right, and we almost hit a rock wall before he turned us away again. With the wall at our backs, and a steep incline to our right, we had little choice but to head back into the dense trees.

A rock hit my helmet, wrenching me sideways. I crashed to the ground, knocking the wind from my lungs. Mason swung the bike around, returning for me just as a berserker stepped into the light, his arm raised to launch another rock.

He was tall—easily seven feet—with long arms that let his hands brush the ground. Hair the color of dead moss covered him. It was matted with dirt and twigs. But that's where the resemblance to the myths of the Sasquatch ended. The berserker's face was oddly hairless, pear-shaped and flat, with a blunt nose and small pale mouth. Black lashless eyes stared at us without emotion. He drew back his raised arm to throw.

"Get on!" Mason shouted. I jumped on the back of the bike. He kicked it into gear and we lurched forward, knocking down the berserker. Then we skidded to a stop at a wall of the flat-faced creatures. They pelted us with stones.

Mason turned the bike, only to find more berserkers blocking our way. He slowed again.

"Can you shoot them?" he asked. I fumbled for the blaster at my belt, pulled it free and fired. The gun clicked, but nothing happened.

Dammit. The pool of magic had fried it. That's why I hated guns. They never worked when you really needed them. I threw it at a berserker. He made a high-pitched squealing noise when I hit my target. More rocks pinged off the bike. One struck my shoulder hard enough that I almost fell off again.

"Ram them!" I shouted

"We won't make it. They'll tear us off the bike."

The berserkers circled us. There had to be twenty of them. Each held a stone at the ready, but they didn't move to attack. Maybe they wanted our bike intact. It would be a treasure to such a primitive tribe. Or maybe they wanted us alive. I couldn't help thinking that freshly killed meat would be tastier than a kill they had to lug for hours to their village. Did berserkers even have villages? I had no idea.

Silently, they closed in.

"We need to stand and fight," Mason said, but he made no move to get off the bike. I already had my knife out.

A shrill caw from above reminded me we weren't alone. Clarence swooped down, breaking branches in his dive. He broke his fall with a spread of impressive wings and raked his talons across the face of a berserker. The beast-man screamed like a stuck boar. Clarence took to the sky only to fall on another berserker. They scattered, screaming and snorting. One was brave enough to lunge at us, and I slashed his eyes before Mason got us out of there.

We sped through the forest with Clarence cawing above us like a police escort. I spied the berserkers loping along beside the bike, but they couldn't keep up for long, and soon we were once again dodging only trees and boulders.

My hands ached from gripping Mason's waist. The spike of adrenaline had left me sweaty and thirsty inside my helmet, but I didn't ask him to stop. We rode for over an hour until the trees thinned and ground leveled out. A few more kilometers and Mason brought us to a halt at a falling-down structure of antique cement. It was the on-ramp for the highway. We stopped for a breather and some water.

Clarence circled high above, then landed on the ramp's metal railing. I got off the bike with shaky legs. I wanted to hug him. I would have hugged the old Clarence, but this new version was too poised and proud.

His curved beak opened.

"Gobble, gobble." He cocked his brilliant red head. His serpentine tail whipped back and forth. I thought he might be smiling. I reached out, ready for him to pull away, but he ducked under my hand, and I petted the silky soft feathers on his neck.

"Gobble, gobble," I said.

He cawed once and launched into the sky.

WE JOINED THE highway just south of what was once Plattsburgh, New York. Terra had done her job here too. Only the tallest buildings crested the lush growth that grew beside the highway. The forest was so green, I felt as if we'd ridden into the middle of summer. To our left shimmered the black expanse of Lake Champlain. The highway followed the shoreline for about fifty kilometers, until the lake thinned to nothing more than a narrow river and we veered west, back into the wild lands.

The road was mostly free of foliage, though the antique asphalt was buckled in many places, and greenery bloomed through these cracks. Mason pushed the bike hard, slowing only to avoid large obstacles like snarls of twisted metal, splintered wood and garbage deposited in the road like flotsam. Old cars were abandoned on the road too. I tried not to think of their last occupants, people who had left their dead vehicles to flee on foot, desperate to escape the inescapable.

We drove on.

In the east, the sky bled from black to purple.

I could feel the tension in Mason as I clung to him.

Just a bit further. One-eyed Father, just get us a bit further.

The road turned east again. In the distance, another lake reflected the pre-dawn light.

"Is that Lake George?" I asked.

"Yes. We're about twenty minutes out."

Twenty minutes to the junction site. We wouldn't make it.

"Just stop," I said. "I can walk the rest of the way."

"Not yet."

I wanted at least a few minutes to confer with Mason before the sun forced him to leave me. The tension of not knowing when he would turn was almost too much to bear. My legs ached from squeezing his hips. He now drove with reckless speed. The engine whined in complaint. Finally, we left the highway, plunging into the trees again until we came to the remains of a village on the edge of the lake. Mason pulled to a stop and killed the engine.

I stumbled off the bike and stamped my feet to bring feeling back to them as I looked around. We were on Main Street of what had once been a resort town for cottagers and boaters who spent their summers on the lake. Run down buildings could have been stores or houses, it was hard to tell. They weren't much more than brick frames filled with debris and new growth.

"Do you have it?" Mason's voice was gruff. I turned to find him talking on the widget Oscar had given us. He listened, nodding once. "Yes, we're here." He listened some more and said impatiently, "Forget all that. I have only a few minutes. Tell me what you found in the schematics." As Oscar spoke, his expression darkened. "That's insane." Oscar must have pleaded his case, because he said, "Fine. Send the specs." Then he cut the call and ran his hand over his eyes.

"Look here." He held out the widget with the train specs displayed. "Oscar says you need to focus your attack on this car." He pointed to the second car from the end of the train. "The golems are here. Gerard won't make his move until after the trains are joined. He needs to take control of both. If you can, disable this first car of golems."

"I get it. Even if I only get to one car, I'll block the other golems." It was barely a plan.

Mason nodded, though he was frowning. "There's just one problem."

"Just one? Oh, that's all right then." I threw my hands in the air and an edge of hysteria crept into my tone. Now that we were here, the reality of my situation sank in. In a few minutes, I would be alone in the Inbetween with nothing but my wits to stop a train full of killer golems. To stop a war.

Mason grabbed my hands and pulled me toward him. "Kyra, you can do this. Look at me!" He cupped my face in his hands and dragged my gaze to meet his. "You fought a rock troll and won. You escaped Underhill on the back of a dragon, remember that? You fought an army of vampires. You. Can. Do. This."

I bit my lip, holding back tears and nodded.

"Good. Now listen. I have only moments. The golem cars are armored. Even the flash bombs will do little damage to them. You have to drop the bomb inside. As soon as the ward goes down. You'll have less than five minutes. Here's where you drop it."

He pointed to an emergency hatch on top of the train car.

"I don't know how, but you must get that open and drop the bomb inside."

"I'll manage." I pushed the widget aside and sank into his arms. He kissed my forehead.

"I'm sorry I can't be there with you."

"I know." We had no other words. Instead, I listened to the slow beat of his heart, letting his magic wrap around me, until he gently pushed me away and stood back.

"I love you," he said, and in the next moment, he turned to stone.

Seeing Mason in stone form was like a dash of cold water down my neck. He seemed so…gone. Then I let out my keening to feel the beat of his magic, slower and deeper than usual, but still alive. That was my Mason. He didn't like me to see him in this state. He thought he was repulsive. So I kissed his forehead, knowing he would sense it even now. If I didn't come back, he'd wrestle with his guilt for abandoning me in the Inbetween for the rest of his long life. But at least he'd know that nothing about him repulsed me. I walked away without looking back.

A block down the old Main Street, a fallen tree blocked the road. Lying on its side, the trunk was twice as tall as me. This wasn't an ordinary tree. It was the kind that could only be found in post-war Inbetween where earth magic ran rampant. I couldn't even imagine the storm that must have brought it down. I considered going around, but a root ball blocked the path on one end and the tangled mass of branches on the other.

Nothing to do but climb.

I used my knife as a pick, driving it into the trunk and digging in my toe before hoisting myself up. Clarence cawed and landed on one of the great tree's branches to watch. As I struggled to find footholds on the rough bark, I thought of how primitive we humanoids must seem to birds, dragons and all those flying creatures who weren't tethered to the ground.

A small body scurried past my head, busy on some critter errand. Another little body ran along the trunk. Then another. Soon furry, chittering creatures swarmed the branches. One stopped right beside me and chirped with a birdlike bill, though its body was squirrel-ish and gray. It sat upright, clutching nimble little hands to its chest.

"Hiya," I said. The critter flicked its fluffy tail and scurried away. I continued to climb. With less than four hours to make it to Junction Point, I wasted thirty precious minutes on that tree.

On the other side, I jumped down to the cracked pavement. This part of town had been completely destroyed. The only remnants of habitation were the road and two squares of broken cement that had once been parking lots. In another few years, even these signs would be gone.

I continued south, then east, until I came to the river that fed the lake. Suddenly, I keened the distinct hum of a ward. The rail line was close by. After the vast quiet of the woodlands, this sound—one I'd lived with for more than a decade—seemed perverse. And it wasn't really a sound. It was a vibration that I felt in my very core. It was the taste of magic on a large scale.

The river was slow and brackish. Trees and vines suffocated it on either side. I couldn't waste time searching for a shallow section to ford it. Instead, I tramped through the thigh-high water trying not to think of all the things that I could be stirring up. On the other side, I paused only to cut off a leech that had stealthily latched onto my elbow. Then I moved on.

I crested a hill and dropped to the ground, using a bramble bush for cover. The rail line snaked across the valley below. Right in front of me sat the platform and newly constructed station that made up Junction Point. The land around the station and tracks was free of foliage. The Inbetween reclaimed cleared land within weeks, sometimes within days, if not protected by a ward. I couldn't even begin to imagine the cost of clearing the way from Montreal to Manhattan.

Red beacons shone from the tops of two towers flanking the station. The Apex stones. All along the rail line, towers like these would connect to the wards, webbing the magic that would keep Terra from encroaching on this reclaimed land. A latticework of wires joined one tower to the next. This was where the "kiss" would happen. When the trains finally met, the wards would join through this nexus. But for a brief window of time, the wards on both ends would be down. I had to get in, drop the bombs and get out in less than five minutes. And if I had any time left over, I'd make pigs fly.

I pulled out my binoculars and turned my attention to the station. It was a long low building made entirely of wood to better blend into this ecosystem. There were no windows on this side, but I guessed that at least part of the building was used as barracks.

Clarence dropped to the ground beside me.

"See that," I said. "How many guards do you count? Six?"

Clarence cocked his head. How I wished we'd had time to outfit him with Gabe's spy tech. But then, a brilliantly hued bird with a snake tail and an eight-foot wingspan might stand out, even in the Inbetween.

A flurry of activity below brought my attention back to the station. A dozen guards poured from the barracks. On the other side of the tracks, the forest camouflaged another wooden structure. I only noticed it because more guards emerged from there. That building was too small to hold so many people, and I concluded that it was an entrance to a tunnel under the track.

Lights on the Apex towers flashed and soon a train appeared on the northbound track, coming in slowly. It stopped at the station's midpoint, leaving room for the Montreal train. I checked my widget. From my calculations, the Manhattan train was almost an hour early.

A station guard spoke to another on the train, but no one got off. When the wards went down, the train would be the safest place for the delegates.

I backed up from the edge of the rise, hiding myself from the long view of the guard towers, and called Oscar.

"Please tell me you have a better way to wipe out those golems," I said as soon as he answered.

"Kyra! You're safe?"

"So far. I'm at Junction Point. Mason told me about your plan to drop the flash bomb inside the train car. I can't do it."

There was dead air on the other end of the line.

"I mean it, Oscar. Find another way. There are dozens of guards here. More will be coming." And when the ward went down, the guards would be on high alert for anything rushing from the woods. No way I could pull it off.

"I'm sorry," Oscar sounded a world away. "I've checked and rechecked. There are no other weaknesses to exploit. Say what you will about Gerard, but he's thorough."

I ground my teeth. My head pounded. When did I last sleep or eat? It felt like a lifetime ago.

"Okay. I'll do what I have to."

"Good. And Kyra? There's one thing more. Something's going on here. The bridges are closed, which we expected. But I can't get a hold of anyone in my office at Hub. The lines are down."

"What are you saying?"

"I'm saying that I have a bad feeling. When you're on your way back north, call me before you arrive. I don't want you coming home to an ambush."

That didn't sound ominous. Not at all.

"Okay. I'll call as soon as it's done."

We disconnected, and I rolled over to lay flat on my back, suddenly exhausted. In less than an hour, the second train would arrive, carrying the Montreal delegation. When the trains kissed, it would signal the beginning of an unprecedented union between two city states. Nothing like it had been tried—not since the war and the collapse of all governments that led to people hiding behind wards just to survive.

And I would have to break that union. In reality, it was already broken. Gerard Golovin had destroyed any chance of a coalition when he filled his train with killer golems. But I had no illusions. If I somehow got past all those guards and dropped my bomb, I would be remembered as the destroyer of the new civilization. The good news was, I wouldn't survive to enjoy that title.

I lay back in my muddy clothes and wet boots, feeling like the sky pressed down on me, and considered my options. In the end, what choice did I have? If Gerard succeeded, we'd be living under a regime with a despotic king and queen who went against everything Montreal stood for. My family—the only family I had—was still on that island.

So I crept back to the edge of the cliff, tucked behind a bush, and studied the placement of guards. A plan slowly spun out in my head.

faraway whistle broke the serenity of the morning, announcing the Montreal train long before it rode into the valley. Guards shuffled around the platform below, preparing for the new arrival. I'd eaten a bite from my rations, then settled down to meditate on my fate. Now I rose, feeling calm.

Clarence had been dozing beside me, his long tail coiled around him. When I stood, he came alert. I ran a hand along his back. He half-closed his eyes like a contented cat.

"Stay here. If I don't come back, find Mason. Do you understand? Mason."

He cocked his head, considering my words. He could probably survive on his own in the wild, but sending him to Mason felt like a last connection to my old world. If things went bad, I wanted Mason to know.

All the activity below centered on the kiss point, but I was interested in the end of the incoming train—the last two cars that held the golems. The whistle blew again, still far away, but it was time for me to get into place. When the ward went down, I had to be ready.

I followed the ridge above the valley, heading north. I'd already scouted a path down the escarpment. It was steep, and my feet skidded out from under me, releasing scree down the slope. I landed on my butt and slid. My hands scraped against rock. The pain jolted my composure, and for a moment, panic claimed me again. I sat in the dirt and took three long, cleansing breaths before continuing, more careful of every footfall.

While I walked, I scanned behind me, keening for anything big coming this way. We were too far south for the berserkers to bother us, but there were a lot worse things in the Inbetween. I called to the trees and bushes to surround me with their essence. I willed my own magic to be quiet, to blend into the surrounding energy. But camouflage would only get me as far as the tree line. I'd have to make a dash for the train and get the hatch open. The guards on the towers would spot me. They would eventually stop me. But I would disable Gerard's army first. After that? It didn't matter. The Manhattan delegates would survive. Montreal would be safe.

The train rolled into view as I hid at the edge of the tree line. The marvelous new technomancy meant that the engine was whisper quiet, and the train pulled to a stop in eerie silence, like the whole world held its breath.

I had misjudged where the second-to-last car would stop and adjusted my hiding spot. Between me and the car lay fifty meters of wide open ground. Anyone looking directly at me would see movement as I ran. I crouched and waited, my legs tense and ready to sprint forward at any moment.

The doors opened on both trains and the delegates emerged onto the platform. Gerard Golovin and Kester Owens shook hands. Flashes of light popped as pictures were shot for posterity. Gerard began his welcome speech that would be transmitted to each ward so the general population could take part in this historic moment.

Where was Polina? Weren't the newlyweds supposed to make the trip together? I scanned the cluster of delegates and soldiers on the platform but couldn't find her.

The speeches dragged on. My legs cramped. I flexed and relaxed muscles without moving from my hiding spot. Finally, the delegates waved to the cameras and turned toward the trains. The engines inched forward, closing the short gap between them. When they were only inches away with Junction Point glowing just above, all movement stopped.

An alarm blared, signaling the suspension of the ward. Three…two… one…and the hum died.

The ward was down. Back home, the island of Montreal was now protected only by Hub's militia, who would stand guard on the bridges and patrol in boats to keep out vampires, marauders and other monsters who might take advantage of this unprecedented lapse in security.

I had five minutes.

I dashed forward, willing my magic to make me small and insignificant. I reached the back end of the second train car and climbed a ladder to the roof, now completely exposed to the guards in the towers. The metal body that I crouched on was a complete antithesis to my green magic, and I could feel my camouflage slipping. The emergency hatch was closed with a lever handle that turned under my grip. Before opening it, I primed my knife with a pulse of magic, feeling it grow hot in my hand, making it ready for whatever came out of that hatch. Then I took a flash bomb from the sack at my waist, ignoring the vile magic that slithered from it. I pulled up on the hatch and it opened to reveal a dark interior. I sensed movement below and pressed the button to arm the bomb.

A distant explosion shattered the silence with a scream of magic.

The entire train lurched, and I fell backward, dropping my knife and only barely hanging onto the bomb with my left hand as I grabbed the ladder with my right. Another explosion shook the train. Junction Point was under fire, but I couldn't worry about that now.

I dangled over the edge of the car, staring at the ticking bomb in my hand and trying desperately to find foot holds on the ladder. Shouts and screams came from the direction of the platform.

The bomb in my hand pulsed with energy, ready to explode.

Shit, shit, shit!

I couldn't release it and, one-handed, I couldn't climb back up to drop it through the hatch.

A raucous caw announced Clarence, but instead of landing on the train, he grabbed the back of my jacket in his massive talons and hauled me onto the top of the car.

I dropped the bomb through the hatch and jumped. The car rocked with the explosion. I scrambled in my belt pouch for the null bracelet that Mason had made for me so long ago, and jammed it on my wrist before the flare of magic in the air overcame me.

Unfortunately, the bracelet also nullified my magic, and I lost my glamor. There was no helping it. I bounded up the ladder of the last train car and scrambled across the roof to the hatch at the far end to drop my last bomb inside.

But I was too late.

A golem jumped from the open car door. Its massive feet crunched on the gravel, arms thick as tree trunks. A black helmeted head made it even more alien. It raised a fist. A blast of firepower shot from its fingers and hit the edge of the car only inches from my feet. I dove off the car, landing badly beside the tracks. My ankle screamed as it twisted, but I had no time for pain. The second bomb—my last weapon—rolled under the train, out of reach. I left it as more shots scattered the gravel at my feet. The guards in the tower had spotted me.

I ducked behind the train and crouched to peer out at the madness. The station platform was a riot of smoke, fire and screaming people. A dozen more golems jumped out of the last car.

Gerard's army was awake.

32

In the smoke and confusion, I only hoped to find Gerard and Polina. The damage was already done. There would be no treaty between Montreal and Manhattan now. But I could stop them from bringing their train of death south and destroying another city.

My flash bomb had disabled the golems in the first car, but dozens poured out of the last car, firing into the knot of guards on the platform. They were a step up from the gencrew that built the rail line. These were killing machines, armored from head to foot with multiple built-in weapons. From the towers, soldiers rained down fire, but even the shots that hit did minor damage. The golems plodded on, their integrated blasters switching out for blades when they hit the miasma of magic from the explosion. Soon even the guards in the towers stopped firing, their blasters rendered useless by all the magic in the air.

More soldiers piled out of the barracks, adding to the general chaos. At least these were sensibly armed with swords and bows.

The delegations cowered behind a knot of soldiers who shielded them with their bodies, taking direct hits to their armor from long range blasters as they inched toward the door of the guardhouse. One delegate panicked and ran for the train, and he was shot dead. The others huddled closer to the guards in response.

I couldn't help them. I had other priorities. Where were Gerard and Polina? Hiding, of course. The cowards were probably waiting out the destruction inside the train.

I dashed toward the door of a train car and almost made it. A golem stepped out between the cars and slashed at me with the razor-sharp edge of its weapon hand. Its creepy, faceless stare churned the fear in my gut. I jumped back and pulled my sword. It lunged, slashing again. I parried and nearly dropped my blade under the force of its strike.

Clarence dove from the sky. He'd had such success with the berserkers, he probably thought he could cause as much damage to the golems, but his talons raked harmlessly across its helmet. The golem slashed upward and Clarence screamed.

No!

The bladed hand morphed into solid fingers that grabbed the bird by the feet and flung him twenty meters along the track. Clarence spread his wings, but it was too late. He hit the gravel hard and didn't get up. I pulled off my null bracelet and tossed it away, not caring if the magic in the air overloaded me.

Instead, I let it fill me and pumped all that power into my sword. It might no longer be a Valkyrie blade, but primed with magic it could still cut through a golem like it was made of paper. With one strike, my loaded blade lopped off its head.

My heart screamed to find Clarence, but my head knew I had to stop this madness first.

I jumped through the open door into the train car. Inside the screams of the dying were muted. I moved up the aisle, checking each seat for lurkers. The car was empty. I opened the adjoining door, crossed the ramp to the next car and slammed the door shut. This was a lounge, with dining tables lining each side and a bar at the far end. I stood and listened. The morning was warm and the hand gripping my sword was slick with sweat. With all the magic flying about, my keening was useless. I waited a full minute, letting anyone hiding in the car think they were safe.

There it was. A tiny flash of a white sleeve as someone shifted to get comfortable.

I pounced.

Gerard was cowering under the third table. I yanked him out and before he could react, I punched him in the gut, putting everything I had into it. He doubled over with a grunt while I shook off the pain in my hand. A whistling wheeze escaped his throat as he struggled to suck in air.

I kneed him in the face, and he went down with a thud, curling into a ball.

This was the man who had ordered Cyril's murder. He'd worked with Prince Alvar to poach the dragons, an act that led to Joran murdering Alvin and Theo. He was also the reason that a mad witch was now free to persecute Mason and everyone close to him.

I jabbed my sword into the fleshy part of his shoulder. He wheezed out a grunt and rolled to face me. I stepped on his chest and dug the tip of my blade into his throat. He should have stared up at me in terror or tried to scramble away. Instead, his eyes were wet with tears and he was laughing.

Laughing.

Blood dripped down his face, staining his white shirt, and he ignored it. I'd seen this mania before. Mason's old friend, Pierre, had displayed the same deranged tendencies. Gerard was no longer at the helm. He might have begun this plot to infiltrate Manhattan and create an empire linked by his rail system, but in the last year Polina had not only taken over his game plan, she'd taken his sanity.

"Where is Polina?"

His laughter turned into a wheeze.

"Where is she?"

"Not…not here." He coughed and the wracking movement pushed him against my blade. A thin red line opened at his throat. I pulled away and waited for his fit to pass.

"Why did you blow up Junction Point?" I asked, when he finally had control of himself again. I knew this wasn't the original plan. The notes on the memory drive outlined an attack on Manhattan. Someone had changed those plans, and it had to be Polina.

"For the love of chaos." His voice was strained, and blood leaked from his split lip as he spoke.

"Is that what we're calling her now? Chaos?"

He grinned and his eyes blazed with madness. What power did Polina have to create such single-minded devotion in her men?

"Tell me. Why did Polina want you to blow it up?" I sent a little pulse of magic through my blade, heating it so the skin on his neck sizzled.

"Tell me!"

He coughed again, but spoke through the spasms. "The junction… connected to the wards…"

It suddenly made sense. The explosion had rippled through the Apex stones back to the source.

Dear all-father! He'd destroyed the wards on the two biggest city states in the northeast. The militia in Montreal had been ready for a five-minute lapse in protection. They couldn't protect the border indefinitely. Already marauders from the fringe villages outside the gates could be swarming the bridges.

And if the opji vampires learned that the island was unprotected…

Gerard pushed my sword aside and kicked me in the ankle. My boot took the brunt of it, but I fell backward against a dining table. Gerard scrambled to his feet, and a knife appeared in his hand.

Instinct took over. I reacted with the reflexes that Dana had pounded into me through years of brutal training. As he slashed downward, my hand whipped up, and I punctured his throat with my blade.

nicked his carotid artery. It happened so fast. Blood fountained across my face. He dropped to his knees, clutching the life that spurted from his neck. I keened the moment his spirit untangled itself from his body and scattered into the ether. His dead eyes were fixed on mine even as guards stormed the car and disarmed me. They dragged me outside. We stepped around the corpse of a golem left to rot in the sun. Its cracked helmet revealed the featureless face beneath that already seemed to be disintegrating back into the earth.

The guards shoved me into a seat in the last car on the Manhattan train. More guards stood at either end of the aisle and outside the door. They confiscated my sword and my belt, but left my canteen. I drank deeply. My hands shook.

I'd killed before, but it never got easier. I took comfort in that. The day that taking a life became easy was the day I became my Aunt Dana.

I leaned my cheek against the cool window and watched the activity outside. The battle was over. The soldiers had stopped the golems, but the price was high. Bodies of men, women and golems littered the ground. Smoke billowed from the station. The wooden structure would be ash in a matter of hours. Soldiers were piling the bodies of their fallen comrades into the fire. Those men and women not tasked with this gruesome detail helped the wounded or stood guard around the train. With no other defenses, the delegations had been secured here.

I strained to see Clarence's body, but he was too far down the line and smoke obscured my view. I sat back and brooded. In a fit of pity, I desperately missed home. I missed Hunter's wet kisses and the way Willow twined around my ankles. I missed the scent of Gita's coffee in the morning and Kur's little cold fingers grasping through the bars of his cage.

I missed Mason.

My legs were restless, and I headed up the aisle to peer through the glass door separating this car from the next. A guard blocked most of my view, but she didn't stop me. Kester Owens debated hotly with another man I recognized as part of the Montreal delegation. No doubt they were assigning blame for this debacle.

"I need to speak to Kester Owens" I said to the guard. She was a stocky blond woman with close-set eyes that narrowed on me.

"He's right there. Just ask him! It's a matter of life or death."

She pinched her lips and shook her head, but didn't answer. Clearly she'd been trained to ignore overwrought prisoners. And I had no doubt that I looked worse than a berserker. My braids had come undone and my hair was matted with dirt and gravel. My clothes were torn and dirty. Blood soaked my sleeve—some of it was mine.

I sat back in my seat and used the last of my water to soak my bandanna and wash off the worst of the dirt and blood. I raked fingers through my hair, combing out the debris and re-braiding it in one long tail down my back.

Kester Owens would talk to me eventually, and when he did, he would see a calm, reasonable woman who had acted in the best interest of her ward.

The morning wore on to afternoon. I watched the sun peak. It was one of those bleached suns that foreshadowed the heat of summer. The sky was just as colorless. The entire world was featureless, as if trying to erase this day from existence. My keening was overloaded, but I could sense the miasma of magic from the bombs dissipating like Gerard's soul had dissipated into the ether.

I shut my eyes and saw his accusing glare locked onto me in death.

An hour later, someone brought me a sandwich and a bottle of water. I hadn't eaten in twenty-four hours, but my stomach roiled at the sight of the thick brown bread, cheese and slice of mystery meat. I forced myself to eat it anyway, choking down every crumb. Whatever came next, I would need energy.

A hand on my shoulder shook me out of a shallow sleep. I stood and the guard nudged me toward the end of the aisle. We crossed to the next car where the delegates were sitting at the dining tables.

Kester Owens spotted me and said, "Sit down."

I took the seat opposite him. We were alone at one end of the car. The other delegates who had survived clustered in two groups at the other end—Montrealers on one side of the aisle, Manhattanites on the other. Either they were exhausted from arguing or they had come to an agreement.

Polina was not among them.

Someone brought us tea and Kester Owens watched me fidget with my mug for a few minutes, then said, "You killed Gerard Golovin."

The man didn't play games. I liked that.

"It was self-defense." I raised my chin and clutched my hands in my lap to keep them from shaking.

"So you say." His enormous brown eyes seemed to bore right into my head. I let out my keening to taste his magic. It was ancient, deeply rooted, and gave off just a whiff of brimstone.

Demon? Fae? I didn't detect a glamor, so I was guessing the former. Many demons had come through the rifts created during the Flood Wars to kill, rape and plunder their way through our world. They were the only reason Earth governments had finally stopped warring with each other and turned their attention to this greater threat. As far as I knew, the last demon had been banished in 1938. And yet, here I was having tea with one.

Even more mind-blowing was the fact that Kester and Mason were friends. We'd have words about keeping secrets the next time I saw him.

I glanced through the window. The sun was still too far above the tree line. Whatever punishment Kester Owens had in store for me, I had to delay it for a few hours. Mason would come. I knew that as surely as I knew the sound of my own heartbeat.

"Why are you here?" Kester asked.

"I came to stop…this." I waved to the destruction outside the window.

"And how did you know?" He made no gestures—didn't lean in or tap his fingers on the table. He was pure calm, and this serenity infected me. I told him everything, starting with Gerard's link to the poachers, through the opji war and Polina's release from the bloodstone, ending with the discovery of the thumb drive with the schematics for the additional train cars and armored golems.

"We thought they were going to kill you—all the delegates, actually—and ride their golem army straight into Manhattan. I planned to stop them by any means." I met his unwavering gaze. "But the kill was self-defense."

"They?"

"Gerard and his new wife. Where is Polina? Is she dead?"

"Not that I know. Unless the flu bug that kept her home has done her in."

Flu bug? Not likely. Polina had changed her plans at the last minute, but sickness wasn't the reason.

Kester leaned back in his seat. He let me stew for a few moments while he considered my story.

"I'm inclined to believe you," he said finally. "About most of it. We found the technician responsible for blowing up the ward, and his story corroborates yours. But we still have the problem of Gerard Golovin's murder."

"Murder in self-defense," I added quickly.

A small smile tugged at his mouth. I thought his face might crack.

"The Montreal delegates are anxious to place blame for this debacle. Many of them are ardent supporters of Golovin, backers in his budding empire."

I could see where this was going. "They want a scapegoat that they can hang from the nearest tree."

"Yes." Kester looked out the window. The station still smoked and a cluster of guards stood around one of the Apex towers. A man perched near the top of the structure. He wore a tool belt and seemed to be working on a box of cables just below the Apex stone. Kester arched an eyebrow toward the scene.

"That's the tech I mentioned—the one who betrayed his people and set the bomb that brought down the wards."

"What's he doing?"

"We made a deal. If he fixes the generator that links the ley-line to the railroad, I won't execute him. But without the ward, the station will have to be abandoned. We'll head home as soon as the line is repaired. I'm not leaving anyone behind. Not even you."

Why did people keep trying to kidnap me and take me hundreds of kilometers from home? Were the fates trying to tell me something?

"What will happen to me when we reach Manhattan?"

"I haven't decided yet. Just be glad that I am the one deciding and not your own delegation."

He raised a hand to get the guard's attention.

I scrambled for something to say as she led me away, some piece of wisdom or leveraging fact that would force Kester to let me go. Nothing came to mind. I'd set out to kill a man and had done just that.

The guard dumped me back in my seat in the adjoining car. I leaned my head against the window and watched the sun take its sweet time to set.

34

All day I watched the soldiers pack up what they could salvage and load it on the train. The tech continued to work on the Apex tower. Without power from the ley-line, the train wouldn't move. And we were sitting ducks for anything or anyone roaming the Inbetween.

In the late afternoon, two black beasts charged from the trees. Big like bison, with shaggy brown fur and horns that curled into points above their wolfish snouts. Their snarling lips pulled back to reveal prehistoric fangs. More bulls crept from the forest to paw at the ground. Then the entire tree line seemed to erupt with them. The beasts stood in the open, glaring at the intruders to their terrain. These weren't docile cows. They looked carnivorous. And pissed. The first and biggest bull raised its head and bellowed—a sound halfway between a wolf's howl and the braying of a donkey.

Then the herd charged. Several made it as far as the train. I felt the impact as their horns hit metal. The few blasters not fried by magic fired from the towers. Other soldiers discharged crossbow bolts into the stampede. A dozen beasts fell before the rest aborted the charge and ran back into the trees. When the guns fell silent, dust from the stampede filled the afternoon light. Everyone waited for several tense minutes, but the creatures must have decided the big metal beast that spat fiery death wasn't worth the effort.

If that didn't give the techs a kick in the pants to get the damned train going, nothing would.

I sat back in my chair, my heart pounding. Sitting around doing nothing wasn't my forte. I stood and paced the aisle, wishing I had my widget, but

Kester's men had taken my belt kit. I couldn't call Oscar, and I worried about his last message. He'd been right to be suspicious. No doubt Polina had timed a coup to coincide with Gerard's treachery. Right now there could be warfare in the streets of Montreal. I could only hope that my family was far enough out of the city to be safe. But I itched to get back to them.

Most of the supplies had burned up in the fire and the train wasn't provisioned for a long voyage. A soldier who looked no older than a teen brought me a supper of nuts, an apple and water.

"When will we be leaving?" I asked, taking the food.

"Soon." Despite his youth, the soldier's eyes were hardened by things he'd seen during his time on duty in the Inbetween. He left without another word, and I sat alone in the darkening car, eating my meager meal and waiting.

I didn't wait long.

Kester had decided I wasn't a flight risk. Who in their right mind would flee into the Inbetween? The doors to the other cars were locked, but he'd left only one soldier standing guard outside the train—the same blond who had taken me to Kester earlier. When I saw her fall, I jumped up, ready to leave.

Mason's head poked into the aisle. I ran to him and threw my arms around his neck. He gave me one quick kiss.

"We have to go. Now." He held up my sword. How had he stolen that back from under Kester's watch? There was no time to ask.

We stepped over the fallen guard. My keening told me she was out, not dead. That meant she could wake up and sound the alarm at any moment. Even so, I was glad Mason hadn't killed her. There had been enough killing today.

Most of the guards stood by the Apex tower, but a dozen patrolled around the train, watching for anything that came out of the trees.

We hugged the side of the train, running to the end of the next car before stopping to peer through the gap. We passed the spot where Clarence had fallen, and I stopped, scanning the ground. Looking for any sign, even a single feather. He was gone. There was no way he could have flown off, not with his wounds. He had to be dead. His body had probably been thrown on the pyre with the others.

"What are you doing?" Mason tugged on my hand. "Come on." I let him pull me away, but I wanted to scream, to lash out and hurt something—

anyone. For Clarence. So when a guard stepped out from behind the next car, I lost it.

A cry erupted from my throat and I tackled him. My shoulder rammed into his gut, forcing a whoosh of air from his lungs. The momentum slammed us against the train. His head cracked against metal and we both fell in a tangled heap. I pushed myself up and away. His hands seemed to be everywhere, grasping my clothes and hair. I stood and kicked him. Mason tugged me into the shadows between train cars.

"Hey, what's got into you? He's out. Look."

I took a deep, shaky breath.

"Clarence is dead." I had to say it aloud. Tears burned my eyes and I fought them back. Now was not the time for grieving. But one tear escaped down my cheek anyway. Mason wiped it away with his thumb.

"Let's go home."

We ran along the train to its end. The pool of magic from my flash bomb had spread into the night. I was too shaky to create any effective wards. Mason could feel it too. The crease between his brows sharpened, and he handed me my sword as his arm turned to stone.

"We have to run for it," I said. The guards hadn't spotted us yet, but once we hit that open ground between the train and the tree line, we'd be seen from the towers. I had nothing left in me to power a glamor.

"Let's not make it easy for them," Mason said. "You run that way. I'll head for that outcropping there. Once we're in the trees, I'll find you."

I noted that he pointed me in the direction away from the towers, while he took the route in closer range for the guards' fire. But he was already sprinting away, leaving me no time to argue.

I ran.

Blaster fire echoed, but I didn't stop to look. My legs felt like pudding, but I kept them pumping until I hit the tree line. I sprinted another few paces until a bramble of underbrush tripped me. Then I doubled over, gasping for air. The gunfire stopped. None of the guards would be dumb enough to chase us into the trees. They were more concerned with things running *out* of the forest.

My breath came in ragged heaves. My reserves were gone. I needed rest and proper food, but I would get neither until we were home. Instead, I turned left and stumbled through the dark until I found Mason.

"I left the bike in a clearing not far from here," Mason said. "I didn't want them to hear me coming."

The hike back was slow. I couldn't have found my way, but Mason's night eyes were better than mine. The trees and ground cover were full of chirps and scurrying feet, but my keening told me nothing bigger than a chipmunk was nearby. The herd of bulls had moved on.

"How did you know where they were keeping me?" I asked. He hadn't let go of my hand since we found each other again, and I was glad for the anchoring feel of his skin on mine.

"Kester told me."

"What?"

"I waited until a guard was taking a piss, then knocked him out and stole his uniform. They're all so worried about deadly creatures like berserkers, they didn't even think about a normal human infiltration."

I remembered the bulls from that afternoon. The guards had every reason to worry.

"Once I got Kester alone and corroborated your story about Polina, he agreed to let us go, but he still had to answer to Gerard's delegation."

"So you staged it to look like an escape." That explained how he'd retrieved my sword. "Why didn't you tell me Kester is a demon?"

Mason smiled. "Didn't seem relevant at the time."

The rising moon lit his face. His dark eyes glinted with amusement. I was about to berate him for keeping secrets, but I spotted the hover bike on the far edge of a clearing, and there, perched beside it, was Clarence.

35

Clarence didn't look good. His feathers were matted with dirt and blood, and he slumped against the bike. He opened one eye when I touched his wing. The other eye had swollen shut.

"Oh, baby." He'd dragged himself here, maybe following Mason's scent. I wanted to hug him, but I was also afraid of hurting him.

"See if he'll take some water." Mason handed me his canteen and then rummaged in the small trunk under the back seat. I tilted Clarence's head and dribbled water into his mouth. His tongue flicked out, and I dribbled some more.

"Just like old times, right?" His good eye tracked me, so I kept babbling. "When I tried to get you to eat hairball remedy, you didn't really need it, did you? You were just busy turning into this magnificent creature." I stroked his head, and he closed his eyes.

Mason pulled out an emergency blanket, and we swaddled Clarence in it. With his brilliant red crest sticking out of the mylar, he looked like a gift wrapped for Christmas.

"He can sit in front of me on the way home," Mason said.

I grabbed his face between my hands and kissed him. He hesitated for a minute, then wrapped his arms around me. His mouth opened to let me in, and I tasted his magic, hot and strong.

After a moment, he pulled away. "What was that for?"

"Because you never even considered leaving Clarence behind."

Mason frowned. "Like you said. He's family."

And so our little family climbed on the bike and went home.

THE RIDE BACK was fast and mostly uneventful. We followed the train tracks east of Lake Champlain, avoiding the berserker-filled mountains altogether. Most wildlife avoided the tracks, even without the ward.

Except for the stubbornly stupid Canada geese. Near the northern end of the lake we had to slow to maneuver through a massive flock. The black and white bodies crowded the space from one edge of the gravel clearing to the other.

"I hate geese," Mason's voice grumbled in my helmet. I agreed. In my line of work, there isn't much that fazes me, but I'd rather face a pack of wolves than a flock of angry Canada geese.

As Mason nudged the bike forward, one large male flapped his wings in an impressive display and lunged at us, his beak open wide to show a black tongue as he hissed in outrage. This set off the others, and soon we inched through a chaos of honking, hissing and flapping. A beak pecked my calf.

"Ouch!" I swatted the bird. Clarence peeked over Mason's shoulder and let out his own hiss.

"Hold on!" Mason revved the engine and the geese closest to us scattered. When we made it to the edge of the flock, he sped up again. We pushed the limits of Oscar's bike, but it had to be near midnight already. Time was precious. Oscar could build a new bike.

While we drove, I worried. What would be waiting for us when we reached Montreal? Polina had some end game other than blowing up the wards, but I couldn't wrap my head around it. I was too tired to strategize.

Mason had tied Clarence to him. The rope ran around his waist and I tucked my hands under it, anchoring myself so I wouldn't fall off the bike. I laid my head on Mason's back and dozed.

Mason's voice rumbling right next to my ear woke me.

"You awake back there?"

"I'm awake." My eyes felt gritty, and I wished I could rub them.

"At least you don't snore." I could hear the smile in his voice. "We're coming into Hedge. You need to stay alert."

We'd left the train tracks and followed a decent road that led into the shanty town outside the south gate of Montreal. Vehicles of every sort used this road, and many camped beside it for the night. We passed vans, mule-drawn carts, rickshaws and even old-fashioned wagons with teams of horses hobbled nearby.

A few eyes followed us as we rode by. Either they were insomniacs or guards posted to watch over family properties. But we weren't the only ones traveling by night. By the time we reached the town proper, the streets were busy with activity.

We parked beside an inn. Mason untied Clarence and handed him to me.

"Wait here," he said. "Dutch should be inside." We'd made plans to rendezvous with Dutch at the inn. Other Guardians waited outside Dorion Park by the western gate, in case we came home that way. Mason had instructed each to wait two days before deciding that we weren't returning.

I nodded, but really I wanted to go inside, get a room, and sleep for a day. I kept the motor running and the hover bike caught more than a few interested glances.

Mason returned looking grim. Dutch followed. He nodded a greeting to me and reached for Clarence.

"Let me take him to Nori," he said.

I clutched Clarence tighter. Suddenly, I didn't want to let go, as if that simple act meant I would never see him again.

"Kyra, please." Mason gently pulled the bird from my grip. "We can't help him here. But Nori can. Let Dutch take him."

"I should go too." I should stay with Clarence, make sure he survived.

Mason shook his head. "We have to see Leighna. Right now."

I handed Clarence into Dutch's arms. He smiled. "I'll take good care of him. I promise."

"Do you have a widget so I can call home?" I asked. "I lost mine."

"The ward is down." Dutch frowned. "So's the ley-net. Widgets aren't working." Then he left, taking my baby bird that had grown into a magnificent creature with him.

"So it's true then." I slumped in the bike seat. "Gerard blew up the ward."

Mason looked grim. "It's true. Dutch says the news in Hedge is mixed. No one really knows what's going on. Hub is guarding the bridge. Hopefully they can get word to Leighna. But we have to go now."

I nodded. We had only a few hours to sunrise. We had to inform Leighna about Gerard's betrayal before the witch made her move. If we weren't already too late.

Mason got back on the bike and we rode on to the south bridge.

36

The south end of Mercy Bridge was blocked by traffic so thick, even our bike couldn't get through. The line of cars and carts stretched back a kilometer or more. People had been dug in for hours, with small campfires burning and tents set up for sleeping. We stopped beside a family of goblins trying to get into the city. It looked like they had everything they owned piled on a cart pulled by a donkey that rested in its traces with eyes half closed. Two goblins sat on the driving seat and watched us approach with guarded curiosity.

"What's going on?" Mason asked. Six goblin children poked their heads from under the canvas covering the cart. They took one look at the strangers and ducked back into their hiding spot. Their father eyed us up and down before answering. He was thin and gawky like most goblins, with craggy, dark-skinned features, an impressive salt-and-pepper beard and bat-wing ears. A younger version of him—probably his son—sat beside him.

"Militia are holding the bridge. Won't let no one cross," the older goblin said.

"For how long?"

He shrugged one skinny shoulder. "'Til they change their minds."

We pulled the bike aside to confer. The donkey had lost interest in waiting for its family to move on and pulled on its harness to reach the weeds by the side of the road. I grabbed a clump of greenery and offered it to the poor beast. No reason we should all starve.

Mason followed me and spoke in a low voice. "We need to get across that bridge."

"Even if we get through this crowd, hub is likely to shoot anyone coming at them on a bike," I said, scratching the donkey's ears.

"We'll go on foot. Talk to the guards and have them take us to Leighna."

We looked at the hover bike. It wasn't the same shiny toy Oscar had given us just a few hours ago. The frame was dented in several places and the paint was matted with dirt. Still, Oscar wouldn't thank us for abandoning it.

Mason walked back to the goblins.

"What's your name?" he asked.

The senior goblin considered him for a moment. "Arriz," he grumbled.

Mason held out his hand. "Henry Mason." The goblin reached out a long, thin hand and they shook. "Is this your son?"

The younger goblin nodded. "Dekar…sir."

"Why are you trying to get into the city?" Mason asked.

"No where else to go," Arriz said. "With the ward down, we'd thought we'd finally have a chance. Tired of living rough."

That had to be the understatement of the year. I couldn't imagine surviving outside a ward with a pack of children. I wondered where their mother was, then thought of all the things that could go wrong in the Inbetween, from monsters to the lack of proper medical care. It was a testament to Arriz's fortitude that any of them survived.

Mason turned his attention to Dekar. It was hard to tell a goblin's age, since their skin was wrinkled like tree bark from birth, and Dekar was no wide-eyed youth. He'd clearly seen too much in his short life. But his deferential manner made him seem younger. I guessed he was in his late teens.

"You think you can drive that?" Mason pointed to the bike. Dekar's eyes widened.

"Yes, sir!"

Mason turned to Arriz. "You know where Dorion Park is?" The troll nodded, frowning.

"My manor house is on the east end of the park. Take the north service road to the end and you'll find it. If you bring that bike back, you can camp there with your family until I get home. I have some business in town, but I'll return in a day or two. If you're still there, we can talk about a job. I need an estate manager."

Arriz leaned back, his eyes hooded as he considered the proposal.

"It's outside the ward," Mason continued, "but close enough to be protected. And the Guardians live with me most of the time. Your family would be safe."

Arriz nodded slowly, but Dekar was already jumping off his seat. Mason gave him a quick run-down on the bike's controls while Arriz turned the cart, not an easy feat in the crowd. The donkey trod on a tent set up nearby, and a rough-looking man jumped out yelling, ready to fight.

I calmed him down with the tip of my sword.

"Just give them a moment. They'll be out of here soon, and you can get your beauty sleep," I said.

The man grumbled but couldn't do much with my blade pressed to his chest. Finally, Arriz and his family were on their way. The children waved to us from the back of the receding cart.

"Do you really need an estate manager?" I asked.

Mason put his arm around me and squeezed. "I'll find something for them to do."

MY SWORD, STRAPPED over one shoulder, was our only visible weapon. I glamored it to be invisible. It wasn't a foolproof casting. Nothing could be made truly invisible, but I could turn someone's gaze away from it the way water slides off oil. Unless they concentrated really hard, the sword would be undetectable. I hoped that we looked defenseless enough not to be shot on sight.

It was almost one in the morning when we finally wended through the crowd to confront the barricade. Armored trucks blocked the road leading to Mercy Bridge. A dozen soldiers stood in front of them or in the truck beds, pointing weapons into the crowd. They wore the distinctive gray on black camouflage of Hub militia. Their uniforms were bulky enough to hide body armor, and the helmets had visors which they kept closed even in the dark. That meant they had scanning hardware in those helmets. Fancy stuff.

They looked serious about stopping anyone from entering the city.

When we left the ranks of the nearest refugees parked by the gate, the soldiers came alert. A dozen blasters pointed at us. Mason raised his hands and called out.

"We are envoys of Queen Leighna with an important message for her."

Nobody moved. They must have been waiting for a communication relay that we couldn't hear. After several minutes, one soldier motioned for us to come forward. We approached the first vehicle. He stood in the truck bed, staring down through that black visor. Nothing on his uniform indicated his rank. He lowered his blaster, but the other guards still pointed weapons at us, trigger fingers ready.

"What's your message?" The soldier's voice was a deep rumble.

Mason stood up taller and sneered. "You don't have clearance to hear what I have to say. I have a message for the queen, and no one else."

Dear gods, he was going to bluff his way through this.

"What's your name?" the soldier asked.

"Henry Mason and Kyra Greene." Mason waved to me. "We are personal friends of the queen and have vital information for her."

Again we waited while the soldier conferred over his communications. The silence was absolute. I could feel hundreds of eyes at our backs, watching this confrontation and waiting for it to explode.

Finally, the soldier swung his blaster toward the bridge, motioning for us to move on.

"Go on. Someone at the ward gate will take you into the city."

Mason nodded, and we walked single file through the tight gap between trucks. One soldier pivoted to follow our progression, gun ready to shoot if we made a wrong move.

Mercy Bridge was a hundred-and-fifty years old and walking over it in the dead of night, I felt every one of its years. Its struts croaked and whined in the wind. Up this high, the air was chilly despite my heavy cycling jacket. I grasped Mason's hand like an anchor. The road angled up toward the first set of arching struts. More guards blocked access to what should have been the gate through the ward. Twin towers rose on either side of the gatehouse, but the Apex stones mounted on them were dark.

The soldiers were expecting us. A car idled, its back door open but not particularly inviting. When I hesitated, one soldier rushed me from behind and shoved. I fell against the car and banged my head as he forced me inside. Mason didn't fair much better. A soldier whacked the back of his legs with the butt of his gun, then two more wrestled him into the backseat.

The doors slammed. There were no handles on the inside. The driver took off at once. I thumped on the glass separating us from the front of the car and yelled for him to stop. He didn't. We raced across the bridge and past the gate on the other side, then followed the ruins of the old highway north and west, cutting through suburbs until we reached another short bridge.

"They're taking us to Buzzard Island," I said, with a sinking heart. Gerard Golovin's estate was on the island.

We drove down a long drive, stopped at a gate and waited for it to open. Ghosts floated along the top of a high stone wall surrounding the estate. Polina's guards. According to Naomi, they were the worst of the worst—spirits that had been locked in the bloodstone with her. And now they submitted to Polina's will only. She could ride their minds, see through their eyes and listen with their ears.

We pulled up in front of the large house with a circular drive. More guards stood by the front doors. These were the usual human kind, dressed in black and carrying blasters. Two of them approached the car. They forced us from the backseat and prodded us up the stairs to the front door.

The foyer filled three stories like a cathedral. A staircase swept up one side and arched doorways lined the other wall. It was dark inside, with only the light from the moon coming through high windows. The guards marched us down a hall, through a kitchen and into a pantry. The door slammed shut as soon as the guards shoved us inside. In the dark, I heard Mason fumbling along the wall, and then an overhead light came on.

I blinked in the sudden brightness and hugged myself. I wasn't cold, but exhaustion was taking its toll.

"You realize, this is Gerard's house," I said. I'd been here before but I wasn't sure if Mason had.

He nodded. "I think his new wife will be very glad to inherit it."

The room was small, windowless and lined with shelves of dry goods. There wasn't even a bare wall for me to slump against. But I didn't have enough energy to stand. My legs crumpled and I sat in the middle of the floor.

"Well, at least we won't starve." I eyed the rows of foodstuffs on the shelves.

Mason grabbed a jar of preserves, sniffed it and handed it to me.

"Strawberry." He found another jar of almond butter and a tray of extra cutlery. He sat beside me, and we ate butter and jam straight from the jars.

He grinned and wiped a bit of jam from my cheek, then kissed the sticky spot. "Mmmm. I feel like a naughty boy sneaking into the pantry for a midnight snack."

I knew what he was doing. We were prisoners. The city was most likely in the middle of a civil war. And he was flirting with me because I needed to relieve the pressure valve of tension, or the constant dread of the last twenty-four hours was going to crush me. So, I swiped a bit of jam across his nose.

"You are a naughty boy."

"You think so?" He stuck his finger in the jar and then teased my lip with it. I took it all in my mouth and sucked it. His eyes widened.

"If you don't stop that, I'll have my way with you on this cold stone floor." His voice was a deep, growling rumble.

I gave him back his finger and grinned. "You could, but I'd fall asleep on you."

"Nice way to prop up a man's confidence."

"It's not that, and you know it." The memory of our one night together on the island was still fresh enough to make me squirm. "But I haven't slept properly in over thirty-six hours now. As soon as this sugar wears off, I'm going to crash."

"Then crash." He put aside the jars and turned me so my head lay across his lap. Then he undid my braids and stroked my hair. "If I know Polina, she'll keep us waiting just because she can. I'll keep watch. I had an entire day to sleep while you battled golems."

I reached up and smoothed the frown lines away from his forehead.

"Didn't your mother ever warn you that if you make a face for too long, it will stick?"

He caught my hand and kissed it.

"I won't forgive myself for letting you go into that fight alone."

"You should. No one blames you. Especially not me."

But he would go on blaming himself. I wanted to convince him not to, but sleep was already tugging me toward oblivion.

I woke after what seemed only a moment—but could have been hours—to the sound of the door opening.

Merrow stood in the doorway. "Come. The queen will see you now."

"What are you doing here?" I blurted as I rose. My right leg had fallen asleep under me and I stamped my foot to wake it. Merrow studied me with a stern expression. Her complexion seemed paler, a sickly yellow rather than her usual olive-gray. For a moment, her glamor wavered and the seven-foot, armor-plated beast peeked through. Then I blinked and the regular Merrow was back, frowning at me.

"Come on. She's waiting."

What the hells was going on? Had Leighna somehow beaten Polina already? But then why had we been kept locked up all this time?

I glanced at Mason. He raised both eyebrows to say he had no idea either and motioned for me to go out the door before him. Four guards flanked us ahead and behind, making it clear we were unwelcome visitors.

Merrow stopped us in the foyer. She held out her hand. "I'll take your weapon now."

I knew she could sense my sword. I didn't want to hand it over, but with the guards watching, I had little choice.

As soon as Merrow touched it, the glamor evaporated, and one guard gasped. Merrow smiled thinly and led us across the foyer to a large room that could have been a ballroom in another era. Now it was bare, except for a raised dais and a massive chair with Polina lounging on it.

She'd made herself a throne room. How eighteenth century of her.

"Kneel for Queen Polina!" Merrow's voice rang out like a herald's.

"Not bloody likely." Mason crossed his arms.

I glared at Merrow, but she stood straight and tall behind us, her eyes glued on an invisible horizon. I wanted to smack her. She'd betrayed her beloved Leighna for this…this fraud?

Polina smiled at us from her lofty height. Her strawberry blond hair was piled on her head with a few long tresses cascading around her face. A glittery tiara topped it all, looking suspiciously like an accessory from a certain popular children's doll.

A tall man wearing the same uniform as her guards stood behind her throne. He had red hair and broad shoulders, and he wore his size with an air of authority. The snaggle-toothed chihuahua paced beside him. Princess wore a purple bow in her hair today along with a bedazzled vest and silver booties. I felt bad for the hell hound and considered calling her to my side. For months, I had been dosing her with my magic. Would it be enough to command her loyalty? Maybe, but then what? Polina would just order her guards to kill the hound. I needed to make my secret weapon count.

"Kneel!" Merrow boomed again.

"Don't bother." Polina sneered. "My dear husband would never abject himself to a mere woman, queen or not. But it doesn't matter. It's not his fealty I want."

I turned my back on the witch and faced Merrow. "Why would you bend to her?"

Merrow's brow lowered over her dark eyes. Then she nodded to the far corner of the room.

And my world fell out from under me.

In the shadows, Leighna was slumped on the bare floor, her legs splayed and clothing ripped. Thick chains ran from iron cuffs on her wrists to bolts in the stone wall. Her eyes were closed and her head lolled back. And she wore a null collar.

"My dear Pierre left me some wonderful treasures to get by in this new world," Polina said. "And the fae were always ridiculous about iron. In truth, I thought the famous Ice Queen would put up a better fight." She shrugged.

So, Pierre had made the null collars that trapped the dragons. He'd been working with Gerard for a long time. And now both were dead and Polina was reaping the rewards.

"What do you want?" Mason said. He reached for my hand and my fingers closed over stone. He was getting ready to fight.

"Yuki." Polina's expression darkened.

"He's not with us. You know that. Your Hub henchmen took us straight from the gala."

"But you know where he is."

If Hub had taken Yuki, he should be at the station or in a hospital if his injuries were severe. I almost said so.

"I don't know," Mason said curtly.

"Your Guardians snatched him from the hospital. Where would they take him?"

I could feel the pull of Polina's power now. She wanted this information badly, tried to coerce it from us with subtle magic. I clenched my teeth so I wouldn't speak out of turn.

After a tense moment, she leaned back in her chair and smiled.

"No matter. You have other resources I can use. Like your blood."

"My blood?" Mason said. "For what? Finally found the fountain of youth spell? I hope so because you're looking a little haggard." He twirled his fingers around his eyes.

Polina's lip curled and she raised her chin.

"I'm already immortal. You made certain of that when you stuck me in that damned stone. What you see here is only the manifestation of my spirit. As I choose to show it to you." She waved a hand down the length of her dress. It changed from red to blue. Her skin turned dark brown and her hair jet black. In another instant, she was blue-tinged with great horns curled around her ears. Then she had the head of a wolf and the body of a gladiator. Next, she was a six-armed red-skinned goddess figure…the forms flickered one after another until she settled back to her desired shape.

Mason shrugged as if her metamorphoses were a parlor trick.

"You're a ghost. Nothing more than illusion held together with magic."

"No!" Polina's voice boomed. It held real power that shivered along my keening.

She disappeared. One moment she was on the throne; the next a column of smoke materialized in front of us and morphed into Polina's angry form. She was taller than before—as tall as Mason. She punched him in the face. Like her voice, she laced the hit with magic. Mason's head snapped back, and he stumbled into me.

"Can an illusion do that?" Polina smirked.

Slowly, Mason raised his stone fist to his mouth to wipe away blood trickling from his split lip.

Polina didn't flinch. She raised her chin as if defying him to retaliate. The little dog jumped off the dais and ran around us, barking.

Polina smiled. "Everyone thinks that cursing is all about destroying. Not so. Curses can create too." She stepped back and held her arms wide. "You freed me to be anything I want as long as I have the power to make it so," Polina said. "You even gave me that power by locking so many thousands of souls in the stone with me."

"I didn't do that," Mason ground out.

Polina waved away his words as if they were meaningless. "But you are right in a way. This body isn't entirely corporeal." She faded to a transparent image of herself, then bloomed to full light again. "It takes a lot of power to keep myself on this plane and in a form that lets me interact with others. It's not sustainable. But with enough blood, I can fix that too. The blessing of long life is nothing without a body to feel. To smell and to taste." She ran a hand up Mason's chest and leaned in to breathe in his scent. He didn't move, except for the muscle that twitched at his jawline.

I slapped Polina's hand away. She turned to me and smiled.

"Don't worry, little Valkyrie. I will take your blood too."

"You won't," Mason growled.

Polina laughed, a tinkling sound like fairy bells.

"Oh, I will. First, I want to thank you for ridding me of that annoyance, Gerard Golovin."

"I killed Gerard," I said. "But not for you."

She turned her gaze on me, and I felt the full brunt of the magic that churned around her like a storm cloud. "Well, you did me a favor. The man had vision. I'll give him that, but he was as horny as a school boy, and I seem to have lost my appetite for the carnal pleasures. Being incorporeal for three centuries does that to a woman." She rubbed her hands down the length of her skirt.

"So for your service, I'll make your death quick. But not too quick." Her grin was edged with ice. "Fear is a powerful medium and we have a lot of work to do."

She climbed the short stairs to her dais and settled back on her throne, taking time to smooth out her ruffled gown. The dog followed and flopped at her feet. Each of her words and actions told me a little more about her power. Why did she walk when she could snap her fingers and appear on the throne? Why bother with real clothing at all? Did her little parlor tricks expend more energy than she let on? And what about the hound? Why did she glamor it here in the safety of her own home? Was that how she controlled it?

Polina had limitations, and I was counting each one of them.

"So get on with it," Mason said. "What are you waiting for?"

Polina waved a finger from side to side. "Don't be hasty. The time is not right. These curses are delicate. Moon cycles and all that."

Mason stepped forward, ignoring the guards who drew their weapons. "You can call yourself queen, but Montreal is a triumvirate, and its citizens will never follow a dictator."

"Yes, I've learned about this new democracy," Polina said. "It seems absurd to me. But people haven't changed that much. All they need is a little motivation. Which I have provided. With the ward down, the city is in danger of being overrun. I already have agents working in those dismal slums outside the gates, stirring up the refugees. And inside the city? Well, with no one at the reins, I expect looting and civil disobedience any minute now. As I said, people haven't changed, but the gadgets they use to kill one another have improved. Once fear makes them start killing, I'll restart the ward and send General Naughton to enforce peace." She waved to the soldier who stood at attention beside her throne.

"And you think everyone will just fall in line and love you for saving them?" Mason asked.

"With a little fae magic, anything is possible." Polina pointed to Leighna. "She's the savior type anyway. She won't mind sharing her power for a good cause." Polina clapped and smiled like a child with a birthday cake.

I let her words sink in. Somehow, she was going to use Leighna to rescue the ward from the brink of chaos that she orchestrated. It was brilliant. Evil as fuck, but brilliant. And it didn't promise a long life for Leighna or any of us.

"As usual, your plans are short-sighted," Mason said. "Soon there will be worse things than refugees clamoring at the gates to get in. The opji are looking for another excuse to attack. They nearly wiped out the entire population before Leighna and her crew created the ward the first time."

"Oh, silly. You think I can't handle a few vampires?"

"No, I don't," Mason said. "I think you'll end up queen of a dead land. Queen of nothing *is* nothing."

She considered him for a long moment.

"Well then, I guess we must reignite that ward before the opji are at the gates. Maybe I'll let them gnaw on those refugees for a time before I swoop in and save them all." She leaned back on her throne and smiled. "And as I understand it, starting the ward isn't a simple task. Gerard's little alchemist minions explained it all to me. Something about boosting those Apex stones. It takes a good jolt of power. In fact, only one person in the entire city was capable of such magic last time." She looked pointedly at the unconscious prisoner. "But with enough blood, I'm sure I can manage it."

Mason shook his head. "You're as stupid as ever."

Polina's lips pressed into a thin line.

"Take them away," she snapped. Merrow turned to leave. I threw a last glance at Polina. She'd sunk back, throwing one leg over the arm of her chair like a sulky teen. Her hand reached to pet the dog, but Princess cowered from her touch.

C H A P T E R

38

Merrow escorted us out a back door and into a wild garden. A path led through a wooded area exploding with spring growth. To the east, the sky blossomed with deep purples and a hint of pink. Two guards followed our parade.

"Wherever you're taking us, you'd better hurry," growled Mason. Merrow glared at him, but she picked up her pace, so I had to jog to keep up.

"You betrayed your queen to put Polina on that fake throne," I said. She didn't answer, but I pressed her. "Why? After all those years…You nearly died to save Leighna when that condo fell on her."

"You know she'll kill you as soon as your usefulness expires," Mason said.

Merrow kept walking toward the sunrise. I thought she wouldn't answer, but finally she stopped at a chain-link fence and turned to us.

"Some things are more important than my life…than even the life of *my* queen."

She emphasized "my." Polina might be *the* queen, but Leighna would always be *her* queen. I only hoped that whatever she protected was worth it.

She unlocked a padlock on the gate and swung it open. We stepped into a bare yard. Merrow shut the gate, locked it and walked away, leaving the guards to stand at attention outside the yard.

Mason and I scouted our new jail cell. The chain-link fence topped in razor wire surrounded a large gravel yard. I knew exactly where we were. I'd dropped by this little compound a dozen times over the last few months to feed Princess, hoping to gain her trust. The yard butted up against an Apex tower. The last time I'd visited, the hum of the ward had been irritating. Now the red stone was dark and silent. To the north, past the tower, the land fell away to a rocky shore filled with debris from the floods. About five-hundred meters into the trees to the east, another creek marked the edge of the property. Beyond that were the floodplains. Another impenetrable barrier. There was only one way out of here, and that was through fifteen acres of forest patrolled by Polina's guards—human and spectral alike.

"What do you think those are for?" Mason point to two doghouses spaced about ten meters apart along the east fence.

"Hell hound." I said. "Just be glad Princess isn't home."

"Princess? You mean that ugly little beast that follows Polina around?"

"Polina glamored her. But I've seen her true form. You don't want to mess with one of those."

"Why two houses?"

"I don't know. I've only seen the one hound."

Other than the doghouses, the only structures were a long building with one door and a stone altar in the middle of the yard. It reeked of death magic and was covered in dark coppery stains. Some of them recent. I didn't care to inspect it too closely.

Instead, I tried the handle on the door to the building.

"Locked."

Mason peered through a small window. "Looks like a lab. Maybe a maintenance room for the tower?"

I squeezed in beside him to look through the window. The interior was dark, but I could make out clean white counters lining two walls and a steel table in the center.

Mason suddenly pulled me in for a deep kiss.

"I have to go," he said. "If you get the chance to escape, take it."

"You know I won't."

"I hate this." He leaned his forehead against mine. "Hate leaving you alone to face whatever comes next without me. You deserve better."

His dark eyes were tormented. He clasped my hips, crushing me against him.

I wound my fingers in his hair. "None of that matters. You hear?" I couldn't keep the waver from my voice.

He nodded, but he didn't believe. I worried that one day he would push me away, thinking it was for my own good. He let me go and sat leaning against the building. In a moment, the sun peaked the horizon, and he was stone.

I WOKE WELL after noon. I'd fallen asleep beside Mason with my back against the wall and legs stuck out in front of me. The sun had shifted. My feet were in full sun and hot inside my boots. I pulled them into the shade. We were alone, but someone had left a tray of food and water on the ground just inside the gate. The guards stood in full sun. They must have been boiling in their black uniforms, but somehow, I couldn't muster any pity for them.

Thirst stuck my throat shut, and I rose to get some water. The tray had also been sitting in the sun, and the water was bathwater warm. I drank half a bottle anyway and left the second bottle for Mason. There were two sandwiches in a canvas sac—not much more than bread, cheese, and wilted lettuce. I gobbled one down and sipped at the rest of my water.

A long stick lay beside the tray. I'd been watching it as I ate. The glamor didn't fool me. Merrow had returned my sword. Why? Did she expect me to fight my way out, past an army of guards? Whatever her motives, I was glad to have my blade back. I picked it up and leaned on it, like it was a walking stick. The guards at the gate didn't even glance my way.

I sat in the shade beside Mason, though the sun would soon take away even that bit of comfort. There was nothing to do but wait. During the next hours, human guards walked by our yard in pairs. Their patrols kept to the same routine I'd already scouted on previous visits. The day was too bright to see ghosts, but I could keen them out there, flitting through the trees.

The weather was hot for May. Or were we into June already? I'd lost track of the days. When was the last time I'd been home? Gita could handle the critters without me, but I didn't want her to worry. And what about Gabe? We'd left things in a bad place. Was he even taking care of Valkyrie Pest Control in my absence? I wouldn't blame him if he'd bailed on me.

A siren blared in the distance, and I smelled smoke. What was happening in the city? Had the looting begun? I wanted to have more faith in humanity, but history has proven too often that when the rule of law is absent, even law-abiding citizens go a little crazy. Polina was banking on it.

Looters would be better than vampires, and I wondered if the opji were already on route from their ward near the Ottawa River.

Mason and I needed to get out of here. I could scale the chain-link fence, but I knew in my heart Mason would never leave me to the tender mercy of a dark witch. And I wouldn't abandon him, no matter how much he begged. Besides, with the river to the north, the flood plains to the east, and an army of guards between me and the main road…No. It was better to sit tight and pick my moment when I had Mason as backup. Then we would face whatever was roaming on Polina's estate together.

I spent the rest of the afternoon watching the woods, analyzing the comings and goings of the guards—human and ghost variety. From the angle of the sun, I guessed it was about five o'clock when the guard at our gate changed. An hour later, I stood with my fingers locked on the chain-link fence, staring into the darkening woods. Suddenly, I felt Mason come alive. I turned just as he stood, stretching his neck and shoulders as if to shake off the last bit of stone. I abandoned my vigil at the fence and pulled him around the far side of the building where I'd tucked our tray of food to keep it out of the sun. In the shadows, we could hide from the guards.

"You should be gone already," Mason growled. "And don't tell me you didn't have a chance."

I handed him the water and said, "Drink. You're going to need it."

Then I watched him eat, with my arms crossed over my chest. The night was cooling rapidly.

"I was too tired to make an effective escape," I lied. "Now, do you want to hear what I learned this afternoon, or do you want to argue?"

He glared for a moment longer, then nodded. "Tell me."

"First, are we taking out Polina before we leave or getting reinforcements?"

I could see him warring with that decision. We were so close and isolated enough that any strike we made would go unnoticed, at least for a while. But he shook his head. "Reinforcements."

He made that choice for me. If he'd been alone, he would have gone after Polina regardless of the danger. I was glad to keep him alive a little longer.

We crouched and I made a quick sketch in the dirt with a stick, showing our compound and Polina's main house. "There are about fifteen acres of woods between us and the estate's perimeter wall, here." I scratched another line. "Only about one acre if we go that way, but that wall borders the river and the beach is barricaded. There are four patrols of guards, circulating in pairs. They aren't random, but loosely follow the same trail." I made another line to show the guards' route.

"Can we get over the barricade?"

I shook my head. "It's debris from the floods—broken metal, glass and driftwood. I tried to climb it the first time I came here and nearly sliced off an arm. We'd never make it in a hurry."

Mason chewed his sandwich slowly, considering. "One day you're going to explain why you've been here before."

I waved away that concern and pointed to the makeshift map again. "So we take the long route here."

We both turned to look at the guards.

"We'll never make it over the fence without being seen," Mason said.

"Then we go through the gate." In the shadows, I let the glamor drop from my sword for a moment.

"How?"

"Merrow. She's a bit wishy-washy about taking sides."

"All right. Through the gate." He pointed to someone coming up the path through the woods. It was Merrow, bringing us supper. "We have only one chance at this. Wait until the gate is open. You take the fae. I'll worry about the guards."

I unsheathed my sword before we headed back to the gate, but kept my arm loose at my side. With any luck, the guards wouldn't see it coming.

"It's about time," I called out. "We're starving!"

Mason stood to my left where he would have a clear line to dart out the gate. One guard fiddled with the lock. The other scanned the forest.

"I hope you brought us something hot at least," I said.

Merrow narrowed her eyes. She could see my blade. Her lips pressed flat. She met my gaze and gave one almost imperceptible nod.

The gate opened. Merrow stepped past the guard and crouched to lay the tray on the ground. Mason jumped through the gate, and his stone arm bashed down on the first guard. I hit Merrow with the butt of my sword. She dropped and didn't get up. At least she'd have plausible deniability about her role in our escape. I didn't know if she deserved it.

By the time I turned back, Mason had already dispatched the second guard.

We ran into the forest, staying away from the path. The moon had yet to rise, and the forest was pitch black. The underbrush hadn't bloomed to its full summer growth, so despite the darkness, we made good time until we hit a boggy patch and had to slow. My foot sank to my ankle in mud and we wasted precious seconds pulling it out. I wiped muddy hands on my jeans and looked around to get my bearings.

"The perimeter wall is about a kilometer that way." I pointed south. "But there will be guards. You might not see them. So, stay behind me."

Mason nodded once and fell into stride. We crept along now, picking through branches.

A hound howled in the distance. The sound itched along my keening.

"What in the hells was that?" Mason said. A second hound answered the call.

"That was Princess and her mate." It seemed that both doghouses were inhabited after all.

The howls echoed again, one from the left, the other to the right, but closer now.

"They're hunting us." Mason grabbed my hand and we ran. Or rather we stumbled through the undergrowth, as fast as we could. I fell. Mason scooped me up and we kept running. The calls came faster. We dashed through the trees into a brief clearing before hitting the wall.

"Give me your foot." Mason held his hands clasped to boost me. Before I could slip my foot into his hands, a beast shot from the trees and clobbered us. I slammed to the dirt with the beast pinning me down. Claws raked across my chest, and I screamed in pain. When my sight cleared, a snarling hound stared down at me with red glowing eyes from my worst nightmares. A growl rumbled from its throat. Grunts and growls from the shadows told me that Mason battled his own hell hound. I struggled to take a deep breath with the weight of the beast pressing down on me, then I screamed one word.

"Hæl!"

I laced it with as much magic as I could draw from the deep well inside me. It burst from my lips, shimmering with power, and slammed into the hell hound like a sledgehammer.

The thing is, hell hounds don't come, sit and heel like regular dogs. My grandfather taught me that. They only respond to power greater than their own. So when I commanded her, Princess jumped back, releasing the pressure on my chest. Her ears perked forward, and she gave me all her attention. She was frighteningly beautiful. Her face was half glossy black fur, half bone-white plating, with a silvery muzzle and silver tipped ears.

I lifted a shaking hand to pet her. The fur around her ear was soft and thick enough to lose my fingers in.

A voice shouted from the shadows. "Princess! Cobalt! Come!"

Princess's gaze snapped toward the new command. The beast hovering over Mason left his prey to run back to his master. General Naughton stood on the edge of the trees with six armed soldiers at his back. I glanced up. A ghost patrolled along the top of the wall—Polina's eyes.

Princess sat back on her haunches, watching me.

"Princess, come!" Naughton shouted again. Princess didn't move. Naughton turned to the soldier on his left. "Bring them. And the hound too."

The guard looked reluctant to approach Princess. He put his hands on her scruff and she growled, her lip curling back to reveal impressive teeth.

Naughton stared at the hound with a frown. He wasn't a man to put up with insubordination, even from a beast.

"Cobalt, kill!" He pointed at Princess.

The second hound sprang, his teeth latching onto the thick fur at her neck. Princess yelped and tried to spring away. They tumbled together in a heap of fur and fangs, snarls and yips of pain. Cobalt was bigger, but Princess was fast and wily. He had her pinned, but she squirmed out to bite him on his unprotected haunch. He whirled. Saliva flew from his jowls as he bit down on her forepaw. Princess screamed and fell. Cobalt paced around the wounded hound. Princess heaved in short breaths, and a gash across her face leaked blood. She watched her death coming for her with hooded eyes. But just as Cobalt dove in for the kill, she twisted and came up sideways, swiping one massive paw across his nose. Before the shock of the strike wore off, she sank her teeth into his throat.

It was over in a matter of seconds. Cobalt lay dead in a muddy puddle of blood. Princess crouched by his body, her muzzle covered in gore. Then she collapsed.

Naughton surveyed the scene. His expression was carefully neutral, but I keened the rage coming off him. He didn't like that one rogue beast had almost foiled his plans. He would have some explaining to do to his queen, when she found out one of her pets was dead and the other compromised.

"Bring the prisoners," he snapped to the guards. "And the hounds. The queen can use their blood."

Naughton's soldiers led us back to the compound with the doghouses and bloody altar. He left us with two more guards at the gate. There was no sign of Merrow or the other guards we'd taken down in our escape attempt, but four ghosts now hovered just outside the fence. The full moon was rising, half hidden by dark clouds.

The soldier carrying Princess laid her on the altar. Another dumped Cobalt's body beside it. As soon as Naughton locked the gate, I ran over to the hound. Her face was criss-crossed with cuts, but her front leg was worse. Blood matted the fur and leaked onto the already stained altar stone.

"Help me move her," I said. Together Mason and I lifted the massive beast off the disgusting stone and let her rest on the ground in the shadow of the lab. She growled when I lifted her paw to examine the puncture wound. With little fight left in her, instinct was taking over.

"Hey you!" I called to the guards. "I need bandages to bind this wound."

One guard glanced at me, then looked nervously at the four ghosts swirling above the fence and shook his head. Interesting.

"Can you see those ghosts?" I asked Mason.

"I see something. Looks like flickering balls of gas."

So Polina had made her ghosts at least a bit corporeal tonight. I wondered if she did that to keep the human guards in line.

I looked down at the hound again.

"She's going to bleed out if we don't treat this wound."

Mason pulled off his shirt and tore it into bandage-sized strips. It was a testament to my exhaustion and worry that I didn't even take time to admire his nakedness before taking the strips of cloth.

Gently, I lifted Princess's arm, but she withdrew it to lick at the wound.

"I'll hold her. You bind it," Mason said. He held the hound down, and when Princess whined and tried to bite him, he turned his arm to stone. I bound her leg quickly, wishing I had antiseptic to clean it with first. Dog bites were notorious for getting infected. Would a hell hound be any different? It was a question for the blog, but not something I could worry about now.

When I was done, Mason let go and Princess flopped on her side. I laid my hand on her chest, feeling for her breath. It was deep and even. She licked me, then thumped her head against the ground and closed her eyes again.

I sat back on my heels and wiped my hands on jeans that were already a kaleidoscope of stains. "I'm worried she has internal injuries, but there's nothing more I can do for her."

A small body scurried in front of my knees and disappeared into the shadows.

I froze.

"Did I just see that?" Mason asked.

"Don't make a big deal or you'll alert the guards."

I stood up, trying to act casual, and stepped around the altar. A little white face poked from a crack in the stone. Whiskers twitched and a long lizard tail flicked back and forth. The squamus had a tiny recording device strapped to its head.

"Smile," I said to Mason. "You're on camera."

RODENT + LIZARD = A CURIOSITY

April 10, 2081

Today on the continuing saga of my life with critters, I bring a truly unique creature. I'm calling it a squamus—squamata (a genus of reptiles which includes snakes and lizards) + mus (a genus of rodents including mice).

I found two of these little guys in the basement of an old church turned rooming house. Their heads are mousy, like the fancy mice kids often badger their parents into getting as pets. The back end is definitely reptile, similar to my bearded dragons. I'm going to go out on a limb and say these aren't native to Terra.

What's really interesting about these critters is that they seem highly intelligent. They understand commands like a dog. My assistant has them in a training regime. I'm curious to see how far he can take it.

Update: Squamice are stinking smart!

So far my assistant has taught the squamice to come, sit and stay. He's even let them loose in the backyard and they come running home when he calls, using a series of whistles. There may be potential to use them on job sites, for scouting tight spaces.

COMMENTS (4)

Those look like a lizard we see here in the desert a lot. We call them dragon rats. They're great for target practice.

BB8 (April 10, 2081)

You shouldn't handle those filthy rodents.
Helen4897 (April 10, 2081)

—•—

They're so cute! If they have babies, can I have one?
Primrose388 (April 11, 2081)

> Sorry, as far as I can tell, they're both girls.
> *Valkyrie367 (April 11, 2081)*

stared into the forest beyond the fence, looking for movement. If the squamice were here, Gabe wasn't far behind. Did he know about the ghost guards? Four of them now floated along the perimeter of our prison yard.

"Let's hope they don't do anything stupid," I mumbled. Mason squeezed my hand, then ambled into the center of the yard, pretending to stretch out his arms and shoulders. I followed him, keeping an eye on the trees.

My keening went into sudden overload and I staggered sideways. Mason caught me at the same time as one of the ghost guards exploded in an array of blue light. A will o'wisp—its mouth open wide to gobble up the ethereal vapors—zoomed by.

The night exploded with blaster fire. The guards panicked. One tried to shoot the wisps tearing through the ghosts. The other swatted at the little glowing beasts as they fluttered around his head like gnats. So he didn't see the vampire sneak out of the woods to cut his throat.

Gabe followed Emil, grabbed the first guard's gun and bashed it down on his head. The guard dropped, and the night fell silent.

Angus strolled from the shadows, holding up the will o'wisp basket. He whistled and the wisps lumbered back to their nest, sated for the moment on ghost ether. Popping the cap on the end of the basket, Angus raised a hand to wave, then shimmered, like a pixilated image breaking apart, and Naomi stepped out of his body.

"Woo hoo! That was a wild ride!" She pumped her incorporeal fist in the air.

Angus grinned. "You can ride me any time, baby."

Naomi cocked a pose with one hand on her hip. "I might just do that."

I ran toward the fence, so glad to see familiar faces. "What are you guys doing here?"

"Rescuing you, what else?" Emil looked as pleased as a teenager out after curfew.

Gabe rifled through the guards' pockets until he found the key and opened the padlock. The gate swung open.

I hugged him. "I'm sorry."

"Me too." He squeezed me back. There was no time for all the things I wanted to say, but he'd come when I needed help. We could fix anything else. He bent down, scooped up Sweet Pea and tucked her into the pocket of his cargo pants.

"I knew these little rascals would be worth the price of their feed." He grinned. "They led us right to you. And we brought you someone else." He pointed into the trees.

Yuki leaned against the trunk of a tall maple. Even in the dim light, I could see that he was pale.

"We broke him out of that hospital," Angus said. "He wants his shot at Polina."

Mason walked over to Yuki and offered his arm. The hand that grasped his elbow shook.

"You shouldn't be here," Mason said.

"None of us should be here." Yuki's words ended with a coughing fit.

"I'm sorry you got caught up in this, my old friend."

Yuki brought his breathing under control and said, "I'm not. Let's get that witch."

We had only minutes before the human guard patrol swept this section of the property. Princess rose on shaky legs to join us. She still wouldn't put weight on the wounded front paw.

"What in the hells is that?" Angus pointed to the hound.

"That's Princess," I said. "She's coming with us." Angus shrugged. He knew me well enough not to argue.

We huddled in the shadows, discussing the best route to take back to the main road.

"How did you get this far without being detected?" Mason asked.

"Well, let's just say the wisps won't need to feed for a while." Angus smiled. "And for the rest, we took care of them." He pointed east. A red glow rose above the trees. "We set the witch's house on fire. That ought to keep her busy for a bit."

I could only hope that, in the confusion, Merrow could get Leighna away.

"Then let's get the hell out of here," I said. I couldn't help scanning the trees, looking for the guards I knew were out there. We had to keep moving.

"No!" Yuki's voice still had some strength. He slipped his hand into the folds of his robe and produced the witch-killer. "I have tasted her magic and only this can defeat her."

Mason took the blade and turned it over in his hands.

I didn't like this idea. Going for reinforcements had seemed like a good idea when it was just Mason and me. But I thought we'd go find the Guardians and come back for a fair fight. Now my "rescuers" would be in harm's way too. Yuki could barely stand upright. Emil and Angus could hold their own, but Gabe was just a guy—a human—and much too fragile for my liking. They had to stop arguing and get their butts out now.

Mason must have been thinking along the same lines. He gripped the blade and said, "You're right. We end this tonight. Me and Kyra. The rest of you need to leave."

I could have kissed him. Once, not too long ago, he would have tried to send me away with the others. But we were a team now. For better or worse, as the saying goes. And we were about to get the worst.

"But we busted you out!" Emil said.

"You did," Mason said. "And I thank you, but we can take it from here."

Yuki pulled himself up to his full height, which barely reached Mason's nose.

"I left you to face the witch alone last time. And still, you came halfway around the world to find me. I won't leave here until we finish this. Together."

Mason frowned at his old mentor, but eventually nodded.

Naomi popped into the middle of our huddle.

"We have to go! Now!"

But we were already too late.

Polina emerged at the head of the path. The light reflecting off the overcast sky gave her a ghoulish cast.

"So touching." She slow-clapped like she just watched a dramatic performance. "I'm glad the entire gang came out to play. Looks like I have more than enough blood to fuel my spells."

She'd come to fight, bringing a dozen men, led by General Naughton. Soldiers fanned out to protect their queen. Naughton snapped a command, and they herded us into the yard. The soldiers were armed with blades, which meant they expected magic to fly tonight. Even so, a dozen men with knives and bows was enough to disarm us. I dropped my sword in the shadows and willed it to be invisible before the soldier frisked me. The witch-killer had disappeared back into the folds of Yuki's robe.

Polina strode through the gate with two soldiers in tow. One carried a box that he set down beside the altar. I pressed my back against the fence, gripping the chain-link in my stiff fingers. Even from a distance I keened the oily, black magic coming from that box. Angus and Yuki also stepped back, recoiling from the scent of death.

The other soldier had Leighna slung over his shoulder. He dropped her roughly onto the blood-stained stone.

Polina hummed a merry tune as she opened the first box and started laying out her implements—knives, delicate glass vials, herbs in bundles and sacks, everything the modern necromancer needed to perform her dark rites.

"You don't think we're just going to stand by and watch you kill us one, by one, do you?" I asked. Princess lay at my feet, still worrying at the bandage on her wounded paw, and Polina frowned at her former pet. Then she flicked a hand at a guard. Even as he swung back for a punch, Mason roared and charged. The guard's fist slammed into my stomach before Mason reached him. I gasped, getting no air, and crumpled to the ground. Angus and Gabe ran to my side. My vision clouded with black and bright splotches. Princess was snarling. The sounds of metal clashing and grunts of pain told me someone nearby was fighting.

I heard Gabe say, "You got this?"

"Go," Angus said. He helped me stand in time to see Gabe and Emil climb over the fence.

Mason had put down two guards, and fought with two more, his naked back shining with sweat in the dim light. Polina ignored us and went back to setting out her implements of death, as if any effort we could muster to escape was insignificant. And against her power and her army, she was right.

"What are they doing?" I hissed through gritted teeth, pointing to Gabe and Emil, who now faced General Naughton and his soldiers.

"You think we came here without a plan?" Angus asked. Then he nodded to Naomi. She pressed herself to Angus's side and melted into him. His eyes widened for an instant, and his grin took on a feral edge. "Are you ready?"

I had no idea what he was up to, but I nodded. Angus crouched in the shadows behind us and began muttering an incantation in Gaelic.

"Remember your promise," Yuki whispered as he slipped something into my hand. The witch-killer.

Polina rose, holding an ornate knife. "Shame the moon is hidden." She glanced at the cloudy sky and frowned. "But I think we have enough blood here tonight to light up the world. So let's get started." She leaned over Leighna's body and raised the knife.

No! She wasn't getting another one of my friends. I raised the witch-killer and leaped, intending to stab Polina in the heart.

But she twisted into smoke and disappeared even as my blade fell.

She reappeared on the other side of the altar. I lunged and she vanished. Again.

"Such spirit," she said, right in my ear. I whirled and she punched me. Or at least I thought she did. I never saw the fist coming, but the hit sent me sailing over the altar. I landed with a shock of pain on my right knee. The witch-killer flew from my hand into the shadows. I tried to rise, but my head spun. Princess slunk from the shadows and licked my face, urging me to get up. Thunder rumbled in the distance. I could hear blades clashing around me. Mason fought one remaining guard. Gabe and Emil had attacked Naughton and the soldiers outside the fence.

And Polina…she raised her knife and plunged it into Leighna's chest.

Polina cut out Leighna's heart and held it up to the moon, now invisible behind clouds. Thunder boomed. Lightning flashed, illuminating a scene I wish I never saw.

She ate it.

Polina's teeth tore into the heart, and I thought of the cute little will o'wisps, eating souls. Not so cute now. She gulped down the last bit of meat and smiled. Blood laced her teeth and dripped down her chin. And she glowed. A fae wind sprang up, whipping her hair, and throwing dust in my face. A bright light radiated from Polina's core—so bright I had to shield my eyes. Her head jerked back, arms raised wide and she rose off the ground, cocooned in her nimbus of light. Thunder boomed again and the light exploded.

Polina sagged against the altar.

"It is done!"

She stood tall and stretched, fascinated with her newly corporeal body, flexing her muscles and ruffling her hair. She leaned over Leighna and kissed her forehead.

"Thank you for the gift of true life. Now we have work to do." Then she shoved the corpse off the stone. It fell with a thud onto the gravel beside the dead hound.

I rose on unsteady legs.

Yuki stood beside Angus who was still deep in his incantation. The last guard slashed at Mason's stone arm in desperation. Mason would wear him down eventually, but we had no time left.

Polina ignored them and turned to Angus, Yuki and I. Princess tried to stand and snarled at her former mistress.

"Now, for my second act. Shall we ignite that ward and save the world?" She laughed and it was a harsh, maniacal sound. "So who's first? Oh, come now. It's for a good cause. Your deaths should create enough energy to jolt that damned Apex stone." She glance at us standing like frightened children around the yard. "Don't make me choose." She pointed her knife at each of us in a silent eeny-meeny-miny-moe.

Yuki stood up and walked over to the altar.

"Oh, good. Just the bit of appetizer I need." Polina pointed the blade to the stone, and Yuki climbed onto it. He sat cross-legged and closed his eyes, the picture of calm surrender.

"Lie down," Polina snapped.

Then three things happened all at once.

Mason swung his stone fist upward, catching the guard under the chin. His head snapped back with a sickening crack, and he toppled over the end of the altar.

Polina raised her blade to spill Yuki's blood.

The third thing was the magic that pulsed from Angus. I should have yanked up my wards as soon as I felt it. I could hear screams from the guards outside the gate. But whatever spell Angus was casting—whatever his grand plan was—it was taking too long. So, I did the unthinkable. I dropped my wards and grabbed one of Angus's hands. Instead of blocking his magic, I gave him mine. I had no idea what he was trying to do, but I trusted him.

He smiled and gripped my fingers, accepting everything I could give. Power surged from him. I felt strangely calm as he hooked into my green magic and used it to boost his own. The brambles in his beard and hair exploded outward. Branches and leaves grew and twined, weaving an impenetrable wall around us.

I look back at that moment of chaos now and think that the world shifted. Everything changed. While tapped into Angus's magic, watching him blossom like a wild hedgerow, I felt a great connection to the lives around me, even the dark presence of Polina, looming like a blight in the bright green growth. But it all happened in an instant.

I blinked and found myself inside the ring of an impenetrable hedge.

Angus had enclosed us inside a fortress of brambles. His face was nearly hidden in the mass of branches. He'd given us this one chance to defeat Polina without her soldiers interfering.

The fighting and screaming continued from the other side.

Gabe and Emil. Oh, gods.

I could only hope they fought their way out. I could do nothing to help them now.

Mason wiped blood from his lip. He'd killed or disabled all the guards, and they lay in a heap beside the altar. Princess was a warm presence against my leg, and I sunk my fingers into her ruff.

Polina's mouth fell open as she turned in a circle, taking in her new prison. Even if we lost today, even if she cut us down, one by one, at least I had the satisfaction that we surprised her. It was cold comfort.

She circled the hedge to where Angus's face peered through the brambles. His eyes were closed, and I didn't know if he was unconscious or deep in the spell. Polina tapped him on the head with one delicate finger.

Then she laughed.

"A clever trap." She turned to Mason and me, frowning when she spied Princess at my side. "But you forget that I am mistress of the dead."

Her eyes went black. Her hands raised. The magic spilling from her should have overloaded my keening, but I was still full of Angus's green magic, and I felt strong.

Polina jerked her hands to the sky as if calling on the power of the night. Lightning flashed, followed by a crack of thunder.

In the shadows, behind the altar of death, Cobalt stood up. He shook out his mane of bloody fur as if awakening from a nap. The dead guards rose. One of them was barely recognizable, his face smashed to bloody pulp by Mason's fist.

Mason yelled, "Yuki! Now!"

The dead guards closest to me attacked. Princess thrust herself in front of me, snarling at the dead men. If she hadn't been wounded, the fight would have been no contest. Two unarmed men—even men with the blind tenacity of the undead—couldn't win against a hell hound. But Princess could barely stand, so even as she puffed herself up to a black ball of fury, I ran to the edge of the yard where I'd dropped my sword. The glamor was long gone, but I no longer needed it. The zombie guards lumbered forward. Behind them, Yuki's head fell back as he cast his last chance spell to stop Polina.

Then the guards fell on Princess, and she turned into a whirlwind of fangs and claws. A hell hound in action is truly a beautiful thing. Scary but beautiful.

When the dust, blood and fur settled, I found the world had shifted. The guards were dead, really dead. As in torn into pieces small enough that their own mothers wouldn't recognize them. Princess panted, her mouth foaming with gore.

Behind them, Yuki lay on the altar, his stomach torn open. Cobalt was eating his entrails.

And Mason held Polina, shoved up against Angus's wall of brambles, the witch-killer blade poised at her throat, ready to spill her blood and end this day for once and all. Polina's eyes were huge and her mouth fixed in a half-frown.

Yuki had done it. His last act had been to release the spell and freeze Polina—the master showing the student she still had a lot to learn.

I thought of Yuki's warning that Mason must not be the one to kill her.

"Wait!" I rushed forward, slipped in the bloody grass and almost went down. Cobalt raised his head and a deep unearthly growl emanated from his chest. Princess answered with a growl of her own.

No! I sliced through the air, and brought my blade down on the undead hound's neck. His head thumped to the ground, but his legs twitched as if not believing they were really dead. I closed my eyes and prayed to the All-father. I hated killing the beast.

Critter wrangler rule number seven: some monsters just need to die.

When I turned my attention to Mason and Polina, the world shifted again. Polina had lost her look of terror. She stood behind Mason, her back to the bramble wall. She held the witch-killer blade to his throat, and he didn't move. His eyes were wide and unblinking and his expression frozen in a frown. It was eerily like seeing him as a gargoyle.

"Yuki always was a fool. And arrogant." She smiled over Mason's shoulder and ran her fingers over his bare chest. Her face was all sharp angles, and she seemed to glow. The storm picked up force and her hair whipped about her head, tangling with the branches behind her.

She leaned into Mason, pressing her lips to his ear. "Maybe once those minor magics would have worked on me, dear husband, but I am infinitely more powerful than even you feared." She held up Yuki's knife and licked the blade. "Mmm. This tastes of power. Yuki's craft, no doubt. It won't help you now."

I took a step closer. Polina jabbed the blade's tip against Mason's neck. He still didn't move. Couldn't move. She'd turned the tables, locking him in the same paralyzing spell that Yuki had tried on her.

"I will kill him," she snarled. "And then I will kill you."

I took another step. "You've got dirt smeared across your face. And your hair is a mess. You look more like a hag than a queen." I circled my sword as if warming up my wrist. Polina glared at me.

"Aren't real bodies fun? No more glamor for you. No more vanishing. In a puff of smoke. You're human again, which means I can kill you."

Polina glanced at my antique hunk of metal and sneered, "That pig-sticker can't hurt me."

"Then why do I see fear in your eyes?"

Angus's green magic still flowed through me. Or maybe it was my magic. I called to the earth and the life teeming underfoot. I pulled, and it came. Vines sprouted from the ground, wrapping around Polina's feet. Branches thrust from the hedge and tangled in her hair.

Polina twisted her legs, but she was trapped. I bet she wished for that fancy incorporeal body now.

"Release me!"

I pulled the vines tighter. Polina struggled, then scowled and pressed the blade against Mason's throat. I could feel her manifesting power again, working at the bindings on her legs. But her magic was all about death. She had no power over the living.

"There is no way out for you." She jabbed Mason, drawing a bead of blood.

His eyes begged me to end this. I could almost hear his voice. *Do it, Kyra. Stop her, no matter what.*

"Yes, my love."

I stepped forward and drove the blade through his shoulder, right into Polina's heart.

And then I kissed him.

How do you reverse a fae spell? Why, with a kiss, of course.

Polina gasped as the sword in her chest flared to life. My bloodthirsty Valkyrie blade tasted her and broke the curse that bound her spirit. The magic she used to cobble together her corporeal body burst. And with an ear-splitting scream, the curse exploded in a hiss of black shadow and smoke, leaving a very scared mortal in its place.

Polina's eyes bulged and the witch-killer tumbled from her fingers. I grabbed it from the air with my left hand and jabbed it into her eye. Her mouth opened in a scream that would never come. There would be no bloodstone to tie Polina to this earth again. And no immortality spell. The witch was dead. Ding, dong and all that.

I'd sent her to whatever hell would take her. Because I was Valkyrie, and that's what we did.

Mason gasped and sagged in my arms. I tugged out the blade and let him drop to the ground, kicking away Polina's corpse.

He was bleeding too much. I'd aimed for his right side, hoping not to strike anything vital, but there was so much blood! He'd already lost his shirt to Princess. So I tore off mine, leaving me with nothing but a thin tank top in the chilly night. I didn't even feel the cold. Wadding the cloth, I pressed it to his wound. Princess paced around our little prison and whined, but I could spare no attention for her.

Blood soaked my shirt and pants. How much blood could Mason lose? I glanced at the sky. Dark clouds churned overhead. I couldn't tell if dawn approached. It had to be soon. This felt like the longest night of my life.

He just had to hang on for the sun.

Mason grabbed my hand. "I'm sorry…"

"You have nothing to be sorry for." Tears flowed down my cheeks. I stroked his face, not caring that I smeared it with blood. He was beautiful to me, bloody or not.

"Sorry…we didn't have more time." He coughed and a fresh surge of blood soaked my shirt.

"Just lie still. Dawn is almost here. The sun heals all wounds. Isn't that what you always tell me?"

He shook his head, a tiny jerk of a movement. "Not this time." He smiled. "You…cured me."

I didn't want to believe it, but I knew it was true. My blade's effect was unpredictable with immortals, but it was good at breaking curses. The minute my magic rushed through the sword, I felt two curses break. The one holding together Polina's corporeal body—life she'd stolen from Leighna—and the one she'd placed on Mason nearly three hundred years ago.

He was no longer a gargoyle.

The looming storm blocked the sunrise, but I keened Angus's magic fall silent. The great bramble bush ring turned to stone. But Mason was still flesh under my hand, his blood oozing between my fingers.

He smiled weakly. "Told you so."

42

Princess crawled across the yard and lay down next to Mason. She'd lost her bandage in the fight, and she licked her leg, causing it to bleed again. I had no energy to stop her. Mason had succumbed to the pain and passed out. Yuki lay like a flayed man on the altar. I couldn't look at either of them. Instead, I stepped over the corpse of the second hound and found Leighna. Her bloody shirt hid the worst of her wounds, and she looked peaceful in death. The tree-of-life medallion given to her by my father lay against her pale cheek. She'd wanted me to have that once. I tugged on the chain and it broke. I tucked the medallion into my pocket. I would examine my motives for taking it later, and no doubt feel guilty for it. But right now, I needed to get out of here.

"Kyra! Are you alive in there?" Gabe's voice came through the stone hedge. I jumped up.

"I'm here. Mason's hurt." I lifted my wadded shirt to check his wound. The bleeding had slowed, but I couldn't wake him. Even in the dim light, his complexion was gray.

In a moment, Emil's head poked over the hedge. He cursed, trying to scramble over the petrified branches, but finally dropped down beside me. Blood covered the side of his face and shoulder, but if it was his, the wounds had already healed.

"Gabe's gone to get the car. Why isn't he stone like Angus?" He pointed at Mason.

"It's a long story." I wiped grit out of my eyes with a blood-covered hand. "We need an ambulance," I said.

"No ambulances." Emil's face was grim. His brown curls were matted to his head with sweat and dirt. "We already called the fire department. There is no one left to come."

"What does that mean?"

"It means that marauders broke through Hedge into the city. Entire blocks are on fire. No one's coming."

"Then we have to get him to Nori. It's his only chance."

When Emil juggled him over the barricade to Gabe's waiting arms, Mason woke up and roared in pain. Then he understood what was happening and bit back his screams.

I turned to Princess. She lay on her side too hurt to get up. The bone-white armor on her face no longer frightened me. She was just a hurt puppy. One who had defended me with her life.

"I have to go." I sank to the ground and ran my fingers through the ruff around her neck. "But I will come back for you. I promise." The hound wuffed out a sigh and closed her eyes.

I climbed over the hedge, ignoring my injuries that screamed for attention.

Gabe bundled him into the back seat of his car, not caring about staining his fancy faux-leather with blood. I slid in beside him and Emil rode shotgun. Gabe gunned the engine, and we raced down the dirt lane toward the house.

A figure stepped into the road, arms waving.

Merrow.

Gabe slowed the car to a stop.

"Ignore her!" I yelled. "Go around!" No one but Mason mattered now. Especially not that traitorous fae.

But Merrow was having none of it. She dropped her glamor and pressed her massive hands on the hood. Deep-set eyes flashed from under a brow of natural armor plating as she glared at me through the windshield.

"My granddaughter is in that house!" She pointed to where smoke rose from the remains of Gerard's old estate.

Mason mumbled something, and I leaned in to hear.

"…help…her…We need her."

"You're the one who needs help now!"

He shook his head.

"Go," Gabe said. "I've got him."

I kissed Mason once more, a sob filling my chest.

"I'll come with you," Emil said, getting out of the car.

That's how I ended up shirtless and shivering in the dawn light with a fae and a vampire, watching my only true love drive away. I didn't know if I would ever see him again.

The storm clouds chose that moment to open up and dump their load. Perfect.

Merrow loomed over me like a giantess. Her eyes were haunted.

"Leighna's dead," I snapped, wishing my words were knives.

"I know." Merrow bowed her head. "I felt her go."

"You could have saved her."

"Save your self-righteousness. I did what I had to. Now are you going to help me find the child?"

"What makes you think she's even here?"

Rain carved a path down the plating on Merrow's face and she wiped it away, shifting from foot to foot.

"Polina set herself up to win the Alchemy seat on the triumvirate, but Leighna didn't trust her. When Polina invited her to come for dinner, Leighna refused. I convinced her it was a diplomatic parlay, a chance to get Polina's measure. I brought her here."

"You led Leighna right into the trap? Why?"

"Because Polina took my daughter-in-law and granddaughter!" Black tears streaked down her face. I considered her for a long moment, then sighed with defeat. I would have done the same thing if my family was threatened.

"Fine." I waved a hand up the road. "Show me." I hugged my arms around me. On a normal day, I wouldn't have found the morning that chill, but exhaustion weakened my defenses.

Emil saw me shivering and took off his shirt. "Here take mine." It was just a t-shirt, a little too wide across the shoulder and spattered with blood, but I accepted it gratefully. He looked better naked than I did, anyway. He winked and followed Merrow toward the house.

The rain let up as we worked our way around the soggy, smoking ruins. The roof had collapsed, bringing down the whole front end of the house with its Doric style columns and sweeping staircase. The back of the structure fared better. We went in through the kitchen. Everything smelled of soot, but the smoke had cleared through a hole in the roof. Part of the ceiling had come down, smashing the counters and stove. The place was deserted. If Polina had servants, they'd taken off the first chance they could. That's the kind of loyalty she inspired.

"They're down there." Merrow pointed to the cellar door. A beam had fallen across it.

"Do you mean to tell me a big, strong fae like yourself couldn't move one little beam?" Emil said.

"Only if I want the whole place to crash down on me. Look." Merrow pointed to the beam propping up more debris, all of which precariously held up an entire wall.

I saw her point. In the end, Merrow used her great size to brace the wall while Emil and I removed debris.

When I opened the cellar door, I heard someone screaming.

"Down here! We're down here!" Merrow vaulted down the stairs and I followed. At the bottom, she produced a key and unlocked a large metal door in the stone wall. A small body flew out of the room and hugged her around the knees. The girl was Merrow's mini-me down to the color of her face-plates and long black hair. Another fae, who had to be her daughter-in-law, came out next.

"She kept us alive," the fae woman said, staring at her daughter in awe. "When the place filled up with smoke, she did something to help us breathe. Like we were in a bubble or something. It was amazing."

Merrow smiled with pride and lifted her granddaughter in her arms.

Outside, the rain started up again, pattering through the leaves. That's when the arguing began.

I WAS TIRED and sick of heart. My brain had no filters left. So, when Merrow told me her plan to restart the ward, I blurted, "Don't be stupid!"

The fae raise one eyebrow at me. "I assure you I am not."

I was sitting under the trees, sipping from a bottle of water Emil had found in the kitchen. I welcomed the water, but my stomach clenched with hunger.

"You don't even know if you can work the magic," I said to Merrow.

"I have to try. The opji might be at the gates right now!"

I shook my head, but she was right. The vampires would come. They had a network of spies and were probably on their way.

"We must get that ward going," Merrow said.

"Then let me do it." I had enough magic if I somehow managed to get the dryad and Valkyrie halves of my psyche to play nice. I stood up, swayed a bit and Merrow caught me.

"On your best day, you couldn't master the magic needed for this spell," she said. "And today?"

She was right.

"There is no one else. Leighna would have gladly given her life to save the city." Merrow smiled sadly. "She told you the story about your father, yes? And how he sacrificed himself to close the door to Underhill?"

I nodded.

"That's the level of power needed to restart the ward. Why do you think Leighna was the only one left from the original triumvirate?" She frowned. "Joe Canta and Beverly Haas were her colleagues. My friends too. We built this city. Joe was a brilliant alchemist and Bev was a witch of uncanny power. But more importantly, they were good souls, willing to give up their lives for others. Nothing is more powerful than the death of a good soul."

She was going to sacrifice herself to restart the ward. And I couldn't stop her. Or could I?

I pulled Emil aside. "I need to make a call."

He pulled his widget from his pocket and handed it to me.

I looked up Oscar's number and waited impatiently for him to answer.

"Are you with Mason?" I asked as soon as the call connected.

"Yes. Nori's treating him now."

Good. He wasn't out of the woods yet, but it was something.

"Oscar, listen. I need you here and fast."

MERROW AGREED TO my plan, if reluctantly. She grumbled about it being her right to sacrifice herself, but that argument didn't get far with her granddaughter—Becca was her name—clinging to her leg and begging her grandmother not to leave her.

While we waited for Oscar, I sent Emil back to check on Princess and Angus. He returned some minutes later frowning.

"The hound is gone," he said. "Must've climbed over the hedge and taken off."

That worried me. Princess was hurt. I'd have to go looking for her.

"We should bury the others." Emil's expression was bleak. "It looks like an abattoir in there."

I nodded. There would be time to bury the dead.

Oscar arrived about the same time as the fae. They came with sirens blaring and lights flashing in the gray morning. Merrow took charge. With Leighna gone, she was the acting prime minister. She might never be able to rival Leighna's regal beauty, but she certainly wielded authority like a queen. She sent her family home and ordered some fae guards to clean up the bodies and secure the house. Another group was sent with Emil to bring back the body of their queen. She would be honored with a state funeral when all this was done.

The chief of security wanted to whisk Merrow away at once, but she insisted on staying to see the ward regenerated. One of the imp secretaries handed her a box. Merrow shook her head and pointed to Oscar. As soon as he opened it, I keened that slithery, restless magic of hundreds of bloodstones.

"What are these?" He dipped his finger in and swirled them around. My stomach lurched. Clearly, Oscar hadn't a whiff of the keening.

"They're bloodstones," I said. "Think of them as little, explosive batteries."

"You mean…" He jerked his hand out of the box.

"That's right. They're souls. Already lost and doing no one any good trapped in there. You studied Pierre's lab after he was killed, right?"

Oscar nodded. I could see the little wheels in his brain spinning out alchemical formulas.

"Pierre was working on a way to harness the bloodstones' energy. That's how he made the golems. Do you think you can adapt his idea to restart the ward?"

"I need a lab and some equipment." He was heading back to his car, clutching the box, but I grabbed his arm and swung him around.

"We've got everything you need right here."

IF NOTHING ELSE, Gerard had been an excellent alchemist. The lab beside the tower was top-notch. While Oscar set up his gear, I sat on a chair by the door, clutching my sword. Only now did I have time to reflect on its reawakening. It felt like having my sight back when I didn't even know I'd been blind. The blade hummed, feeding me its joy through our bond.

I sat with my back to the only window, not wanting to witness the clean up taking place in the yard or gaze at the stone hedge that was once my friend.

One of Merrow's imps brought tea. From where, I couldn't guess, but I was grateful for the warmth. I dumped three sugars in mine, hoping for a boost to get me through these last few hours before I could crash.

Soon, Oscar had a device rigged to the Apex stone.

"It works like a spark plug," he said, "only this spark will be a lot bigger." He showed us the machine that was too similar to the blazing alembic that had taken Jacoby from me. My hands started to shake, and I clutched the bare blade of my sword, taking comfort from it.

Oscar looked thoughtful and turned to Merrow. "Are you certain that once we activate the ward, it will stay up?"

"It will. The ward is still there. Buried deep in the land. Nothing can truly break it. The Apex towers just draw the power from the earth. Once flowing, it will keep flowing until something stronger comes along to shut it off."

"Well, let's get this party started then." Oscar rubbed his hands together. "You might want to clear the room."

"I'm staying right here." Merrow sipped her tea. Her calm assurance was an anchor for the rest of us. Even so, she sent away all her aides. I opted to stay. This was my idea, and I wanted to see it through. I still couldn't stop my hands from trembling.

"Have some more tea." Merrow leaned over and added a hot spot to my cup. "When this is all done, you will tell me of her last minutes." It wasn't a request. The image of Polina eating Leighna's heart was forever burned in my memory, but I would never share that with Merrow. I just nodded. I would think of something to tell her.

"I'm ready," Oscar called from the other side of the room. "Hold on to your lug nuts!"

He pulled goggles into place over his eyes and picked up the box of bloodstones. I avoided the thought of all those lost souls—or rather, I took a

Valkyrie's view. We were doing a good thing, releasing them from an eternal prison. It was all we could do for them. And if their release saved the city, maybe their deaths had meaning.

Oscar dumped the stones into the blazing alembic.

I had my personal wards ramped up to full capacity, ready for the explosion of magic that would restart the ward.

Or so I thought.

I woke in an unfamiliar bed. The room was dark, but the sheets smelled familiar and comforting. Mason! I turned, expecting to find him beside me. The bed was empty except for my sword that lay under the covers within my reach. I was in Mason's house, in one of the many guest rooms he kept for the Guardians.

Clarence perched on the night stand, his beak tucked under one wing as he dozed. I struggled to sit up. Clarence woke, fluttered his wings and hopped to the mattress. I reached up to scratch the feathers behind his ears and he bent low to take the caress.

"Missed you too, buddy." My throat felt raw.

"It's about time you woke up," Nori said from a chair in the corner. "That bloody bird has been standing vigil over your bed since you got here."

"How long have I been asleep?" My thoughts were still groggy and my voice croaked like a moon-frog.

"Nearly twenty-four hours." She rose and laid a hand on my face. "You have no fever. As far as I can tell, you collapsed from sheer exhaustion. When was the last time you ate?"

I took a moment to remember and she frowned.

"Your well of energy was depleted. I've never seen anything like it. And that too." She pointed at my sword. "You have some weird tie to that blade. I think it was the only thing keeping you alive for a while there."

I ran my finger along the dull metal, feeling that familiar low hum of magic and realizing how much I'd missed it. I vowed never to silence it again.

"I'm going to get you some soup." Nori turned away.

I grabbed her hand. "Mason?"

"He's unconscious. His body has a lot of healing to do, but I fixed the worst of it."

"I need to see him." I swung a leg out of bed and the room spun. Nori gently pushed me back into bed.

"Soup first."

I opened my mouth to protest, but she held up her hand. "No arguments. I'll have Dutch come sit on you while I force feed you if necessary." She gave me her best fierce-doctor look. It was a work in progress. She was too young and too pretty to pull it off, but I complied, because my legs felt like hollow sticks and I wasn't sure they would hold me.

She returned in a few minutes with a bowl of steaming broth and a hunk of bread to dip into it. Even though I was ravenous, the first few bites threatened to come back up.

"Slow down," Nori said. "If you vomit, I'm sending you to the hospital for an IV."

I nodded and sipped the broth.

"I'm sorry about your grandfather," I said. She nodded, and her eyes glittered with tears. She quickly wiped them away. "Emil and the fae buried him in the yard where he fell. I would like to go see it."

"What about Angus?"

"He's still there." Poor Angus. It was bad enough to spend half your life as stone. Now he was stuck to one spot as part of a hedge. "We're going to cut him out tonight, as soon as he turns," Nori said. "I wanted to do it sooner, but the Guardians were all in the city last night and I…" She waved a hand around the room. And she was here taking care of us.

While I ate, she continued to catch me up.

Oscar restarted the ward, though Nori had to treat his hands for burns. He'd been so enthralled by the magic combustion, he couldn't resist touching the blazing alembic. He'd wear bandages on his hands for the next few weeks.

Merrow was already locking down the city. Hub enforcers were rounding up looters and marauders. Grandill prison would get an influx of new inmates. Marauders had breached from the south end, and Hub cleared Hedge as a punishment. The taverns were shut down, and the village of shacks and tents emptied. Hedge was a ghost town for now. It wouldn't remain that way. The lure of the south gate—of safety adjacent to the ward—would bring outsiders back eventually.

Outside the north gate, the town of Barrows hadn't fared so well. Fae soldiers had let no one through, but the fighting had been brutal. Then the vampires showed up just as Oscar reignited the ward. They took their frustrations out on the residents, killing many and carting off the rest to fill the opji breeding farms.

Merrow had other worries, closer to home. Jean-Paul Tremblay, the human Prime Minister, had been injured during the uprising and forced to abandon his post. That meant all three branches of the triumvirate were now led by acting prime ministers. Elections could be held when things were back to normal, but until then, the city needed strong leadership. I had no doubt Merrow could step into that void, but she would face opposition at every turn. I didn't envy the work she still had to do, repairing ties with Manhattan and rebuilding people's trust in the efficacy of the ward and the government. She would need to conduct a complete review of Hub and all its officers and militia to root out those on Gerard's payroll.

When I finished eating, I asked Nori to lend me her widget so I could call Gabe. Add another thing to my to-do list: replace my lost kit.

When Gabe answered, he seemed relieved to hear from me.

"Don't worry about anything here," he said. "Emil and I are staying in your apartment until things clear up. You just rest and take care of Mason."

Gabe and Emil together in my apartment. Hmm. I decided not to comment. Instead, Gabe told me how looters had smashed the window to the office and stolen our computers. Add another expense to the growing list. But they took nothing from the apartment. I could imagine how that had gone. The looters, thinking they'd found an easy target, broke in to find one severely pissed banshee and a plucky pygmy kraken ready to defend it. It was a story they'd tell their thieving friends for years.

Gabe and Emil had boarded up the window and even checked on Mr. Murray upstairs.

"He was waiting just inside the front door with a shotgun," Gabe said. "Something from before the war. I'm not sure it could even fire, but the old coot looks pretty menacing when he waves it about."

The Sayntanne police were making an effort to be visible in the streets, and that had calmed down most people. The west gate, which was only a few kilometers from my house, was the only one that hadn't seen trouble with marauders or vampires.

I told Gabe I'd be home the next morning.

"I'll take the bird downstairs to feed him," Nori said when she was satisfied that I had scraped up every drop of soup. "What kind of bird is he anyway?"

"Your guess is as good as mine. Roc, maybe."

"He's very pretty." Clarence stood nearly as tall as her waist and looked like he could snap her thin arm with his beak, but he let her pet him, then he followed her downstairs, hopping rather than flying in the narrow hallway.

I got out of bed, not daring to look in the mirror. Mason wouldn't care what I looked like. As I walked across the landing to his room, I could feel my strength returning, but when I saw him lying unconscious, my knees gave out and I sagged against his bed. Sunlight streamed through the window, accentuating his paleness and the dark circles under his eyes.

I brushed the hair from his forehead and drew my finger along the laugh lines around his eyes. He'd get more wrinkles now. Someday, his hair would go gray. And the sun would no longer heal his wounds. He'd wanted to be rid of his curse, but I didn't feel like I had given him a gift.

"I thought I dreamed it." His voice startled me. He was awake, dark eyes watching me intently.

"What?"

"I thought I dreamed how beautiful you are in the sunshine." His hand stroked my hair that hung in a mess around my shoulders. "In the dark, I never saw the fire in your hair."

Tears stung my eyes. I crawled into bed and wrapped myself around him.

He was alive. Everything else would be all right.

I STAYED IN bed with Mason until the sun waned.

"I need to see about Angus," I said. "Has he ever done anything like that before?"

"Turn himself into a living barricade, you mean?" Mason's eyes glinted with amusement, and I dropped a kiss on the edge of his lips, where they hinted at a smile.

"No. I've seen him grow and shrink his branches, but never to that extreme."

"Nori says we have to cut him out."

Mason nodded. I kissed him again and left the warmth of his bed, promising to come back as soon as Angus was safe.

Nori insisted on coming with me. She wanted to see Yuki's grave. I couldn't deny her that right. In her place, I'd do the same.

Dutch needed to stay with Mason, and I didn't feel strong enough to get behind the wheel. So we took Mason's car and let the AI navigate. The silence on the drive would have been awkward, except Nori and I were lost in our own thoughts.

We drove by the ruins of the house to the edge of the property where the Apex tower now blazed brightly. The familiar hum of the ward settled over me like a hair blanket.

The fae had cleaned up the yard. Only the bloodstains remained to mark the violence that had taken place here. But in another month, summer grass would grow over it, obliterating even this memory. That was how Terra worked her magic.

The sun hadn't quite set and the hedge in the middle of the yard was bone white. I turned to scout the forest.

"Princess? *Kom her!*" I laced my words with magic. If she was nearby, she would come.

I waited. Nothing. No whine or the sound of paws through the underbrush. I was too late. I shouldn't have been so selfish to spend that hour with Mason. I should have come right here. Maybe then…

A huge black body tackled me to the ground. I landed flat on my back staring up at Princess's half-fluffy, half-armored face. Her tongue lolled out the corner of her mouth, and her eyes were bright. Blood still matted her fur, but she seemed whole and mostly recovered.

"You need a bath." I could barely breathe under the weight of a hell hound on my chest. She gave me a doggie grin and licked my face.

"Eeeww! And a breath mint."

I fed her the bag of sausages Dutch had forfeited for her. She gobbled them down in less than a minute, then sat primly with her tail wagging, looking for more.

"You'll have to wait until we get home." I rubbed her behind one ear where the armored plating met fur. I didn't know how I would fit a two-hundred pound hell hound in my little apartment, but I'd find a way. Willow was going to be pissed.

I left Princess and Nori eyeing each other warily and climbed over the hedge. Angus was dormant. Leaves and branches reached from all parts of his body, twining into the intricate hedge. He was a true green man. It wouldn't be easy to cut him out.

Merrow's people had cleaned up in here, but the smell of blood still hung in the air. Cobalt's body was gone, along with the remains of Polina and her guards. A fresh grave had been dug beside the altar for Yuki. Someone had scrubbed the blood from the stone and lain fresh flowers on it. Already, I could feel the green magic of the flowers cleansing away the dark rites that had taken place on that stone.

There was no sign of the will o'wisps or their basket. The fae might have taken them, or they'd been freed during the fight. Either way, they were no longer my responsibility.

"Well, aren't you a sight for these sorry eyes?" I turned to find Angus smiling at me. The hedge had turned from white to earthy brown and green. "Why don't you do an old man a favor and cut me out of here?"

"You sure that won't hurt?"

"Oh, it will hurt like a devil's kiss. But you gotta do it anyway."

So, I primed my sword and hacked into the branches beside his head. He screamed when I made the first cut, but there was no blood.

"Keep going," he said through gritted teeth. I pruned until Angus broke free. He cracked the last branches, and as soon as he stepped away, the hedge turned back to stone.

"A fitting monument to remember a terrible day," he said somberly, then jumped and laughed as if someone had tickled him.

"Stop that!" He scolded. I turned around, looking for a ghost or something else that might have tweaked him.

"Where is Naomi anyway?" I asked.

Angus thumped his chest. "Right here. She jumped into me when I started the spell. Gave me a right decent boost of power. But now it seems she stuck."

"Stuck how?"

"Not sure, I can feel her in there, but I can't communicate with her." He rubbed his stomach the way a pregnant woman communes with her unborn child. "We'll figure it out."

We would. What was a little possession among friends, after all?

NORI SAT ON the stone beside Yuki's grave and sank into contemplation or prayer. Angus had wandered away, saying he needed some "forest time," whatever that meant. I sat on the ground and leaned against the stone hedge, my face turned up to the rising moon, until a scratching noise disturbed me. I opened my eyes to find Princess digging up Yuki's grave.

"No! You leave that!" I snapped. The hound looked wounded. She flopped onto the grass and put her muzzle on her paws.

The sound roused Nori. She opened her eyes and stretched. I had used a bit of my magic to call up yellow flowers around the grave. They were just buttercups, but even in the dim light, they brightened the yard. Nori smiled at them.

"He knew he wasn't going home. He wanted to do one great thing before he died."

I rose and sat on the stone beside her. "Well, he did. At least it was a great thing for Mason and me. He saved us."

Nori nodded, her expression somber. "You know, he would never have punished me that severely for what I did to you."

I wasn't so sure of that. "He seemed adamant that death was the only way to save your family's honor."

"It was all bluster. In the end he would have found an excuse to spare me." She smiled slyly. "That wasn't the first time I've been in trouble with him." Then her expression grew serious again. "But I want to say how sorry I am for my part in all this. Please forgive me."

She had changed in a few short weeks. Gone was the impulsive, spoiled girl. In her place was a serene woman. I wanted to hug her, but I resisted. She wasn't another one of my rescues, and I didn't think she would appreciate the gesture.

"That means a lot to me. I hope we can be friends, I mean…if you aren't going back to France."

"Nothing in Marseilles is worth risking that terrible journey again." She sighed. "You know, I thought I loved him. Mason." She looked me right in the eye. Maybe I had jumped the gun on the friends thing. "Now I realize it was just a silly crush." She seemed uncomfortable. "I saw how he feels about you."

"What do you mean?"

"When I heal someone, it's not like conventional healing. I sort of sink inside a person's energy, and I get a glimpse of their true being. Of their soul, I suppose. And when Mason was dying, all his thoughts and worries were for you. I can only hope that one day I will find someone to love me like that."

I hoped she would too.

Nori stood and swiped at her pants to get rid of the dirt clinging to them. I rose too and called Princess as we left the stone ring.

"I've been thinking a lot about your proposal to help the dervish," Nori said. "You wanted to go after his spirit, to see if he could find his way to you."

I nodded. "You said it couldn't be done."

"No, I said your spirit would be torn apart if you tried. But in theory, it's a good idea."

I eyed her, suspicious about any idea that meant I could turn into a disembodied spirit.

"No, really. That giant bird is bound to you, and your sword too. Even that damned hound looks like she would follow you anywhere. Mason too," she finished quietly. I could see how much this cost her to say. "You might be the dervish's only hope of finding his way back to his body."

"So, you'll teach me?" I asked.

"I can teach you the magic, but it won't be enough. You need an anchor, something to keep you tethered to this realm."

I frowned. "Like what?"

"Something rooted to this plane so deeply that not even Terra could topple it. The Bodhi tree where Buddha attained enlightenment is such a place."

"A tree of life?" I took Leighna's medallion from my pocket and showed it to Nori. "My people have a tree like that too. Yggdrasil. Its roots and branches cross into nine different worlds."

"Yes! That is exactly how you could anchor yourself." Nori's voice became animated. "Can you access this tree of your people?"

"No. The way is closed to me." But as the medallion warmed in my hand, I had another idea. "Does it matter what world the tree is rooted to?"

Nori shook her head.

Then I knew where I had to go. My father, Timberfoot Greenleaf, had sacrificed himself to close the door between our world and Underhill, all because of his love for the Queen of the Fae. My father's tree still stood. Its roots pierced the veil between our worlds, ensuring that one day the fae could go home. It could be my anchor while I let my spirit roam free in the ether. I would find Jacoby. And I would bring him home.

I squeezed Nori's hands in mine, startling her with my sudden excitement. "How would you feel about a road trip?"

Dear Reader,

You probably know that authors love reviews, but do you know why? Reviews are important because they help other readers know what to expect from the book, they let me know how my books are received by readers, and they help booksellers decide which books to show to new readers.

If you enjoyed this book I would be grateful for your honest review. It can be as short as you like. Even a few positive words will go a long way. And I'll try to make it as painless as possible. Use this link to find the review site of your choice. http://kimmcdougall.com/review-hell-hounds-dont-heel.

And thank you for joining me on Kyra's adventure!

Kim McDougall

Want to find out more about Kyra's world?

Learn more about the Valkyrie Bestiary series at KimMcDougall.com including deleted scenes and more series fun.

Or join Kim McDougall's reader group to get the latest release updates and a free eBook at sendfox.com/wrongtreepress.

Poke around at Kyra's blog at ValkyrieBestiary.com.

Other places you can follow Kim McDougall: Amazon, BookBub, Goodreads, Facebook, Twitter, or Instagram.

About the Author

If Kim McDougall could have one magical superpower, it would be to talk to animals. Or maybe to shift into animal form. Definitely, fantastical critters and magic often feature in her stories. So until she can change into a griffin and fly away, she writes dark paranormal action and romance tales, from her home in Central Ontario. Visit Kim Online at www.KimMcDougall.com.

www.ingramcontent.com/pod-product-compliance
Lightning Source LLC
Chambersburg PA
CBHW061612100726